RIVER FRONT TOWER

The Tower of Souls

Mary E. Wilson Stephenson

authorHOUSE®

AuthorHouse™ LLC
1663 Liberty Drive
Bloomington, IN 47403
www.authorhouse.com
Phone: 1-800-839-8640

Published by AuthorHouse 12/28/2013

ISBN: 978-1-4918-4167-9 (sc)
ISBN: 978-1-4918-4166-2 (e)

Library of Congress Control Number: 2013922542

Fiction, all characters are not real and based only from my imagination.

Special thanks to Pamela Stephenson for editing.
Special shout-out to Charyn Smallwood for encouraging
me to stop perching and start publishing.

Dedication goes to husband Ernest Stephenson for love and support.

PROLOGUE

The River Front Tower is a twelve-story beige color high-rise apartment building, constructed of concrete and steel. It sits magnificently on five acres of land. This construction is rooted on the bottom east-end of the city, several hundred yards off the bank of the James River. It doesn't sit alone in the perimeter, there's the park and other tenements. Other unburnished Subsidized Housing and some neat single family homes with the sameness in construction staunch near by. The magnificent Tower can be seen at least two miles away, depending on what direction you are traveling in the city. It's wide steel frame picture windows gives its tenants a breath taking view of the James River. A fabulous row of Maple, blossoming Myrtle and Oak trees shaded the foot paths leading to the shore. They were intentionally planted spaced equally enough apart, so as not to spoil the view of the ocean for the people who live on the lower levels of the Tower.

For nearly three and half decade the River Front Tower has been a receptacle of sorrow and pain, a mastery keeper of secrets, lies, and violence. In it's historic resilient physique it has also been a container of dreams, laughter, and prayers.

PART ONE

CHAPTER ONE

Entombed

Mona sat up in bed gasping for air. She looked desperately around the tiny bedroom, trying to connect herself with the familiarity of the dark brown drapes, and the cheap antique dresser and chair. She collapsed back onto the soft coil mattress and tried to go back to sleep. The small clock with the decorative pink glass frame, that her nephew gave her confirmed her intuition of the time. It was three in the morning, and it was always the same time that she would awake in the middle of the night, every night for the past thirty three years.

At first she would lay awake for hours before drifting off to sleep, wondering why that particular dream hunted her. She venture to think that it had something to do with her accident over thirty years ago, but she had no all-inclusive memory of that day, and she didn't want to depend on a dream to give her closure. No one, not even her doctor would speculate what happen on that day, and he encourage her family to let her piece things together herself. She laid there reliving the months she spent in the hospital trying to recuperate from her injuries. She regressed back to the year she was in and out of that horrible clinic, visiting psychiatrist. Reflection of those days were perplexing and wore weary on her brain. And just like every night she would finally drift off to sleep.

The morning brilliant yellow light pushed through the tiny fabric openings of the sheer forest green panels, and place a vivid glow on the revolting dark green carpet, and the ' sixty style' maple finished livingroom furniture. The luminescence of the sun also reached the dinning area of the room, and cast it's wonderfully warm beams over the top of the square yellow Formica top dinetté table with matching vinyl cushion chairs.

A combination of gray thin smoke and grease escaped the confinement of the small kitchen and past through the stream of light before traveling through the rest of the apartment. The smell of fried bacon and eggs enticed the roaches to come out from hiding in the seams of the counter, the cracks in the floor, and from behind the refrigerator and stove. Mona was weary of their constant intrusion, but tried to ignore them until after breakfast.

She piled the two plates with the crispy bacon, and scramble eggs that was mixed with New York style sharp cheddar cheese. She placed four slices of toasted raisin bread on a blue flowered salad plate, and then pour steaming hot coffee into the two porcelain tea cups.

She didn't realize how hungry she was until she sat down at the table. She quickly filled her mouth with two heaping spoonful of the succulent cheese and eggs, and carefully sipped on the hot sweet black brew to wash it down. She looked across the table and frowned.

"It's the same with you at every meal. You hardly eat enough to keep a bird alive. Even as a child you were very picky, Mama use to threaten to take the switch after you if you didn't eat." For a moment a storm infused across her face.

"Suit yourself, it makes it more for me. I grow tired of taking care of you and worrying about your health."

She wanted to make light conversation to ease her worried mind, but the same disturbing dream during the night weighed heavy against her brain and she had to talk it over with her or she would be plagued by it's present the rest of the day.

"I had the same dream last night. Now Clara don't give me that look. I know that you're probably tired of hearing about it, but it gives me a sense of peace when I am able to talk it through with you."

There was a whisper. "Speak louder Clara, I can barely understand what you'll saying. You know very well that I don't hear that well, especially in my left ear."

There was another whisper, and it irritated Mona. "For crying out loud I can see that you're in one of your shitty moods this morning. No matter, I'm gonna to tell you about my dream any how."

There was silence . . . . and then Mona crunched down on a slice of raisin toast.

"It was at night. Pitch black. We were driving on a lonely road, at least I was the one that was doing the driving as usual. It was a tar paved road with a double solid yellow line dividing the two lanes, and the headlights on my light blue sixty-one Rambler was the only light illuminating the road. You were sitting next to me in the passenger seat yelling and swearing at me about something, I could never remember what it was. At the time of the dream I understood what it was that you were mad at me about, but as soon as I awoke I forgot. Except for the pitch blackness of the night everything inside the car was in vivid color. Your Afro was glistering from the Afro sheen you sprayed on earlier, and the large white hoop earrings went splendid along with your white rayon pant suite. With you around there was no need for a mirror, I always knew how I look, just by taking one look at you. I use to like that, we were twins, people always marveled at how identical we were and nobody except mama and papa could tell us apart, not even your husband Alfred."

Something gave her pause when she mention Clara's husband name, and she couldn't remember why. She finished the rest of the scrambled eggs and sipped again at the now tepid coffee.

"And oh, I even remember that in my dream the O'Jays song, 'You Got Your Hooks In Me" was playing on the radio. It use to be one of our favorite songs. Anyway you kept shouting at me at the top of your voice, calling me a bitch and a whore, low down and dirty. It was disturbing, even now telling it to you I feel a little shaken by it. I began crying uncontrollably, and then we both were wailing at the same time. I remembered that I wanted to crawl under a rock and hide, I don't remember why, I guess I was ashamed of something that I did. I remembered telling you that it was not all my fault, and that I was sorry, but you were unwilling to listen. You just kept on yelling obscenities at me, and then you slapped me across the face and yanked at my hair, and I cried out in pain. I tried to defend myself and doing so I lost control of the car and before we both knew it the car was racing toward the side of the road and toward a huge tree. That's when I woke up."

She paused a few minutes and looked across the table. "Don't look at me like that, like you could ram that butter knife up my ass. I told you I don't know why I keep having this same dream night after night . . . . Anyways, I'm done talking about it for now, and I feel much better. You see sis I knew once I told you about my dream I would feel better afterward."

She cleared the dishes from the table and put them into the sink. She took down the can of Raid from the kitchen cabinet and sprayed around the counter, the stove, and the floor. She looked toward the kitchen entrance.

"You see Clara, it don't do no good to spray, it don't kill them, just make them dizzy and paralyzed for a few minutes, and then they just get up and walk away. I think they like the stuff, like a" Crackhead" like crack. Besides I ain't gonna let nothing break my spirits today. You do know what the day is, don't you?"

She waited for the whisper. "That's right it is the first of the month, the day our check is automatically deposited into our account. The day our boy comes to see us, bringing with him all the things, we had on our list."

She pulled at her ear to make sure she heard her right. "Amen to that Clara, having him was the best thing that ever happened to you. Hell fire, he is the best thing that ever happened to the both of us. He's a blessing, a heaven sent."

Mona's lips curled, like something foul smelling just entered the room. "Why do you keep throwing that in my face? I can't help it if I wasn't able to conceive a child, you promised to share him with me. Now you gone and upset me. You always know how to push my buttons. Always getting your 'digs' in, stressing me out, and ruining my day.

⁓

She recognized his knock, it was the only knock that she would answer to. She hurried to comb her kinky gray hair. For the hundredth time in her life she cringed at her disfigured face in the mirror. She grabbed her metal cane and hurried to answer the door, cursing the hindrance of her lamed left leg.

"Hi Auntie." He kissed her on the cheeks. "How's my favorite aunt?"

"Kicking, but not too high. How's my handsome boy?"

"I'm good." He walked pass her. He headed in the direction of the kitchen, pulling the white two wheel cart full of grocery behind him.

She looked at him as if she was looking at him for the very first time, admiring his smooth chocolate skin, his thick mustached that nearly hid his thick black lips, and his bald head that he shaved every day. She never noticed any signs that he was going naturally bald. She found it hard to understand why he preferred to keep his head shaven. She did admit to herself that he looked extremely handsome that way. She thought, that he was almost the spitting image of his father even without the hair.

She heard the whisper. "Yes I know Clara, he's as tall as his father, and just as good-looking."

"What was that Auntie?

"Nothing son. Your mom and I were just agreeing about something."

He looked at her dumbfounded, hunched his shoulders, and then went back to putting away the grocery.

"Listen Auntie, I know that you don't want to hear this, but on my way up here I stopped at the rental office downstairs to pay your rent. I talked to the manager about getting you an apartment on the first floor."

He looked at her sternly. "Now don't give me a hard time about this. We have talked about this for the longest time. It's not safe for you here on the tenth floor. What if there's a fire? You could be trapped up here. You don't associate with any of your neighbors, and most of them probably don't know who you are."

She gave him that same fierce look whenever he suggested that she leave her apartment. He knew that she was raging inside.

She reminded him so much of his mother, but he remained firm. His heart was yearning to make her happy even if it was the wrong thing to do.

"Auntie, you can curse and rant all you want, this time I am not giving in. It's for your own good."

She signaled him with a quick smile to let him know that she forgave him, in fact she could never stay mad at him.

"Al J (Alfred Junior), let's not argue about this again. The only way I am leaving this apartment, is if they were to carry me out in a body bag. I been locked away in this haven for nearly thirty-five years, and I am not leaving. Conversation about me leaving has ended !"

"Chill out Auntie, it's just that I feel responsible if anything bad should ever happen to you. One of my main concern in life is knowing that you are safe and happy."

"Al J, you are a good man. You do a lot for me as it is, and you need not worry about me. I can take care of myself."

At that moment she realized that Clara wasn't around, and she thought that maybe she went for a walk. It was one of her habits of leaving without telling her. Usually it would irritat her, but then she thought that, she was glad to have the time alone with her nephew.

With his hands behind his back, he walked over to where she was sitting on the couch. He bend down and kissed her on the forehead. "I got a present for you." He pulled out a square red and white box from a Wal-mart bag.

"What's that?"

"It's a converter box."

"Why will I be needing a converter box?"

"To help with the reception of your old antenna."

"Why will my old antenna need help? it works fine."

"For one thing it doesn't work fine, unless there's several layers of aluminum foil wrapped around it. For another thing, starting next year you won't be able to use it at all, because your old antenna by it self won't be able to receive a signal.

You are being technically forced into the twenty first century whether you like it or not. Don't fight with me on this, just be quiet and let me quickly install it."

She watched as he pulled the old style console T.V. from the wall, and connected the converter box cable to the component in the back of the T. V. In a matter of minutes the digital box was set and ready to receive a signal.

"Its amazing that this old set is still working." The grooves inside the plastic knob that came with the television has long since worn down. He used the plyers that were on top of the television to turn it on. "There you go, a clearer and sharper picture. I saw that quick smile, no use in turning it upside down."

He sat next to her on the couch, and instructed her on how to use the remote control. He surfed the few optional channels until he came to the evening news.

"What do you think of President Elect Barack Obama?"

"I like him. He's smart and good-looking, reminds me of you. The first African American to become President of the United States. I'm glad that I lived long enough to witness such an historical event."

She pressed the power button on the remote.

"I'm tired of all the political mumbo jumbo." nonchalantly she change the subject. "I want to know about those wonderful twin boys of yours. Why is it that you never bring them over anymore?"

"Don't you remember that I told you that Chandrise don't want the boys to come to this part of town because of all the crimes that take place down here. Every time I come here, I see young punks out there in front of this building hustling drugs."

She grabbed her cane, and hoisted herself up. She went to the window, separated the sheer panels and stared out at the clear blue water that surged back and forth against the white sandy shores. The picturesque scene was mesmerizing, and she thought that if she tried hard enough she could smell the salty sea. She thought about the long hours she spent sitting in the soft comfortable high wing chair next to the window in her bedroom, just staring out at the ocean. She especially like to see the sun rise and set on the Amytal waters. On particular mornings she would watch the mystical mist dance flirtatiously above it. She remembered on foggy nights, she could hear distant ships fog horns warning mariners of it's present. The sound of the fog horns would make her melancholy, and filled her mind with fantasy.

She spoke to him without turning to face him. "Chandrise is a snob."

"That's unfair Auntie." He said with a flat voice. "Chandrise is a good person, and . . . a compassionate person. You're forgetting that with her type of job, she works all day assisting and providing services for underprivileged people."

She turned to face him again and she could see thin chocolate folds of flesh crease his forehead and his kindly light brown eyes darken with anger. She sat down beside him on the couch.

"Al J, let's not ruin the day by arguing. It's just that her attitude has been like a bee in my bonnet for some time now. I miss seeing the twins."

"Well even if they were to come, they wouldn't be much company for you now. They keep their ears pressed up against their cell phone, or their fingers and mind committed to the Desk Top computer. Other times they are engrossed with their PSP. It's hard to get their attention, unless you'll an electronic toy. They live on another planet and it's difficult getting tickets to board their space ship."

She patted his cheek with her stiff arthritic fingers, that looked like light brown knotted twigs. "I understand, kids now-a—days don't have time for old people." It was a failed effort to make him comfortable, and so she changed the subject.

"Did I tell you about the time, long before our brother Kenneth was born. Your mother and I were little girls, and on Sunday's our mother used to take us to Church, or for a strolls in Lincoln Park. People always stopped us and made a fuss about how cute we were and how so much we looked alike. They were amazed that there were no distinguishing marks impressed on our golden skin to tell us apart. Our hair was always comb in the same style. Our mother always dressed us the same, and it became a game with people to try and tell us apart. It was exciting for us then. We use to love the attention."

She remembered that she had told him the story many times before. A huge smile thinned his luscious lips and made him looked like he did when he was a young boy, and so she decided to continued to tell the story again. A whisper came from the kitchen, and she looked past him in that direction.

He couldn't help but notice the annoyed look on her face. He turned around to look in the same direction.

"Although we liked the attention, at early age we couldn't quite figure out why people would make a big too—do about us, more so than they did with other kids. It wasn't until we reached the age of five that we realize that we were mirrored images of each other."

She grabbed an antique brass frame with an old black and white studio photo of them as children. Although the dress they wore appeared white in the photo, she remembered that it was pastel green. It had puffed sleeves and a ruffles skirt. Their r mother had brought at Nachman's department store. To match the fancy dress they wore white lacy socks and black patent leather Mary Jane shoes.

For anyone who looked at the photo and saw them for the very first time, they would only see two adorable twin girls. They would not see the difference in personality. They would not notice the anger and longing in Clara's eyes. Not even their mother noticed the difference.

"Growing up we were inseparable and protective of each other. We had the same social skills, liked the same type of foods, and the same type of boys. Our family doctor once told our mother that he never before seen a set of twins with such strong genetic tendencies. Strangely enough when I had a tooth cavity, my sister Clara would have a tooth cavity in the same area of her mouth. There was the time when I fell off a swing and hurt my shoulder, and we both cried from the pain. Then there was the time in High School, I was held back by a teacher to complete an assignment. Clara was outside playing softball. She was on the outfield when a batted softball hit her in the head, knocking her unconscious. It must have been at that very instance that I fell unconscious onto the classroom floor."

She placed the picture back in the same spot. "Our parents and friends were astonished by the freaky events, but not Clara and me. We felt special. It was like we shared something nobody else had the power of sharing."

She moved from the couch and walked toward the kitchen. Her eyes were glassy and focused on a sphere between the kitchen cabinet and the refrigerator.

"I remember when Clara became pregnant with you, it was as if it was just yesterday. For the first three months we both had morning sickness, and even my monthly friend (menstruation) stopped visiting me. When Clara had strange cravings, I found myself craving the same things. One example is we both crave Argo starch, ate it like they were coconut bon bons. Sound stupid I know, but it's true. Frankly I was surprise to see that you wasn't born with the white substance on your skin."

She turned to face him and tears were streaming down the side of her face. Her tears moved more slowly down the right side of the face that was scarred, and momentarily paused inside each cradle of flesh.

"On the day that Clara went into labor, I suffered with the same severed spasmodic cramps. Clara was dilating at a slugs pace. It was six excruciating hours of labor, but it was all worth it when you was born. Yet after you was born I didn't have the perk of taking you home, Clara rightfully claimed the prize."

She looked piteous at him, and he moved towards her to comfort her. The tune 'La Traviata' splintered the few moments of silence between them, and closed the divide between past and present. He reached down to release the cell phone from the little black pouch that was attached to his belt. "I'm at Auntie Mona's." He grunted some words of agreement, and then place the phone back in it's pouch. "I got to go."

She wanted to tell him more, but he had a concerned look on his face, and so she decided that it could wait until he come back.

He kissed her on the forehead and headed out the door, promising her that he would call the next day. He did not hear the soft whispers that follow him to the door, nor did he feel the coldness at his back.

Hours after Al J left an ominous mood stayed in the apartment.

A white and gold porcelain tea cup was taken from the three tier curio, and thrown against the wall, shattering into tiny fragments before it landed on the carpet.

It startled Mona and she looked down at the fragments with sad eyes, that quickly harden within seconds.

"How could you? There's only few pieces of mama's fine china left, and you knew how much mama took pride in owning them. Daddy brought them back with him from Japan after the war."

She held up a piece of the bottom of the cup to the light hoping to see the image of the Geisha girl with translucent skin, and mountain high black hair piled on top of her head. She wept because it was the only cup that was left to the tea set. She also wept because with the exception of a few faded photo's the now diminishing set was the only reminder she had of her parents. She wept harder because it was a hurtful thing that Clara had done to her.

"Not even Kenneth, God rest his soul, would touch mama's tea set. Not even when he was on that stuff. Not even when he would come by with the pretense of helping out around the place, all the time stealing anything he could lay hands on to make a quick buck. Not even then would he touch mama's tea set, because he knew how much I cherished the set. He also respected of mama's memory."

She collected the pieces and placed them on the lonely matching saucer.

"I won't forgive you for this Clara."

There was a whisper and she turned to face the space between her and the kitchen.

"I am not trying to take your place with Al J, how many times do I have to repeat that. I . . . I was just telling the boy . . ." A whisper. "No it's just not true, I wasn't going to tell him about his father." She lied. "It's our secret."

A copied portrait of Martin Luther King was removed from it's place on the wall over the console TV, and flung to the floor. It was then that she started to feel the foreshadowing threat in the air. She knew what Clara was capable of and she started to tremble with fear.

"Clara, stop this shit right now." She tried to sound assertive. She remember how Clara was always trying to boss her around, especially during their childhood. People would refer to Clara as being the extroverted twin and Mona the introverted twin. It was the only way they figured that they could tell them apart. That's when Clara became cagy as they grew older and would never reveal her true side when ever she was out in public.

The whispers were becoming more tempestuous, and Mona wanted to shut it out by turning on the television. It was around eight in the evening, and Tyler Perry's 'House of Payne' was on. She turned up the volume to drown out the menacing whispers, but it was doing no good, and besides the tenants next door were drumming their fist on the wall, for her to turn the volume down.

She yelled at the tenants on the other side of the wall. "Alright I'm turning it down." She looked beaten and she tried to cover her ears against the whispering sounds. "It's not my fault. It's your fault, you did it not me. I'm not the one to blame."

Mona went to the medicine cabinet and took out the bottle of Tylenol PM, and swallowed two gel tabs with a sip of bottle water. It occurred to her that she had not eaten since breakfast, but she was to weary and had no appetite. For fear of falling again in the bath tub, she did her usual birdbath in the bathroom sink. She removed her partial plates, brushed them with fluoride toothpaste and placed them on the night stand. She slid between the clean smelling sheets and tried to block out the memories of her past. The whispers had ceased thirty minutes ago, and she wanted to quickly make her escape through sleep before Clara started to taunt her again. She laid there trying to think about anything that didn't involve her past. "Not tonight, please God not to night". She solemnly prayed, she was to depressed, too tired. Never the less the memories rushed through the fissures of her encephalon, like water rushing through a crack in a levee.

She thought about the time after Al J was born how Clara had change. She no longer wanted to share her life with her. She wanted to live her life independent from her, have her own views about life, her own social circle of friends. She wanted to keep Al J to herself, even after she promised her that she would allow her to play an essential role in raising him. She remembered that after Clara and Alfred got married, she started accusing her of trying to steel him away from her. She would make snide remarks about her being alone with him when she wasn't around. She remembered that she would say things like. "I don't like it when you try to get Alfred's attention all the time. Always trying to make him believe that the two of you share things in common."

She had to admit to herself that Clara wasn't wrong in thinking that she was secretly infatuated with Alfred. In fact she was never interested in any of the boys that flirted with her, only the boys that Clara had an interest in.

She could never understand her fearfulness of not having what her sister had or the fear of being in an existence without Clara. She was driven by this fear when she set about to seduce Alfred.

It wasn't hard to get Alfred into bed, she always suspected that he had a hidden desire to make the comparison between Clara and her. She had lost her virginity years ago, and there were many lovers after Alfred, however the first time that she made love to him was like she was on an amazing journey. She thought how wonderful the way he use his fingers to arouse her, and how different it was from the caresses of the other men she made love to in her past. They played with her perky brown nipples and throbbing clitoris of course, but it was no way equivalent to the way he taunted and teased. She made a heavy sigh when she remembered how he parted her legs and slid his huge pulsating cock rhythmically against the walls of her uterus. She became submerged into an amazing world of sexual paroxysm, unlike anything she ever felt before. She thought. 'Even now after thirty three years, the memory of our lovemaking still arouses me.'

She massaged her 'little man in the boat' until she climax. After she felt ashamed that a woman her age would do such a thing.

At first she had a series of fitful flash backs that last a few seconds and then they turned into a more concise order of sequel memories

She began to remember the night of their thirtieth birthday party when they had that final altercation over Alfred. Clara's voice was echoing in her head as she laid there thinking about that night. Clara had first confronted Alfred about their affair earlier that day, in which he consistently denied. When Clara approached her about it, she of course first denied it, but Clara had her ways in making her tell her the truth. She had irritating ways of coercing her into battle.

In all honestly she was glad to get it out in the opening. She felt exulted to be able to throw their affair in her face, give her the low down as to how she felt being excluded from their world.

"It was a mistake Clara and I'm sorry that I let it happen. We just found ourselves caught up in a situation, and I've regretted doing it." She lied.

"You whore, I knew as much, always sniffing around him like some bitch in heat. Always thinking of ways to get him alone with you."

She remembered trying not to show her delight in seeing Clara's face looking wretched and twisted in a weird way.

"It was only the one time, I swear."

"You are a liar Mona. One thing or one time doing anything was never enough for you." A waterfall of tears streamed down her cheeks. "And you know that I know you pursued Al. It has always been your intention since the day Al and I met."

Clara grabbed the knife that was lying next to the birthday cake. She remembered being shock at first in seeing the knife in Clara's hand, but then she became angry that her own sister would try to kill her over a man. They began barking at each other like rabid wolves.

The atmosphere in the room became more intense, and the light in the ceiling exposed the heat of their souls. Tunnel sounds of family members concerns and pleas surrounded them like an aura, but they didn't care.

Alfred tried to grab the knife from Clara's hand, but she was too quick for him, and move a short distance away, making it difficult to get at her without being cut. "Clara you don't won't to do this. Honey put down the knife. We can talk this shit over like civilize people."

In retrospect, Clara was beyond the point of reasoning. She waved the knife in Alfred's direction.

"You foul motherfucker. You think that, what you did to me was minuscule. Wasn't I enough? Didn't I do enough to make you happy?"

A nervous strain veiled Alfred's face, as he tried to plea with Clara. "Listen Clara I know that I fucked up. I know this, but we can work it out, just put down the knife and lets talk about it."

He moved closer, but Clara wasn't ready to be consoled. She didn't intend to cut him, she was wildly, and forcefully slashing at the air, but the knife did find Alfred's jugular vein, and his life fluid moved rapidly from the deep wound, soaking his clothes and the plush carpet beneath his feet. He collapsed to the floor, holding his neck with both hands in a useless effort to stop the blood from leaving his body.

There were screams and chaos, and someone had tried to stop the bleeding by pressing a towel against the wound.

She thought that she would never forget how his handsome face looked frozen in death, and how her heart pounded hard against her chest. Mona tried hard to remember what happen after that, but she was starting to feel the effects of Tylenol, and instead she drop steeply into a dream world.

When she awoke, it was pitch black in the room. As always she had the intuitive about the time, but out of habit she would always look at the clock on the side table, it was different tonight, she couldn't see the clock. She was irritated at the inconvenience of the darkness and she could not understand why there was no stream of light coming from the bathroom. She remembered turning it on before she went to bed, in fact it was used as her guiding light enabling her to reach her bed safely at night.

The moon refused to break the clouds that night and so none of it's welcoming beams penetrated the thick curtains. Her apartment was at the back of the building, and the only light post on the premises was at the front of the building.

She feared the darkness every since she could remember.

A startling noise came from the direction of the kitchen, anxiety griped her by the throat. She tried hard to remember the familiarity of the sound, and she thought that, maybe it was the mouse trap that she position in the bottom of the kitchen cabinet directly underneath the sink. Then she thought it was no use in trying to convince herself that it was the sound of the spring snap of the mouse trap.

She knew for certain that, it was not the humming and subtle clicking sound of the refrigerator, nor was it the low consistent roaring of the heater.

There was a soft sound of movement coming from the foot of her bed. She laid still, holding her breath in wait of the sound to recur. There was another soft rustling sound, but this time it seem to be nearing.

She called out. "Is that you Clara?" The rustling sound stop for a second or two, and then started again, moving closer. She frantically felt for the lamp on the side table, her slow shaking fingers made it's way up the cold ceramic base until they reached the light switch. When the light did not work she felt around anxiously at the head of the bed for her cane, clumsily knocking it over. By this time the rustling sounds had ceased, but there still was an eerie feeling in the darkness. After a few minutes on her knees searching she was able to reclaim the cane. With the aid of the cane and side of the bed, she was able to stand.

Next to her was a faint moan, and then a soft snicker. It was so swift and faint that she thought that she had imagine it.

"Clara?" There was another, but much deeper guttural consonant. She felt a chill, and it motivated her to move quickly, as quickly as her physically impaired body was allowed.

She made her way to the bathroom, and flip at the unaccommodating light switch several times. With unsure steps she reached the kitchen and ran her hands across the smooth surface of wall, expecting to find the circuit breaker.

"Perpetrator." The word was softly spoken, yet it was potent.

She wanted to answer with reproach, but her body was now cloaked with fear.

"Clara stop trying to frighten me. You always like to play these sick games when ever you'll upset with me. Stop it now."

"Perpetrator. Imposter."

A fierce force shove her and she fell forward hitting her head against the edge of the counter, and then her face slapped the cold linoleum floor, and unconsciousness devoured her.

Tiny tingling sensations were invading different areas of her body. Her mind was lazy, and did not want to submit to consciousness. However the crawling and biting encroachment against her skin made it impossible for her brain to languish in the comfortable slumber any longer, it sent signals to her hands to scratch and hit at what ever it was that was causing the discomfort.

Although Daylight exposed her milieus, she was still confused as to how she ended up on the kitchen floor. She moved to get up and was forced to lay still from the excruciating pain on the side of her head. She touched at the puffy wound with her fingers, wipe the blood on her robe, and then gave herself a few moments of pause, hoping that the pain would subside. While she waited she watched the roaches run back to their hiding places after leaving her body with red spots from their carnivorous impaling. The phone rang and she was prompt to bare the pain, and pull herself up and answer it.

"Auntie. Listen I was thinking about what you said yesterday, about wanting to see Malcolm and Malik. I'm bringing them by for a visit this evening, right after I get off from work."

She listen to the comfort sound of his voice, staring hard at the phone as if she could see Al J's chocolate face and broad smile.

"Al J". There was a few seconds intermission.

"Yes Auntie".

"Al J. Was there a storm last night?"

"Not that I know of. Why?"

"My lights went out last night."

"Are they on now?"

"I don't know, let me check". She open the refrigerator door. "The light in the refrigerator is on. It's strange because last night I woke up and the house was pitch black, but the refrigerator and heater was on. I left the light on in the bathroom, I know I did, but when I woke up it was off ".

"Maybe the bulb blew out."

"Maybe."

"Anyway I will be there later on and I will change it for you. Are you ok? Your voice sound a little strained."

"Just a little woozy. I must have slipped on something in the dark, and I fell and hit my head against the kitchen counter."

"I'll stop by on my way to work."

She didn't want him to be concern, and so she try to sound as if the whole matter was trivia.

"No. Don't go out your way. I'll take a couple of Ibuprofen, and put some ice against my head and I will be fine."

"Are you sure?"

"Sure I'm sure."

"I'll call you later."

When she hung the phone up, she retrieved her cane from the kitchen floor and made her way to the bathroom. In the plain square mirror above the small beige porcelain sink she looked at her image. A hideous mass of folded and raw flesh stared back at her. She was glad that she convinced Al J not to come over that morning because she was ashamed at the way she look. Besides the facial scar, and the gaping gash on her forehead, she looked and felt old. The pain of her disabled body had made her body bend and feel unsteady.

She was convinced that her whole appearance was horrifying.

She could see Clara pretty narrow face behind her own twisted image, staring at her in the mirror, with a dull and frosty glare.

"I can not forgive you this time Clara. What you did to me last night was vicious and cold. What's gotten into you lately?"

She waited for a response, in it's place was a deafening uncomfortable silence that wrecked her nerves.

"There's no point in denying what you done. You played the same nasty game with me when we were coming up you know how much I hated the dark."

The sharp click of the light switch sounded the room, and a the yellow light fused the unburnished natural light. She was shocked that the light came on. Out of habit she had tried the switch just minutes ago, just as she entered the bathroom. She turned to face Clara just in time to watch her melt into the wall. She felt relieved, and glad that for now she didn't have be subservient to Clara's hawkish scrutiny.

She peeled off her robe and nightgown, and bathed her golden wafer of a body with the tepid water from the sink. Afterwards she grabbed the bottle of alcohol an hand full of cotton balls from the vanity and blotted at the red insect bites that nearly covered her entire body. She then put on a soft light blue long sleeve acrylic sweater, and a vintage navy blue pleated skirt. Afterwards she then dressed the painful wound on her forehead with peroxide and a cotton gauze.

She was disturbed to such a degree about what transpired last night that she had no appetite for breakfast, but did decide to percolate a pot of coffee. The dark hot brew was her only true addiction. It's warm stimulating effects lifted her spirit and made her more lucid.

She perched her weary wreck of a body on the comfortable arm chair at her bedroom window. Staring out at the ocean, she thought about how upsetting it was that Clara was acting so vicious lately, and she was perplexed as to what might have brought on these unforeseen tantrums.

She remembered that Clara started acting strange when ever she mentioned anything of significance about their past.

The waves crashed the shores, and as she watched the mist evaporate into the

air, she thought why it was that she was having so many photo flashes of Alfred, and split second memories about her relationship with him. It was as if certain parts of her brain had laid dormant over the years, holding back some dark secret, and now some unforeseeable force was compelling her to evoke those memories.

One thing for certain, was that thirty three years ago she was injured in a car accident and she stayed in the hospital for a long time. Most of her memories of that night was lost along with the wreckage of her car. However it did seem that after the accident, Clara became like her moving shadow, and it made her happy that they were close again. She refused to give it much thought back then, but in retrospect, there was a strangeness about Clara.

They went about their life, locked away in her dismal apartment, hiding from the rest of the world. It was if their life was in suspension.

She thought about the ugly scar on the one side of her face, and the weakening folds of flesh that draped her body, and she thought how the years faded fast like the flavor of a stick of gum. What was so inaccessible to her conscious mind was that Clara's beauty remains the same.

Angry raised voices vibrated the walls of her apartment, lifting her out of the wellspring of retention. A child was crying, furniture was tempestuously thrown about, doors were slam shut, and the intensity of the cacophonies beat against her brow.

She forced down two Ibuprofen with the assistance of a glass of tap water from the kitchen sink, she then went to front room and turned the volume up on the television to muffle the disturbing noise coming from next door, and laid back against the arm of the sofa, blanking her eyes with a wet warm cloth.

The vociferate expletives and baby crying moved to the hallway then lessen in degrees as the voices echoed further down the corridor.

Her mind drifted in a space of wondrous recollections, discombobulating at first, but then things began to be fall into place like a puzzle.

With almost complete clarity she remembered the time she spent in the hospital. She laid in the ICU for three weeks in a coma. She remembered on one particular day that her brother Kenneth came to visit. In fact it was exactly two days after she awakened from her coma.

He looked older than twenty five, the drugs had taken it's toll. Her heart bled for him, and she wished that she could comfort him, and hold tight to his shaking hands. The pain from her injuries would not allow her to move her body to different positions in the bed, and it was nearly impossible for her to lift up her arms to give him a hug.

He sat next to her bed, with a dark look of concern on his face. She had first thought he was in need of a hit, but instead she found out that he came to tell her that their mother had passed.

She had suffered a heart attacked the day after the car accident. He went on to tell her that the doctor and nurses advise him to wait until a couple days after she had recover, before he told her for fear that the shocking news would cause a relapse. The doctors was right, hearing the news of her mother passing was so devastating she did relapse, although she did not sink back into a coma, she did suffered with severe headaches, memory lost, and depression. After she left the hospital, they sent her to a nursing and rehabilitation home, and when she improved enough for them to release her, she was sent as an outpatient to the Health Clinic for psychological evaluation.

She was now beginning to remember everything, the affair with Alfred, the argument with her sister, and the car accident. Everything was coming back in quick and steady flashes, but something in the room change, it was if something evil had walked into the room. Then it came like a a shot to the head, a vicious whisper that pierced her conscious. "It's all your fault that she's dead."

She dare not to remove the warm compress from her eyes, there was really no need to. "Go away Clara. Leave me alone."

"Broke Mama's heart is what you did."

"I refuse to hear any of your lies."

"She's in heaven with Papa now, looking down at your piteous and deceitful life."

She remove the damp cloth from her eyes and faced Clara and matched her maddening glare with her own.

"Mama and Alfred death are not my sin, the blame lies with you, and it is not the whole of your sin and you know it. No matter how much you torment me with your lies, I will never admit to something that is not true."

"The fact is you would not know the truth if it bit you on the ass. You wont allow yourself to think hard about the night of the accident. You are afraid to face the horrible truth, and expose the real you."

"I don't understand, why is that, lately you seem heated with the desire to destroy me."

An epiphany mantle her brain, and she thought that it was debilitating trying to refute Clara's accusations.

It was no point in her refuting Mona's accusations.

It was no need to hide from herself anymore.

No need to hide from the truth anymore.

She had knew for sometime about Mona and Alfred. She had planned all that week to confront them both at her birthday party, in front of all their friends and relatives. But things got out of hand, she was mad evil that night, grabbing the knife and slashing Alfred's throat. She did not intend to kill him, but he kept advancing upon her, telling her to calm down, but she wasn't ready to calm down.

When he fell to the floor holding his throat, she turned to face Clara. It was all her fault she thought, and she felt that she needed to confront her again. Mona must have seen the crazed look in her eyes, and ran for refuge. She ran after her, yelling obscenities at her back. She caught up with Mona just as she was getting into her car to drive off. She was able to slide in on the passenger side, but barely, because Mona already had the car in motion. She drove recklessly, almost hitting oncoming cars. Mona turned off the main road to a dark side street. They were at each other, striking out at each other. Mona lost control of the car and they crashed into a tall Oak, and they were thrown from the car.

"Yes." She whispered out loud. "No need to hide from the truth anymore."

It was a terrible thing that she did, and she escaped from any atonement by falling into a well amnesia. She knew now that she needed to tell someone what she did nearly thirty four years ago. Painfully she thought, that she needed to tell her son the truth about who she was, and what she did to his father.

However the thought of how the truth would effect Al J, and the consequence of not having his love anymore was too stressful and painful.

Just the thought of losing her son's respect and love made her blood pressure rise, and her head felt fuzzy and light. There was a crushing pain in her chest, and it was difficult for her to breathe. Her vision became blurry, and she thought that she heard faint laughter, and then the light left the room.

CHAPTER TWO

You Got To Hold On

Climbing the ten floors up to his apartment was part of his daily regiment, it was a continuance from his routine workout at the gym. Keeping in shape was an obsession with him. To him a weak body, and a weak mind were fallible conditions, and not an option in his life. Although his compulsion to be superior in body and mind was a fallacy, he just did not see it that way.

His apartment was three doors from the stairwell and he was glad that he didn't have to walk any further. The bag of groceries that he gripped securely in his arm were beginning to feel very heavy and bothersome. He noticed a lot of people going in and out of apartment 1002 near the stairwell. It was the first time since he's been living there, that he could recall, ever seeing anyone going in and out of that apartment other than a tall bald handsome brown man. However it was probable that the maintenance man went in the apartment on occasions, but he has yet to see him enter the apartment.

As he past the door to get to his apartment, he recognized Elaine, the assistant manager of the building. He also recognized the same tall bald handsome man that he seen frequent the apartment, and along side him were two light brown boys who look to be in their teens and identical to one another. They stood almost in a full circle around the two White male paramedics who were trying to resuscitate the elderly woman. He could see the graveness in the face of one of the paramedics, as he looked up at the handsome bald man and shook his head.

He stood there shamelessly glaring inside the apartment.

Today he was breaking one of his rules, by becoming one of those snoops that he so hotly hated. Yet he was captivated, he had heard references about the woman's mental state, about how she kept herself locked away in that apartment.

She lived in that apartment longer than most of the tenants in the building, or so he was told and no one in the building other than the landlord knew exactly how long she's been living there. There were all kinds of speculations about who she was, and why she kept to herself, but nobody really knew the woman's story.

His first glimpse at the woman's mutilated face and he understood why she kept herself locked away. A pang of pity for the deceased woman twisted his heart and he immediately was ashamed of his presence there in her doorway, and so he left and headed for his apartment.

He could hear the phone ringing inside his apartment, as he slip the key into the key hole. He heard his answering machine accept the call.

"Hi this is Harold, I am sorry that I am not able to take your call right now, but if you leave your name and number, I promise to call you back." He spent a couple of seconds thinking about the mediocre message he recorded on his answering machine, and thought that if things go as plan, that he would include David's name into his answer machine. He also thought that maybe by then he will have a cute catch

phrase, like 'hi David and Harold are too busy makin' love right now to answer your call, but promise to call you right back as soon as they culminate.'

The message from the caller interrupted his thoughts.

"Harold, this is Melba. I just wanted to call and let you know that last night was off the hook. It was the best time I had in a long time. If you want a repeat for tonight, I'm available, give me a call sugar."

The loud beep echoed the room and the caller was disconnected. He yelled at the

phone. "Hell to the No! Melba or Melvin what ever the fuck you call yourself now days. You were just a tool, a useful means to make my man happy."

He check the machine for other messages, and the only other message was from Lacy inviting herself over Friday night for a game of "Trivial Pursuit".

His mind went back to last night. He remember telling David early that evening, that he had invited Melba over for dinner and a night of fun.

"Melba? Your "slutty" friend that you introduce to me at Jason's party a few months back", was his response.

"Melba is ok." He threw back at him." She's flamboyant and charismatic, and I can not see anything wrong with being strong will and entertaining."

"She's an emotional confused trollop. Remember now, that this is your analytical phrase. You told me that any given day that you may run across her, and that she maybe dressed in drag, and any other possible encounters, she may be dressed in regular hip-hop clothes. And, did you not tell me that she had slept with nearly half the men at Jason's party."

"Yes I did tell you that, and that's the real reason I invited her over tonight, I thought it would be fun to have a menage-et-trois night, if you scared of catching something wear a condom for goodness sake."

"Why for fuck sake would you want another person in our bed? I thought that you wanted a monogamous relationship."

"I still do, it's just lately I have been getting the feeling that you're bored with me. We have been together for more than a year, and I am starting to feel that things are not as great between us like it was in the beginning. Our relationship seems to be dull and dried up.

Sometimes I have to throw myself at you to get you to make love to me, and then its as if you're not there just going through the motions."

They were having the conversation in the kitchen, and he turned around to remove the roasted chicken from the oven.

He wanted to ask him a question that has been tormenting him for the longest time, but he was afraid to face him, afraid that if he did he may see something in his face that he was not prepared to see, afraid that he may be able to read the truth in his eyes.

"Don't get me wrong, I am a sexually driven man, and to say that I would not be ravenous to any crumb you throw my way would be a lie, but I want back the hot steamy passion we had before. I want to know David, do you desire me in the same way anymore?"

He took too long time to answer the question and he thought that if he didn't let air back into his lungs while waiting for his answer, that he would loose consciousness, and to blackout out like a sissy would be insufferable.

"Of course I still desire you, shit there are times that I crave everything about you, but there's more to a relationship than sex. And there's times when I come home I would just like to be in your company. I would like to just be able to enjoy the peaceful atmosphere of our apartment, to read and try to understand one of those thick and profound books you got on the bookshelf."

By this time he was inhaling and exhaling at the speed of a passenger train. His eyes followed the direction in which David had fixed his stare.

They both stood looking at the massive white book case that spanned across three fourth of the wall facing the comfortable brown suede couch. On the shelves were several African pieces he got from friends as gift, and a few he had brought from a specialty shop in the mall. However the most impressive collection on the shelves were his books. It was his intention for those who came to his home, to be impressed by them, for indeed he had read every one and each volume left an impressionable scar in his mind and soul. He had meticulously categorized the books according to type of book and author, for instance most of the shelves contain hard copies of fiction, prose, and literary genre by authors like Dante (English translation of La Divina Commedia), Ernest Hemingway (The Sun Also Rises), John Steinbeck (Of Mice and Men), James Baldwin, Gordon Parks, James Weldon Johnson, and folk lore and short stories by Langston Hughes and Zora Neale Hurston. A small section at the bottom of the massive shelf were three copies of Factfinder, Books on Herbs, Gay Rights, a copy of Taber's Cyclopedic Medical Dictionary, and five editions of Laurence Perrine books on literature. He was proud of his small library, and he hoped that to others it defined the type of man he really was.

He was glad that David expressed his yearning to express his love for literature, and it made him breathe a sigh of relief, thinking that it maybe a promising sign. Yet he stayed committed to that prior evening as planned, and it wasn't until this morning when he awaken that he thought he may have made a mistake. Although the" menage-et-trois"was fun and they had great sex, it left him with a bitter aftertaste of jealousy.

A can of mushroom rolled off the counter and landed painfully on his foot, jerking his mind back from last night recollections. He realize that in his haste to answer the phone, he had mistakenly placed the grocery bag in a slanted angle on the counter and the bag fell over causing some the items to spill over unto the counter.

He removed the rest of the items from the bag and placed them next to the other items on the counter, and then threw the paper sack into the recycle ben. He decided to make for dinner David's favorite Spinach Salad with black olives and thin wedges of fresh home grown tomatoes, (or so the grocery sign claimed) and let it chill in the plastic Crisper for an hour inside the refrigerator.

He looked up at the clock on the kitchen wall, and he said amusing out loud.

"Shit! David will be coming home in thirty minutes. I better hop into the tub and shower the funk off my fine tight ass."

Before stepping into the shower, he caught a image of his naked body in the full length mirror on the bathroom door.

Unrestrained of any false modesty he admired his masculine anatomy, crediting his body perfection to proper diet and to the time he spent on the press bench and the tread mill. He leaned closer to the mirror to peer at the tiny pustule on his Amerind nose, and with the tip of his clean manicured fingernails forced the yellowish pus out from it's infectious bed. Needless, yet excessively he worried that the red spot left on his face would turn dark and mar his honey complexion. He smiled at his image, thinking gravely how much he and his sister look so much alike. Their intercrossed straight and curly hair and light skin are the hereditary sampling from their father side of the family. A pang of longing to see his family swiftly swept through his conscious. He decided that sorrowful memories of his estranged family should stay deeply rooted in his cerebral cortex, and he focused once again on himself.

As always during his intimate time alone, especially his time in the bathroom, he would proudly run his hands over the curves of his body, and grip and adjust his penis. Before stepping into the shower, he inflated his ego by thinking smugly to himself. "I am truly blessed." He stepped into the shower and jerked off.

There relationship still remained at a simmer, even after last night menage-et-trois. For three weeks he has tried hard to make their nights as pleasurable as he possibly could.

That night in particular he started out the evening with a deliciously hot meal, that was painstakingly planned and prepared during the day. He was glad that when he first moved into his apartment that he had chosen the spot in the livingroom in front of the wide picture frame window to position his dinning table and chairs. It was the quintessential romantic spot to partake an intimate meal with someone special. To be able to look out at the river, and watch the tide hit the shore was enchanting. Tonight there was a full moon and the moon beams illuminated the ocean, and wigged along with the waves, and the scene heighten his mood for lovemaking. The only thing that would have embellished a romantic evening would be if there was a fireplace with high fitful sparks of flames.

He thought to himself. "Harold you'll such romantic dope. Too much of residuum from Morquez book 'Love in the time of Cholera', that he finished reading that morning.

David sat across from him with a tedium look upon his face. Harold thought how perfectly handsome his face is even with the look of discontentment. The red polo shirt he wore and the flickering candle light were comparable enhancements that radiated his flawless coffee bean complexion. His hair was freshly cut into his favorite wearing Caesar style. He had a "five-o'clock shadow" and Harold wondered if David forgotten to shave that morning, or if he was planing to grow a beard, and if he did would the Navy approve. Irregardless of David's intentions or lack of, he approved, in fact he was aroused by it.

He recalled reading once in a poem or short story that;" The mark of the beast is not indelible upon a man until he goes about with a stubble".

His impetuous eyes then scanned his upper torso, and he was overtaken with delight at the way the red polo shirt fitted tightly against the muscular curves of his chest and arm, and it didn't take much imagination to picture his scrub board ribs underneath.

He watched him stab at one of the shrimps in the Shrimp Scampi, and move it in circles around the orzo and green onions.

"What's wrong David? You seem preoccupied. Is there something you want to tell me?"

"No. It's been a long day, and I'm just exhausted. I think that I am going to go to bed early."

"You haven't eaten you dinner. I thought Shrimp Scampi was your favorite."

"I'm sorry, I'm just not hungry."

A weak smile stretched across his face. "As you can see I ate all of my spinach salad."

"David we need to talk. You need to tell me what it is that's bothering you. If there's a problem concerning the two of us, you need to share your feelings with me."

A quick painful look veiled David's face. "I don't want any drama tonight. The day has been too long and tedious, and as you know that because of our little twist between the sheet, I didn't get much sleep last night."

In an effort to subjugate the laughter he had building up inside, Harold made a spurting sound from the back of his throat and little droplets spittle shot through his nose and ran down his top lip.

"Our manage-et-trois was never between the sheets. Just about every where else in the house, but never between the sheets."

"You know what the fuck I mean. Don't get it twisted, I am not saying that it wasn't enjoyable and entertaining, it was just hard on the body, and this morning I had to drag myself out of the bed to try and beat the east bound traffic on I-64 to Norfolk. I barely made it on the Navy Base by 0700 hours.

Harold was burning with the desire to have it out with David, to force him to open up to him. He convinced himself that it would be a mistake, and that it would probably make things worst between them.

"The only time we really spend time together are on your days off, and it seems that lately you have been working overtime. What's up with that?"

"It's a lot of stuff going down aboard ship lately, a lot of preparation for deployment. There's been a lot of equipment mishap, and a lot of bull shit entanglements."

"Hell. I knew that it would happen sooner or later, I was hoping for later. When did you learn about the deployment?"

"We got our orders in October."

"That's over a month ago! That means that you won't be here for Thanksgiving. Shit! Why didn't you tell me about it back in October?"

"I don't know. Shit. I guess I was waiting for the right moment. I been a little fuck up about it myself. I sure as hell don't want to spend six months out at sea with some of the fucking 'Flamers' (officers) in my crew, they have been brutal in reaming out most of the 'newbies'.

I know that it is part of their political bull shit, but some of the shit that they do is really foul, and I doubt that the Admiral knows about every thing that goes on aboard his ship."

David squirmed in his chair, and he changed his slump muscular frame to a defensive stiff statue.

"What kind of shit are you talking about?"

"I don't want to go into it right now, besides I have a fucking headache and I'm going to bed."

"I got just the right remedy for a headache."

Harold moved swiftly to David side, and with ardent skill, massage the side of his forehead, the nape of his neck, and the muscles around his shoulder and upper back. David's body yield to the consistent rhythm kneading, and Harold jumped at the opportunity to advance further down his body.

Heatedly he massage David's manhood, and he drooled with satisfaction when David's member quickly swell in response. He unzipped David's pants and ran his fingers through his kinky black pubic hairs and gently rubbed his scrotum.

He got on his knees and moved his lips towards David's throbbing member, and the stench of it was like an aphrodisiac, and he could feel the swelling of his own cock pressing tightly against his Dockers, begging for release.

With his hot wet tongue he lavishly teased the head of David's penis as if it was a sweet tasting popsicle. His tongue massage the shaft of his phallus for what seem a blissful eternity, extending his tongue as far as he could, and with repeated and forceful movement of a oil drill he forced the member deeper down his throat until it explode.

He couldn't concentrate on his assignments. Years ago he had contended that he was never self righteously motivated into thinking that he had to rub the hair off his head against the walls of some prestigious and costly college in order to accomplish some prescribed self-worth. Being a Medical Transcriptionist requires meticulous skills and pharmaceutical knowledge, and he always thought that it was the type of job that well suited him. However today he could not stay focus, because today or rather tonight would be the last night he will have to spend with David until after the end of his six months deployment.

Last night they invited a few of their friends over for a farewell party, and the little get-together lifted David's spirt, but tonight he wanted him all to himself.

He had to admit to himself, that when he first met David it was during his "slutty period", and he had no intention in getting committed to anyone so soon after his breakup with Anthony. And especially not to a married man, he just wanted to get laid with no emotional strings attached. He just wanted to be "buck wild, a fuck'm then leave'm Wild Bill, and that's all. He didn't want any of that "I'm so into you" bull crap, or any other of the bull shit that guys feed you, just to get you all emotionally crippled and wrapped up into their world. He remember his train of thought back then was the 'old school' way of thinking and that was;' all I wanna do is a boom boom, and a zoom zoom'. Silly little amusing and entertaining expressions were always floating around in his head.

He typed in a few more medical instructions, did a couple more applications, and then closed the screen. He thought it was no use, to continue with this rainy cloud hanging over his head, sooner or later he would make some serious mistakes, and this was not the type of job that you were allowed to many mistake. One great thing, he thought, about working at home, is that your hours were flexible, and it suited him just fine.

It was still early in the day, around noon to be precise, five hours before David would be walking through that door for the last time, until next spring. He felt like a thousand butterflies were madly fluttering around in his stomach as he thought of the possibility that after six months is up, David might return home to his wife.

He marinaded a pound of flank steak with pineapple juice, teriyaki sauce, and honey and placed it refrigerator. His mind drifted back to that particular day at the gym where he first met David.

Other than some of the gay clubs, that particular gym was surreptitiously a place to meet gay men or men Harold laughingly call men with gay tendencies. David was such a man, he was on the 'downlow'. He had the desire to be openly gay, but was still mentally struggling with the repercussions of coming out.

He remember feeling very horny that day and when he saw this tall dark-skinned buffed man awkwardly cruising the room. He made his move, smiled at him and offered to give him instructions on how some of the equipment work, not that he really felt he needed to be instructed because it was so obvious that he had already been conforming his body to a habitual rule of weight lifting.

"Are you familiar with the Power Line?"

"Like the palm of my hand."

Harold gave him a glance of approval.

"I can see that."

"Then why ask."

An impish smile crossed his face.

"It was a rhetorical question, a weak attempt at starting a conversation."

He noticed a wedding ring on his finger, and thought for a moment that his "Gaydar" was off it's mark, until he caught him eyeing his crouch.

Harold walked over to the Press Bench. "I wonder if you could spot me?"

"Sure. How much are you lifting?"

"I usually start with one-fifty."

"Are you sure? You look like you can handle more than you weight."

"I'm not pushing to be like Lou Ferrigno. I just want to look athletic without looking to brawny. How much do you lift?"

"It depends on my day. Some days I do a lot of cardio, and so I might only do one eighty, it depends on my energy level."

After about dozen lifts, he switch places with David.

"What do you think of the Redskins? Do you think that they might make it to the Playoff"s again this year?"

"I seriously doubt it. They had a rough season in 2006, finishing the season at 5-11. Maybe they will do better this year, but I wouldn't bet on them making it to the Playoff's."

He stared into space remembering how mundane the conversation went at first, and he recalled how he was hoping that they could get to the real "nitty gritty".

"A few of my friends are meeting at my place for a game party this Sunday to watch the Skins play against the Lions, and I would like for you to come."

"Sorry, I'm on duty Sunday, but keep me in mind for the next party."

"You in the military?"

"Yeah the Navy, unfortunately."

"I notice a ring on your third finger. How long have you been married?"

He could see that the question made him uncomfortable, but he figured that if

he didn't want any one to know that he was married, then he shouldn't have worn the ring.

"Five years. I got a wife and daughter living in Atlanta. I haven't seen them in almost a year. I talk to my little girl once or maybe twice a week, and she's always asking me "daddy when you are coming home? Every time she ask me, I' m always lost for words. The truth is my relationship with my wife is a little strained right now, and I am really dreading going back there."

He remember at that particular moment being grateful that David changed the conversation from being pleonastic to being more personal.

"Look why don't we just take a break, I'm exhausted and thirsty. Why don't we go to Harpoon Larry's and get a couple cold beers and make it an early lunch and order two seafood platter."

"I can't I got to report back to the ship at thirteen hundred hours."

"Well since you don't have but ninety minutes to spare, why don't we go to my place it's just ten minutes from here. Pushing all bullshit aside, we might as well get down to the 'nitty gritty', we both came here today for the same reason."

David's face altered from an anxious radiation to a pleased and relieved expression.

"You drive and I will follow you."

In his recollection of that day, he recall that when they entered his apartment and closed the door, there was no more diplomatic bullshit, or rotted conversation about who will

29

make it to the NFL finals, or who would win the Super Bowl, it was just lustful probing and kissing. And when they finally made it to his bed, he couldn't remember the task of undressing, he could not remember if they started to undress at the same time, or if he lead and David follow. What was so engraved in his mind was the love making. He corrected his thoughts. It was hardcore fucking. It was so intense and feverish that he ejaculated twice within minutes apart. He guess that it must have been thirty minutes at least, not that he made time to look at a clock, but it felt like an eternity of unadulterated blissfulness. Afterward he felt as if David cock was still in him, analytically he thought it was like when he was a kid and would go roller skating for several hours, and when he finally took off his skates, he still felt like he had them on and that he was still inches off the ground.

He remember after they showered together, he convinced David to let him fix them a quick lunch before he left. He smiled thinking that there must be something compelling in a person to make them talk about their personal life after they had a good fuck, and a satisfying meal. Unremittingly David talked about his marriage, the birth of his daughter, and his enlistment into the Navy.

He said that other than having a stable job, that there were dismaying reasons why he joined the Navy. His mood change and went dark and disturbing, and nervously with cynicism he sang a verse from the Village People song.

They both laugh and sung a few more verses to the song, and he mellow out, but a worried look veiled his face again then he truthfully said. "All my life I have been living a lie. Since I was little I knew that I was different from father, but I kept it a secret, afraid that I would lose his love. We lived in a big house along with Big Mama, my mother and my three older sisters, and so I was like his blessing replica in a family pool of nothing but females. In a family pool of nothing but females, I was like a blessing, a replica of him. I just could not go to him and profess that I had feelings for my best friend Sean, or my having wet dreams about Billy Dee Williams.

For years growing up I did the things he expected me to do. I participated in sports at school, and excelled well in Basketball. The truth is I grew to like basketball, and maybe that's was why I did better in that particular sport, than I did playing Soccer and Football.

I wanted to join the wrestling team, but my father wasn't having that, he would often say that it something about wrestling that rubbed him the wrong way. I had my obscure reasons for wanting to join, and I suspect that he had his secretive reasons for not wanting me to join. Anyway it was like that with my father, I went out with girls that I had no real physical attraction to, just living the lie among my family and peers.

I remember that my first sexual encounter was with this gay nerd at high school. We both were the same age, I think we was sixteen at the time. Shit I know I was sixteen at the time, something like that live with you for the rest of your life. Something like that you don't ever forget, you remember where it took place, the time of day, and you even remember world eventful moments that took place.

He was good looking, nearly as tall as me, shit I was unusually tall for my age. Anyway he was always watching me, saying provocative things to me. It was like he knew my inside, my desires, my secrets. I thought I hated him for that, and every time he approached me I would make fun of him just like the rest of the group of boys I hung out with. For some reason maybe a divine intervention, no maybe not that, maybe it was more like serendipity, or karma, whatever the fuck you want to label it. We came together even after all the flirting he would do and the Homophobic demoralizing I would do.

It was amazing, but afterward in stead of befriending him, I beat him up and threaten to kill him if he told on me.

It was the first time having sex with anyone, and like I said before it is something that stays with you for the rest of your life, and the fact that I beat him up was disdainful, and horrific and it stayed embedded in my mind like black mold, you can bleach it up with superficial feelings and think that it's gone for good, but it returns."

He poured David a glass full of cognac. "You need something a little more potent than a Bud Light. Let me tell you about my coming out party. I was caught locked tight in the arms of Kevin Green by father in the basement of his Church."

He wore a sheepish smirk like a tight fitting sweater, when the memory of that day conquered his nous. "There I was, just a few week past my twelfth birthday, with raging hormones, and as the old folks would say 'smelling the must of my underarm'. I was locked in the passionate folds of honey sweet Kevin Green, trying my hardest to swallow his hot probing tongue when my father found us.

When my father got me home that evening, he practically skinned me alive. He was spitting out scriptures from Genesis, Romans, and first Corinthians all the while he was tanning my ass. When he got through with me he turned me over to my mother. She spared the rod but just to see the shame and hurt in her eyes was worst than any whipping I ever had. I was her shining star, her precious angel who happily followed her to church three times a week. I was her prize possession who zealously helped her at church function and trailed behind her like I was in bondage. The rumor that I was with Kevin Green in an unholy way went through the church grapevine faster than boll weevils can destroy several acres cotton. My mother and my aunts prayed over me for weeks, and as far as I know until this day they could be still on their knees praying over me, hoping that I would change my ways as if it was easy as changing my socks.

Back then even with all the prayers, the sermons and brow beatings on the abomination of homosexuality Kevin Green and I still got our groove on."

"Was he worth it?" "Well hell yeah! At first it was like we were two playful kittens, just groping at each, kissing, and experimenting, not really sure what we were doing, but it was sweet and satisfying. The most important thing that came out of Kevin and my relationship, was that it was liberating, as if I was Dorothy in the Wizard of Oz stepping out of the poppy field and entering the world of Oz. It was a new stage in my life, and I was not fearful of the future, I accepted who I am. I figure that my parents would come to their senses one day and accept me as I am, but mean while, as in a quote from Shakespeare's Hamlet, 'to thine our own self be true'."

The light in the rooms of his apartment change from a lustrous yellow to a grayish blue, and the furnace popped on. The chill in the room and the mechanical sounds of the gas chambers stirred his conscious mind. Cognitively he returned to the very spot his body was standing before his mind was reminiscently annihilated. An hour had past and he didn't know that he was lost to thought that long.

He had plenty of time before David returned home, and so he decided to go for a run. He quickly changed into his jogging suit and New Balance and left the warmth of his apartment.

The hallway stank of over flowing garbage in the garbage drop-off, and the temperature in the hallway was frigid and he guessed that outside was at least ten degrees colder. He ran the one flight down and walked briskly to Lacy's apartment. He waited almost three minutes before she answered the door.

He thought how white she looked with her straight raven hair in a disarranging frame against her oval face. She was dressed in tight fitting jeans and a lavender sweater, and she looked pretty pasty skin and all. She had a fetish for lavender, every thing in her apartment was either lavender or purple. He once asked her; "how in the hell you manage to find a purple couch and chair?" He soon learned that if she didn't purchase things purple or lavender, she would find ways to have it dyed or painted. Lavender fragrance was stifling throughout the apartment. She even dressed her two adorable bronze little boy and girl in lavender. This he know did not set well with De'Aundre, Lacy's boyfriend for seven years.

"Where have you been all morning? I have been calling you and calling you, don't you fucking answer your cell phone any more. No point in calling you on your house phone because you don't answer that either."

"I had my cell on vibrate. You should have rang me on my house phone, because I have been home all day. Where's ' Ass Hole' ?" He didn't like De'Aundre, as a matter of fact he didn't like the wasted energy it took to hate anyone, but it was energy well spent when he devoted a few minutes of his time in hating him. He still seethe over the several altercations he had with De'aundre about his relationship with Lacy. In his mind he conjured up the imagery of the ebony beefy man with threaten looks and hateful demeanor. Harold often thought himself a fool for not being intimidated by him.

"I couldn't tell you, he left couple hours ago, probably mixing it with his with some his gangster friends."

Harold knew exactly what that meant. He was doing re-ups.

"I guess it would be to much of a real hardship for the son-of-a-bitch to find a honest job."

"Don't even go there! For Christ sake don't even say anything like that to his face, unless you're looking to get killed."

"I ain't scare of that gorilla. I might be a ' queer' to him, but I assure you that I have mad boxing skills.'

Lacy flinched at his naivete. "Stupid. You do know that De'De carries a ' Burner'. He carries it around tucked in the front of his pants, like a second penis. I tell him all the time that I didn't want him packing around the house, especially around the kids. I might as well been talking to the walls, cause De'Aundre is gonna to do what De'Aundre wants to do regardless."

Harold grew weary talking about De'Aundre. "You know how I feel about the bastard. What you need to do is kick the bastard out. Anyway I am done talking about Dé Dé." There was a note of sarcasm in his voice when using Lacy's pet name for him. "That's not what I came down here for. Come go jogging with me, I will slow my pace down to equal yours. I want some company today, I need to get out of my place for a while. Get some fresh winter air into my lungs, and get my mind off of David's leaving, if only for an hour or so."

"My bad. I forgot that David is being shipped out tomorrow. I know that it's gonna be hard on you when he leave." She touched his cheeks tenderly. "Sure I'll go jogging with you, but I can only stay gone for one hour, the kids will be getting out of school by then. It will just take a few minutes to change my clothes, and I will be right back."

He looked around the neat apartment trying to fix his mind on something that would entertain him while she changed her clothes. He flipped the pages of the November issue of People magazine. On the cover was a picture of Jennifer Hudson with a grievous look on her face and underneath her photo was the sub-title: Family Murdered, Jennifer's Agony. He read and was touched by story of the artist famed life and about the brutal murders of her mother, brother and young nephew. Yet he could not help but thinking that People magazine use to have fascinating article about people, extension and follow up stories of breaking news. Now he dislike the magazine. He thinks of it as being a 'rag', with no real substantial articles, only superficial information and pictures of celebrities, and the majority of them were White. He sigh heavily and placed the magazine back on the coffee table.

"I'm ready. How do I look?"

She wore a purple velour jogging outfit with white sneakers adorned with purple lilacs painted in parcels all over the shoe. He thought creative but sickening. He responded

"Appropriate. Lets hurry up if you want to be back in time to get little De'Audrey and Kobe off the bus."

He spoke adoring of them and his lips and face relaxed into a glowing smile.

One of the reason that she like Harold was his soft heart when it came to children.

In the grayish blue sky a small cattle of white Egrets flocked towards the direction of the marsh, and Harold noted the beauty of their flight. He then expanded his chest and filled his lungs with the heavy frosty air. The ground was hard and dry, and the grass was brown and dying. He had a particular route he like to follow every time he ran and so he headed towards the back of the building, looking back to see if Lacy was on his trail.

"Move your fat ass Lacy."

"Fuck you Harold ! It's fucking cold out here, colder than I thought it would be." She marked him. "What happen to, I'll run at your pace Lacy'."

"I am . . . . It's you that's not running at your full potential."

He slowed his pace to match her trot. He could see that even at that pace she was having a hard time maintaining. Her cheeks and nose were red from the harsh air, which he secretly though was an improvement from the deathly pale look.

"I should have told you to stretch for fifteen minutes before starting out. Breathe normally, don't try to take in to much air."

"I'm breathing normal."

"You're not Lacy! You're breathing to fast and hard. Slow your breathing down and your heart rate will decrease, and you will be able to run at a steady pace."

They headed down the footpath that was almost completely blanketed with the leaves of the tall Maple trees, the proud Oak trees, and the elegant Myrtle trees.

He sadly yearned for spring when the trees were rich with sap, and plumped with shiny green leaves. When there were obvious signs of life taking up residents in their bark, on their limbs, and feasting on their leaves. It was the time of the year, where Mother nature apologizes for the bitter winter.

Lacy had her breathing under control, her energy level was up, and she thought she was an equal competitor for Harold. She increased her speed and gave him the California greeting when she past him. He smiled and was glad to see that she was in a mood for a race and so he increase his speed, confident that she was no match for him.

They moved from the footpath to the shore, kicking up sand as they ran towards and past the tall hard woody stems of the bamboo plants.

The beach varied in formation and sloped in various degrees, and they were delighted and invigorated at the variations. They then climb the embankment and ran to the park, taking on the one mile run in the park on the sidewalk with ferocity before settling down on one of the wooden benches.

"We should have brought along a bottle water, this crisp dry air makes you thirsty."

She nodded in agreement.

"It's serene here not a soul in sight. I'm glad that I tagged along, I feel cold and exhausted, but I also feel renewed. Without realizing it, I really needed the break from my apartment."

Three miles away they could still see the River Front Tower, looming over the acres of land and trees that surround it. From where they sat it look peaceful,

and unrefined by the actual violence and drama that took place inside it's walls. Harold recalled that some of the tenants referred to it as 'the tower of anguished souls'. It was a circulated truth among the tenants, that during the three decade stretched through time, the River Front Tower was once a home for patients of Eastern State.

They sat a few minutes in tranquillity enjoying the scenery.

"Do you have a big meal planned for David?" The question was a casual breakage of the silence that had developed between them.

"Yes. Marinated flank steak with pineapple, serve over wild rice, and a side portion of baby carrots."

"Sounds to fancy for me. You couldn't just fry up some chicken, whipped up some mash potatoes?"

Pretentiously he replied.

"Too high in cholesterol."

"Are you going down to the pier tomorrow morning?"

"Doubtful."

"Why?"

"I don't think that David will feel comfortable with me there."

He got up from the bench, did a couple of stretches, ran for a few minutes in one spot, and motioned her to do the same.

"Do you love him?"

If it was anyone else other than Lacy, that asked that question, he probably would have been evasive in answering. Most likely he would have joked about it. He thought if he was to dissect the word love he would have to admit that he do have deep affection for David, but how deep was the question he often asked himself.

"I'm not completely committed to that word yet, the word love. Do I feel passionate about him I would have to say yes. I think that when he's gone, that I would crave his body the way a baby craves his pacifier.

I don't know. If I am to be completely honest with you, I don't know if I could be Celibate the whole time he's away.

I want to say that I will be loyal and faithful, while he is gone, but with the same token I know that I will be plagued with questions like; Is he being faithful to me? Will he come home to me? Or, will he go back to his wife? I have been the poster child for unrequited love before, and that's not the route I want to travel anymore."

"As you know, I have been in David's company lots of time, and if it's one thing I know for sure is the look of love on a person's face, and I noticed that on David's face every time he looks at you, every word of reasoning that slip through your lips is like the bible to him. I would say that he is your homing pigeon and that you have nothing to worry about."

He could see the sincerity in her brown speckled blue eyes and her words were spiritual food for his soul, and mind, and he savored them and locked them away into the depths of his cerebral cortex, only to be released during rainy days. He kissed her cold pink cheeks.

"Damn Lacy, that was some well thought out shit."

He gave a her a loving shove, knocking her off balance. He ran leaving her behind, challenging her to catch up.

"Come on bitch, no more leniency shit for you any more. Show me that you can do better, or eat my dust the rest of the way back home."

He laid securely in his arms, afraid to move, afraid if he did, it would spoil the moment. He was caught up in an afterglow, still salivating over what took place just minutes ago. It was the most explosive and the best act of sexual copulation that he ever thought was possible between two men. His brain couldn't get past the way he moved so smoothly and tenderly inside him hitting his ' G-spot', inflaming and fully stimulating both the prostate and the perineum. He got aroused again just thinking about it, and he wanted more.

It was as if David read his thoughts, because he gently gripped his phallus, tugging at it slowly and with such rhythm that it cause his member to throb and swell hard enough to cut diamonds. He then straddle him backward style for a good I do yours and you do mines fellatio.

Minutes later they laid close to each other, feeling completely exhausted and fulfilled. Sweat glowed like fire on their naked caramel and chocolate bodies, two sweet combination.

Harold concluded that this will be the night to remember for rest of his life, and that no other night or man can compare.

This night is a spoiler for him.

This night he could say with all certainty that he was in love.

He look into David's dark brown eyes and searched for the same adoration he was feeling for him. His heart danced inside his chest with delight in what truth he found there, and he felt confident and whole, and the smile on his face out shined the silver stream of moon beams that penetrated the aquamarine sheers that hang from the window.

"I wish that this night could last forever. Lying next to you is where I want to be for the rest of my life."

All of a sudden David's body became ridged, and Harold sensed that his mood had change. He thought that the talk of a future with him may have agitated David. He wanted to quickly let him know that he was not trying to convince him to consider taking another step into the future with him, if he didn't feel comfortable doing so.

"But there is always the next day, the anticipation of the so call normality and reality of it hangs aloft above our dreams."

"Yes". He sadly agreed. He held onto Harold tighter. "There's something I need to tell you. Something that I have been keeping from you for while."

Harold begin to think of the days that David moped around the house, shooting arrows of discontent straight into his heart. He was afflictive of the nights that David had denied him sex. His eyes moisten and he choked on the moan that cauterize the back of his throat. He had heard the predictable lines to a breakup before, but he thought how cruel it was for him to make 'out of this world' love to him and then tell him that he wanted to end their relationship. How could he have been so wrong in thinking that he saw in his face the same adoration that he felt for him. He held his breath.

"Two months ago I witness misconduct by an Officer and mischief behavior by some members of my crew that may have resulted in a crime. By not coming forth and cooperating with the investing Officers, I may have broken some laws." He hesitated for a few moments before continuing. But that's not what is really bothering me. What tormenting my mind is the fact by keeping quiet I have been having this major morality battle with myself."

The sigh of relief seethed through Harold lips like the steam from a tea kettle.

"Do you remember the night that I came home from work on edge and intolerable? And we had this huge fight about something as trivial as me leaving my underwear on the floor next to the hamper."

Harold thought of the many evenings that they argued about a lot insignificant things, yet he refrained from being his usual sarcastic self.

"Yes . . . er . . . of course it's coming back to me. You came home that particular day like 'a bat out of hell', ticked me off too, but please finish telling me what happen that day.

"Let me start off by telling you about the events that led up to that day. We had this 'newbie' in our crew who just finish boot camp, and was still green behind the ears when it came to the politics aboard ship. But that's not all. It was so oblivious that he was gay. It was the consensus of the crew that he was planted there by one the recruiting officer's as joke on the Navy Corp. I wouldn't go so far as to say that he was as flamboyant as Melba, but it was his mannerism that gave him away. And he was smart as hell, knew all there was to know about electronic. This evaluation is coming from my perspective, and I'm no slouch when it comes to electronics. In fact one of the reason that I was assigned to this crew, was because of my skills in electronics." He spoke with pride.

Harold smile at David's moment of self confident, yet he said nothing, even though he was overly anxious for David to finish telling him about what happen, he thought it best to let him take his time.

"He reminded me of a copper penny, all shiny and new, handsome, very neat and intelligent, a little to intelligent according to some of the members in our crew. I personally thought that he was a great access to the Navy, and I wondered a many of times, that since he had formal education, why he didn't go to the U.S. Navy Academy.

His main fault was his arrogance though, particular in his approaches and response, and that definite did not set well with any of us, and especially certain ones."

"I thought that there was sought of a rapport developing between the two of us, mainly because of our common interest in electronics. I tried to warn him. I told him once to just 'be cool' and ' go with the flow'." David could feel the adrenalin sore through his body. "I told him that it would be plenty of opportunities for him to prove himself once he finish technical training. I could sense that he thought himself superior in our tentative relationship, and my warnings to him went in one ear and out the other. He acted as if he wasn't worried about it. I said to myself fuck it, if he wasn't worried about, why in the fuck should I worry about it. But I knew that there was going to be trouble, I mean big trouble.

Especially when one day the C.O. gave him a command, that he felt was not in relationship with his duties, and he he barked back at one of the Officers."

He stared into the night as if he had envision that person in the same room with them.

"Lieutenant Brad O'Ryan was a Kentucky 'redneck'. In the past, he and I had a few altercations, but he knew that I was a force to be reckon with. He knew that he was not a physical match for me, and that I had the comradery and respect from most of the crewmen aboard ship. Officer O'Ryan figured that since the 'newbie' had burned all of his bridges, that he had a free hand to handle him anyway he choose. And that's just what the fuck he did to. He started by giving him bullshit assignments, none of which was conducive to the type of work that he was assigned to do. Then there were the pranks, and the usual colorful slangs and distasteful jokes, and gay magazines left in his 'rack'.

I thought; 'there, but for the grace of God go I', and I did nothing to intervene.

I could tell by the 'newbie' demeanor that he was having a difficult time trying to stay afloat. He never confided in me, but word got around that he went to one of the Senior Officer Commander to complain.

Stupid! Dumb ideal!

We shared a cabin, along with two other mates, but I hardly spend my nights there because as you know I am usually here with you. That week we were on 'Peak and Tweak' alert, and we had a lot of technical problems, and so no one in our crew was allowed to go ashore for at least forty-eight hours.

On the second night around 'zero dark thirty' I went to the birthing area, and before I climbed up to my 'rack', I noticed that everyone was there in the cabin except the 'newbie'. I tried not to think much about it, because I figured that he was probably in the latrine. I popped in two Tylenol PM, and tried to relax so I could fall asleep, but there something about ' newbie' absence that was nagging at the back of my head.

For one, I didn't know how long he been gone, but I know that I had been lying there for almost an hour. Another thing was that his bed had no creases, no signs that he had been to bed. Most importantly was his eyeglasses that he wore all the time, was on the floor beside his ' rack', and that was alarming to me. Although these things were pestering me, I tried to lay there hoping that I could fall asleep.

No such luck, so finally I got up and went to the latrine looking for him. There was blood on the floor near one of the urinal. It look like someone had tried to wipe it up, but they missed a smear on the line of the floor near the base of the urinal. I tried to tell myself that it could be anybody's blood. Someone could have gotten hurt on the job and came to the latrine to cleanup."

He looked at Harold, but he was invisible to him.

"I sneaked up to the 'Mess Deck', wishfully thinking that he may have gone there for a late night snack.

There was no one there except the Wharf rats and so I gave up and went back to my cabin hoping that he had return. I laid in my 'rack' for I don't know how long before falling asleep, cursing the 'newbie', cursing the situation, and shit, cursing myself for giving a damn.

I over slept the next morning, so when I awoke, I was alone in the cabin, I suspected that everyone was at the 'Mess' eating breakfast. I picked the 'newbie's' glasses up from the floor and placed them on the table, thinking later that it might have been the wrong thing to do if anything foul had actually happen to him.

I asked some crewmen if they seen the 'newbie' around. I got a lot of irritated and indifference replies, until finally I said fuck it. When he didn't show up for duty at all that day, I felt duty bound to report his absence to my commanding Officer.

I was glad that the leave to shore for our crew was lifted, and was I comforted in knowing that I was coming home to you."

He caressed Harold's chest and stomach, and Harold moan with delight.

"Days later he was reported AWOL. I was questioned a few times. I told them nothing of course, but it didn't matter anyway because no one seemed to give a good goddamn.

Lieutenant O'Ryan continue being his same old ass hole self, but I suspected that he knew something about the missing of the 'newbie' and that he was good in hiding the fact that he knew. I decided that I just couldn't deal with the guilt any longer so I went to the Chaplain for counseling, and I confess to him everything I knew about the Lieutenant's misconduct towards the 'newbie' and I even went so far as to tell him of my suspicion about the alleged AWOL of the 'newbie' Private Timothy Kinnard.

These sessions, I thought was suppose to be confidential, but somehow the Lieutenant caught wind of it, and he and his buddy crewmen started harassing me. Some of the guys that I thought were my comrades treated me like I was not to be trusted. As you well know, 'closet gay' I may be, but one thing for sure I'm no 'punk', and I pride myself in taking just about anything that they may throw my way.

I wrote my wife for the first time in a year, telling her what she and my daughter got legally coming to them in case something happen to me. I'm sure that she's got another man in her life by now, but I can't concern myself with that right now, I just want to make sure that my daughter is provided for if anything was to happen to me."

"David you got to go to the Senior Officer and tell him what you know. Maybe he will see to your safety until after the investigation is over."

David smiled at Harold's naiveness, and then kissed him long and hard.

Harold look searchingly into David's dark brown eyes.

"Promise me that you do the right thing to keep your self safe, and come back to me whole." There was a teasing grin that spread across David's smooth ebony face.

"No shit now David, you got to promise me that you will hold on until you come home." Fear flooded Harold's face, as a tear rolled down his cheek, and his thin lips repeated the phrase . . . ."You got to hold on."

CHAPTER THREE

The Professor

Words like antebellum, assimilation, manifestation, and legions of other related and equivocal terms were whirl pooling around in his head. He kicked around some of the hardback books that cluttered the plush beige carpet to make a pathway to the other side of the livingroom. He rummage through the old roll-top desk in search of his unfinished Thesis on Moorish culture and the Proscription of the Muslim Faith, and inked in a few concepts on the outside margin of one the pages.

He scratched at his scalp, loosening the soft reddish gray curls that darn the top of his head and then he smoothed out the kinks in his red and silver goatee. It was an unconscious ritual with him, a habitual practice he slumped into when ever he was in deep contemplation.

He then became anxious about something, of what he could not remember. It was frustrating to him to think that it must have been important. He tried more word games, but nothing came to mind. He open the bible to the book of Genesis and read chapter nine verses twenty through twenty-five, and he tried like so many times before to equate the mystery behind the reason for the justification of slavery. "The curse of Ham", the curse that Noah placed on Ham's son Canaan. He pondered over the curse that was used by members of the Abrahamic religion, which theorized that Ham begotten the dark skin branch of mankind, and it was the Rabbis pedagogy: that there were three copulations in the ark, and they were all punished; the dog, the raven, and Ham. He devoured the part about the dog being doomed to be tied, the raven expectorates his seed into the mouth of his mates, and Ham was smitten in his skin.

He thought ; what about the theory that it was Cush, Cannan's brother who was the progenitor of the African race? Rationalization. Enslavement of the Canaanites."

With ferocity he slammed the bible shut, open it and slammed three more times and he mouthed out loud to the off white walls, and the vast emptiness of the apartment. "There are no explanation in the bible as to what 'the smitten of Ham's skin' meant." He shouted a thundering roar. "How was it then that the Islamic race, and the European race could use, something that was written around 1000BC to justify racism. Well we have the Rabbinic scholars to thank for the misinterpretation to the equality of the Black race."

He pulled open his brown metal filling cabinet and fingered through the folders of ancient articles. Articles about the riots in Watts, and Detroit. Yellow frail articles about the Black Power Movement, the march on Washington, and the march from Selma to Montgomery. Tear stained articles about the assassinations of John F. Kennedy, Bobby Kennedy, and Martin Luther King. The bottom draw of the filling cabinet had names, addresses, and phone numbers of NAACP, SNCC, CORE, SCLC, other related organizations He closed and then open the cabinet draw four times. Whispered words pressed passed his thin pink lips and exploded into particles of dust into the sunlight that had enveloped the room.

"Systematic disenfranchisement of the American Negro. Oppression. Exploitation. Political Lynching." He looked passed the piles of old newspaper that lined the wall like bottom paneling. Staring at nothing in particular, his mind was lost in thoughts about improving his dissertation on the breakdown in the moral fiber of the new Renaissance African American.

Many of such unfinished dissertations were scattered through out the apartment, most in obscured places, dismissed from his mind until he felt the need to excavate them. He lost his train of thought. He looked at his watch, removed it from his wrist and knocked it four times against the side table, made a mental note for the hundredth time to go to Wal-mart for a replacement battery. His stomach growled, and he went into the narrow kitchen to check the refrigerator for eggs. There was just an empty egg carton, that he had absent mindedly left on the inside door compartment. He thought to make some butter and toast, but there was no bread, in fact the only edible thing in the refrigerator was a yellow onion and a small tub of margarine. He cursed out loud. "Shit! I forgot to pick up a few things from the store last night to tie me over until my check come in the mail." He re-collected his thoughts. "Or maybe that was two nights ago and today is the first of the month." He couldn't remember. He quietly closed and open the refrigerator door four times.

He made sure that he had his door keys in his pocket before leaving the apartment to go downstairs to the mail box. He cared nothing about his disarranging attire, or the potent odor of his body or his scabrous bare feet. He commissioned the elevator to stop on the six floor and he settle inside the eight by eight foot square box with walls of black marble. He then pressed the plastic one button on the metal panel.

"Good afternoon Professor."

He looked at the familiar petite brown skin woman with surprise. She had deep black piercing eyes, that he imagine had the ability to read a person and sum them up with one glance. Although it was cold, She was dressed in skimpy attire and her hair was done up tight into small black and red micro braids.

"Don't even try it Professor, you know you saw me standing here."

"Shanita! How you doing ? I'm sorry that I didn't notice you right off, my mind is miles from here. What's up with you? You been behaving yourself?"

"Fuck no! You know better than that Professor."

"The question was rhetorical. I do know you better than that."

The bell sounded and the elevator released it's captives. Shanita kept in pace with his steps as he headed down the hall towards the mail box.

"Professor, I ain't wanting to ask you, but I'm hurting. Can you let me hold ten bucks til I get paid Friday. I'm good for it, I promise."

He could see how anxious she was, and he knew that when Friday came around Shanita would be no where to be found. The sickness had her in a tight hold, and he was familiar with the feeling, and he felt sorry for her.

"What day is today Shanita?"

"Monday. Man I promise to bring the money to you as soon as I get paid."

"No that's not what I meant. I just could not remember the day. Is it the fifth day of January?"

"Shit yell. Professor what you been smoking? And, do you have any more that you care to share with a sister?" She smiled a crooked smile.

He laughed and turned the key in the mail box. He was happy to see that the check was there, between a stack of delinquent bills and advertisement. He tried secretly to place the check back in between the bills, but Shanita piercing eyes caught sight of rectangle manila envelope. He open and closed the small door to the metal box four times.

"You know Professor I ain't trying to get into your business or nothing, but don't you think that it would be safer is you had direct deposit?"

"I don't trust banks. I don't trust banks, the FBI, or the IRS. I had my dealings with them in the past. I will take my chances on the postman."

"You know what it's like around here. People are up and down this hallway all times at night. Some of them would steal a penny off a dead mans eyes. I ain't just talking about the tenants. You know we don't have security round here no more. It didn't make much difference when we did, there still were all kinds of people hanging around."

Dissentious shouts and vociferous expletive reverberated the hallway from the direction of the rental office.

"I fucking dare you to put my shit out on the sidewalk, I fucking dare you!"

An angry looking tall husky ebony woman hovered over the desk of Cheryl Lucas (the office manager). Although Cheryl out weighed the woman by at least a hundred pounds, she felt intimidated by the woman's size and threatening demeanor. Although Cheryl was pretty in the face, she was morbidly obese and if the woman decided to make true her threats and lunge at her she could not move her body fast enough to escape her attack.

She had just finished gorging down a Whopper, large fries, and a diet Pepsi, and was opening up a pack of Hostess Jewels for dessert, when the tenant walked in, shouting obscenities at her.

"Miss Johnson you can shout until the roof caves in, what's done is done. It is now out of my hands. This is your third time being served with an eviction notice, and you knew that this was going to happen. I have given you a lot more chances than I have given to my other tenants."

"You ain't gave me shit, but a bunch of lawyers fees, court fees, and late fees. You fucking knew that I wouldn't be able to catch up. You white whale. Fuck you Jabba The Hutt."

The women's boisterous confrontation rented the stale air and was attracting a lot of attention. People started coming in by ones then twos, and soon enough there was a small crowd that had gathered at the front entrance inside the building near the office. The maintenance man and the assistant manger Elaine squeezed by the on lookers and enter the office. Cheryl felt a little more confident with both of her associates being there to witness what was going on.

"Miss Johnson you got until the end of the day to move all of your stuff off the property. If you're still here tomorrow morning, I will have the Sheriff come out and physically remove you."

The small crowd grew in size, and people understanding the situation started a heated conversation among themselves, some were even bold enough to shout comforting phases to the tenant, but it didn't help, it just added fuel to her fury.

Miss Johnson snorted and leaped on top the huge cluttered desk, knocking papers and office supplies to the floor. She grab Cheryl by her double chin and tried to pull her heavy body off her swivel chair. When that did not work, she tighten her wide man like fist, and punched Cheryl up side her head. Cheryl yapped like a wounded dog and fell to the floor.

For a tall husky woman, Miss Johnson moved swiftly and unerring to the big mass of flesh and fabric that rested helplessly on the floor.

"I will fuck you up. You don't give a flying fuck about me and my kids being out on the street. You'll a heartless tub of lard."

Cheryl frantically twisted on the floor, trying desperately to get to her feet. Miss Johnson knew that she had an advantage and she wasted no time in her attack. She kicked Cheryl in the face and stomach.

The Professor and two other men grabbed Miss Johnson by the arms and they pushed and pulled her, moving out of sequence with each other, but they finally was able to get her through the narrow office door and through the crowd. She had the strength of a raging bull and she struggled against them still cursing the office manager.

The Professor tried to reason with her. "Miss Johnson I know how you feel, we all know how you feel. We been there and done that, but beating Cheryl up is not the way you should have handle the situation. I'm sure by now Elaine has call the police, and they are surely going to arrest you for assault, and probably call in CPS if you don't have anyone to watch your kids."

She looked at the Professor light-brown freckled face and into his chromatic eyes that seem to switch from orange to reddish brown every time he blinked.

She had happened upon him many times before, in the elevator, in the hallway, in front of the mail box and in passing to and from the building. He was always kind and polite to her. They had conversed once or twice about trivial matters. The beast inside of her was subsiding and the sweat dripped down from her forehead and cool her face. Her sensibility was mounting and she realized the graveness of the predicament she gotten herself in.

"You don't know Professor what I have been through these last few months. That no good son-of-bitch of a man left me four months ago, left me footing the bills, and trying to feed three kids and myself on the little bit of money I make at my shitty job."

Tears ran down her face and mingled with the sudor.

"I hear you sister, and I am not trying to be presumptuous, and tell you how to handle your business, but the dye has been cast, and you are in a heap of trouble. You might can save yourself from being thrown into jail, if you go in there and apologize to Cheryl."

"Hell would freeze over before I apologize to that stubborn cunt. When my man left me, I went to her like a woman. I said to her, Cheryl, Jessie left me, you can take his name off the lease. I asked her to give me some time so that I can try and get some help from the Housing Authority to help pay part of my rent. She say's to me; well Miss Johnson you have been here nearly two years, and you have been late with your rent almost every month. And I said to her I pay it don't I? I never miss a whole month, now do I. And even though it's hard on me financially, I pay the late fee's too. Now don't I ? The next thing I know when I got home from work one evening there was a notice of eviction taped to my door.

I appreciate your words of reasoning, I really do, but you can't image what it's been like for me. Shit like this happens to me all the time, and I'm just tired, tired of being tired. No I ain't gonna apologize, if the bitch wants to send me to jail, then fuck her, shit I need the rest any how. Hell fire, my mother can take care the kids for a while, she owe me for the times I use to sell my young pussy so she could get her fix on."

She turned away and walked loosely down the hallway towards the elevator.

The Professor knew very little about Miss Johnson, just some collective comments made in the past by neighboring tenants. They said that she had a hard life, and that the man she was living with was not the children's father. There was also talk among the neighbor that they would often hear them arguing, shouting obscenities, and throwing furniture around inside the apartment.

Shanita called his name and he turned his attention away from Miss Johnson.

"Do you think that you can lend me the ten bucks?"

"Sure Shanita, give me two or maybe three hours, I should have the money by then."

He could see her body trembling and perspiring and he knew that her pain had gotten progressively worst.

"I don't know if I can last that long. Can you lend me a couple bucks and I will try to bargain with that." He reached deep into his pants pocket and collected lint, three bills and some coins, and handed them to Shanita.

A big burst of wind brushed his cheek, and tugged at his overcoat, as he hurried his tall thin frame from the bus stop, and across the hard brown lawn to the front entrance of River Front Tower apartments.

The 'mares' tail' moved across the blue sky at a snails pace, and the Professor took notice of the feathery and threadlike formation, and he made a mental prediction of more cold weather to come, with a possibility of snow.

A strong coffee colored hand pushed open the door to let him in. He recognize Raheem, his neighbor on the third floor.

"Assalamu Alikum Professor. Come in before you freeze your testicle off."

"Assalamu Alikum Wa Rahmatutah Wa Barakatuh brother Raheem.

'They pounded' (soulful hand shake and hug).

"It Looks like we may get some snow."

"How can you tell my brother?"

"The Cirrus clouds tell's it all."

They both settled into a comfortable silence as they peer at the sky through the glass double doors in the small lobby.

"I haven't seen you in a while Professor. I miss our meetings on the park bench, and our long discussion about the Etymology of the Holy Qur'an."

"I have a low tolerance for the cold weather, so I pretty much hibernate during the winter, except on days I have to go to my doctor or to the store for provisions."

"In that case Professor you must come to my apartment on the third floor, apartment 301 and we can continue our discussion on the Qur'anic guidance."

The words Meccan revelation, kalamallah, dhikrallah seared his brain and he tried hard to discount them.

"All due respect to you Raheem I am a little used up with the discussion of the bible and the qur'an.

I did time in State prison, spent eight years of my twenty years, close with prison inmates who practice the Muslim faith, some of them, like myself were sycophantic, just there in pretense, under the protected group. The truth is, I am agnostic. I have a Graduate degree from Howard University, and I am by no means an ideologist, but an infinite student of many notions and theories."

"In all honesty Professor, I often wondered about you. How a man of your intelligent could end up living in a place like this, not to knock every tenant that live here, because there are some pretty decent folks that occupy this building. People like myself, who are striving every day to make their life better and move out of this place."

"I wasn't aware that I was such an enigmatic fancy in your mind. I have always candid about my life, so if it was anything that you wanted to know about me, all you had to do was ask."

"Well for one thing, I would have never guessed that you been to prison, Professor. Never would have guessed in a thousand years. You don't appear broken in spirit like most convicts. Or ex-convicts."

"That's because my body was in prison, not my mind. I had access to the library,

and was able to do tremendous amount of research. Besides prison is a vessel to a smorgasbord of human suffering. I've always said that if you wanted to learn first hand about human behavior, you can learn a whole hell of a lot in prison. I will tell you about that someday. I don't mind purging, it's cathartic, good for the soul."

He exited the lobby through the second set of double doors, opening and closing them four times. He did not look back to see the puzzle look on Raheem face. He had seen the look before on many faces. Faces of many ages, sizes, and different shades of skin tone.

Raheem yelled at his back, trying to catch him before he was devoured by the elevator.

"What about Friday night? What about coming to my place Friday night? I can get my wife to cook us a good home meal"

"What time?"

"Seven."

He stepped into the mouth of the elevator, before shouting out his final reply.

"I will be there. However I don't eat red meat or anything with whole wheat."

∽

After being in their neatly decorated apartment for over and hour, he surmised that he like the Mahdi's, they treated him warmly. Seven year old Sakeena and six year old Zaina, the two Mahdi girls, had superlative shiny mocha faces with curious glowing eyes and they were genetic replicas of their parents. They were normal rambunctious children with inquisitive minds and loving deportment. He had very little experience with children their ages and he felt out of touch with the appropriate verbiage, and so he left it up to them to ask what ever questions they may want to ask and he answered with as much passable information that he could. They soon got bored with him and locked themselves back into their own little world.

Raheem's wife, Ayeh was a silent woman, and the Professor guessed that she was a private woman that kept all her secrets locked up inside. She was very attractive, with deep dimples that would capture the heart when she smiled and she smiled a lot that night. The Professor was secretly envious of Raheem. Although she wore a modest ecru long sleeve shell, you didn't need X-ray vision to see the shape of her perky round breasts and protruding nipples. And her black cotton skirt with three layers of pleats that started at the waist and ended at the tip of her flat shoes, even that stylish skirt could not disguise her shapely hips.

He looked greedily at her, wishing that she was his. In some ways she reminded him of his wife Rochelle, whom he hadn't thought of in years.

"Ayeh you are a great cook, I really enjoyed the Korma." When Raheem first introduced her to him, she had insisted that he called her by her first name.

"Thank you Professor." She said, boosting his heart with her gentle smile.

He dismissed the urge to tell her that Curtis is his given name, and confess that he never went to post graduate school, (although for years it has always been one of his goals)ed. People started calling him the Professor because they perceived him as a person who seem to have many answers on certain subject matters.

"It's an old recipe that my mother-in-law gave me. It wasn't to spicy for you?"

He threw her a warm smile.

"I did have to drink a lot of water, but it was delicious."

"My family like a lot of chilli powder and pepper corn in their food, but I think that yogurt kinda' balances it out."

She dismissed Sakeena and Zaina from the dining room table. The two girls looked relieved and ran to the entertainment center and cut on the flat screen television, and flopped down on the plush carpet in front of it.

She accidently brushed his shoulders with her tender breasts as she was clearing the table, and it sent an electric shock wave through his body. He discretely placed his hand over his groin to hide his shame.

He remembered that he had not been with a woman in almost a year, he knew it was because he has been so immersed with anxiety and manic depression. And then there was his research for his book, that is if he could finally determine which of his thesis was worth while. Maybe he should do like his psychiatrist suggested, and pick another field of study, since writing about racism, and the African American plight was too personal.

He thought about cultural diversity, ethnicity, apartheid, and other similar words that incarcerated his brain and he forgot where he was until Raheem called out his name.

"You ok man? You looked like you was lost in thought. Ayeh wanted to know if you wanted dessert. Tonight is your lucky night because she made raisin pudding, which she seldom makes unless it's a religious holiday."

"Well I am truly grateful that she thinks that much of my visit to go out of her way to make such a delightful meal, and it would be insufferable of me if I was to turn down her raisin pudding, so lay it on me my man."

Raheem put two scoops of the congeal dessert on a small glass dish, and slid it within the Professor's reach, and then poured them both a glass of cheap port.

With satisfied bellies and a relaxing atmosphere the two talked of current events, they talked of the upcoming President Obama inauguration. And they talked about how proud and exuberant spirit of the African American are now because of Obama. They talked about the war in Iraq, and situation with the economy. They talked late into the evening.

Ayeh sent the kids off to bed, and grabbed a soft spot on the living room couch and listened attentively to the two men as they went back and forth about their opinions concerning political topics.

The Professor could tell by the expression on Ayeh face and her wide infectious smile, that she was impressed with his wisdom.

Later into the conversation, both Ayeh and Raheem became his student, and their attentiveness caused him to pause and reflect on his past life.

He said to them. "It's been such a longtime since I had such a captive audience. You make me feel important and I haven't felt that way in a long time."

He did not know if it was the friendliness of the Mahdi's or the red wine mixed with his medication, or the combination of all three, because he felt wired, and did not want the night to end.

He decided to extend his visit with the Mahdi's by given them a crystal ball look into his personal past. He knew that Raheem wondered about it but tonight he must have felt too polite to ask him.

"Raheem you asked me the other day, how I came to live here, in other words what particular set circumstances torpedo me here. For you made it seems as if the River Front Tower is some dreadful and unconsolable asylum."

He did not give Raheem the chance for rebuttal. "But I don't share your opinion of the people that live here. However for now, let me start off by saying that I was raised in a middle class family with a father who was employed, and worked hard everyday as an Heavy Equipment Operator. My father was a common man, with common habits. He may have an occasional can of beer on weekends in front of the television watching his favorite sports program, he was not by my definition an alcoholic.

My mother, well my mother as the old folks would say was a God fearing woman, She also worked hard everyday as a teacher at Springfield public school.

I remember that earlier on in my life my parents struggle to make ends meet, and for a while we move from tenement to tenement in D.C., and believe me if you can live in the tenements in D.C. you can live in any tenement in America.

I was brought up knowing four simple things that was impounded into my brain from as long as I care to remember. One, was that I had the potential to be successful in life and to be what ever I wanted to be. Well actually that was two things, but you try to argue that with my mother. Two, to keep a positive attitude in life. Three, you are judged by the company you keep, and four, if you lay down with dogs you get up with fleas.

For a long time I was dedicated to the tutelage of my parents and their guidance, and it was what kept me off the D.C. streets and away from gangs.

I focused on school, and worked hard to keep my grades high, invested my time in some academic programs that helped me to earn a scholarship from Howard.

College life was a far cry different lifestyle than I had at home with my parents. From the time I stepped foot on campus ground I felt like an alien.

Like myself there were some nerds there of course, but it didn't take me long to change hats. I gravitated towards the more radical liberal minded group of students.

It was an exciting time for me. It was the early seventies during the war in Viet Nam and every conscious thinker on campus had their way in expressing their views and dissatisfaction about the war.

We, that is the group I became involved with, entertained ourselves with discussion of the Viet Nam war, Communism and Socialism in any place that seem suitable for us to do so. We gathered for long debates, in our dormitory, at Raves, night clubs, and even at picnics in the park.

We got together with the main purpose to stimulate our minds and spirits, and smoking hashish, swallowing Peyote button, and sugar cubes soaked with LSD was part of the social scene.

I manage to graduate and not long after graduation I was fortunate enough to land a job teaching. It was during that time that I met my ex-wife. Also during that time I crossed the line from doing drugs socially to abusing drugs heavy drugs like meth and cocaine."

He didn't want to look at their face, afraid that their faces would be draped with disappointment or disapproval. He gulped down the last bit of wine that was left in his glass and forged on.

"If someone was to ask me back then about why I hooked up with Portia, other than the fact that she was good looking, I would truly have been lost for words."

He laughed because he knew how inconceivable that was to Raheem and Ayeh because they knew him well enough now to know that he loved to talk.

"To be honest I really don't know why I married Portia. She was good-looking, but I have dated better looking women than her. Sex, well I'm not going to go into our sex life, but I've had better sex with other women.

Portia was very maternal and demanding and she had this griping hold over me, that even now, right now, today I can not fully explain. Maybe I thought that she was the 'ying to my yang'. I really don't know what coin of phrase that would fit, all I know was that I was so infatuated with her.

One thing I knew for sure was that she made me forget the normalcy of life. The both of us became swooped up into this ruinous affair with cocaine.

He looked directly at Raheem.

Cocaine is a terrible drug my friend, don't ever try it. It's a drug that offered a false sense of confidence, a sense of well being and Portia and I spent a lot of our time chasing after that first high. I spent so much time getting high with Portia that I lost my teaching job. We had to think of a way that was feasible for the both of us to support our habit and that's when we decided to sell drugs."

Vivid memories of the things that they had to do and the methods they used to transport and market the drugs were flooding his brain.

"I was like a dog chasing after his own tail. I thought that I was being smart by learning all there was to know about buying and selling cocaine. I was doing pretty well for a while, even became enterprising. As lone dealer, I was able to get financial backing from Black

Entrepreneur, who wanted to make some fast money to get or keep their business going. It was a good arrangement that lasted about a minute.

After five years of moving contraband from Harlem to Maryland, my luck soon ran out. On route back to Maryland I was stopped by a state trooper, who found six kilos of cocaine in the hollow of my spare tire.

It took me five years to build up a small empire, and it took only me five weeks to lose it all." He breathe a sigh of despair. Raheem pour him another glass of wine.

"I had good lawyers, but even with the best lawyer we could not disprove the impacting amount of evidence I had stack against me. Things was not going well for me during my trial and the proverbial 'nail that sealed my coffin shut' was when Portia testified against me." He decided not to gulp down the wine this time, instead he sipped at the smooth liquid slowly.

"I never put all my eggs in one basket. I had in my possession at one time three quarters of a million dollars. I had it hidden all over my apartment and even a great deal of it I hid in my old bedroom at my parents place."

Raheem and Ayeh were both wide eye in disbelief. Raheem whistled, "wow three quarters of a million dollars. I can't even fix my mind to imagine what that amount of money look like."

"I spent a lot of time in prison reflecting on how much money went through my hands. I had it buried and waiting for me inside appliances like the vacuum cleaner, under the burner on top of the stove, taped behind the refrigerator, in the washing machine, and dryer. Of course Portia knew of all the places I had the money hid and as part of her deal with the District Attorney she was to help them find the money I had hidden away."

Because of Portia cooperation with the police she received a light sentence of five years. Eighteen months of her sentence she had already served in jail while waiting for the trial and she was out of prison after three years."

He looked intensely into Raheem eyes. "Now check this out. Portia had her faults, but stupidity wasn't one of them. She gave up all of my hiding places, except the one at my parents house. She managed to con my parents into believing that she was remorseful, and that the District Attorney had tricked her into testifying against me. I got a letter from my mom, and in that letter she mentioned that Portia had been there. She mention the conversation they had between them. Of course she made off with the money and I have no idea where she is, and I am glad in away. I remember thinking after I read that letter, how much I hated her, and how much I wanted to hurt her. I wanted to strangle her with my bare hands. All the years of dealing drugs, I never had to use force or violence, but at that moment and for months later I wanted to kill her."

He checked his watch, removed it from his wrist, and knocked it four times against the Mahdi diningroom table. He made a mental note to purchase a battery the next time he shopped at Walmart. It was getting late, according to Raheem clock on the wall. It was nearly eleven, and even though he could see that Raheem and Ayeh were eagerly digesting every word of his morally decayed history, he decided that it was time to go home. And if the Mahdi's wanted to invite him back for more self purging, he was certainly willing, and most importantly it would give him a chance to see Ayeh again.

His thoughts of pluralism, cultural and racial assimilation were losing their place in his encephalon. For several weeks thoughts of Ayeh were predominate now. He imagine her with him, kissing him and loving him. Yet he needed more, if nothing more than still images of her. He searched anxiously in his bureau draw for his old Polaroid six hundred camera. He retrieved it from beneath a pile of knotted white ankle socks, which he neatly arranged and rearranged back in place four times.

He was glad that his apartment was located on the westside of the building facing the front courtyard, in that way he saw her when she left or returned from where ever she went each day. He even saw her a few times on the playground with Sakeena and Zaina, and he snapped pictures of them. Her scheduled leaving and returning home varied, but he did notice a certain routine, and scratched down these habits on a piece of paper.

He took pictures of her on the mornings when she put the kids on the school bus, and then again when she caught the city transit two hours later.

One day in particular he knew that she would be gone for four hours, and so he busied himself in the apartment until she came home. He made his bed up four times, making sure of the hospital corners. He cleaned and rinse the ceramic tiles in the shower four times, giving special abrasive attention to the mildew and soap scum. With out any technical aid, he organized and reorganized his filing system, changing his files by date to files by related issues, from related issues to source and reference, and then back to files by date.

He looked at the, metal square frame clock on the wall. It was close to the time that Ayeh will be getting off the bus, and he went to the front window to look for her.

She stepped off the bus with two other women, and they were absorbed in a cordial conversation. They laughed lightly at something that was amusingly said between the three of them. The camera made a short mechanical sound and then ousted the still shot, and he took three more pictures of her. They left fresh footprints in the dusting of snow, and within minutes Ayeh and the two women disappeared inside the building.

He compared the photos that he had taken of her that day and the days before. He decided that they were just not good enough. He felt the need to be near her and he decided to pay her a visit.

When she open the door to her apartment, she still had on her gold silk Hijab.

"Professor. You must been born to live a long life, because Raheem and I were talking about you this morning. He was saying that he wanted to get your 'take' on a certain article in the Sunday's newspaper."

"An article in the Sunday's paper?"

She motioned for him to enter.

"Come in Professor, it's cold in the hallway. Sorry I should have invited you in right away. I was just so surprise to see you today."

Although he had not been outside the whole day, he rubbed the soles of his shoes against the straw welcome mat in the hall four times.

He followed her to the living room and sat next to her on the sofa.

He thought how pretty she looked in the light of the afternoon sun that filtered through the power blue curtains. And he thought "God I would like so much to kiss her right now. Too hold he tightly and never let her go.

She could feel a particular energy bounced off him and on to her, and she was in awe of the feeling.

"Forgive me, I could be so dingy at times. You came here for a reason? Did you wanted to talk to Raheem about something?"

"Yes. I missed his company in the last few weeks, and I thought I would come over and we could just hang out for few hours."

He lied. He knew Raheem schedule well, he watched him get into his car around six that morning leaving for Thomas Nelson community College. He also knew that around two o'clock he would report to work as a Coordinator at a telemarketing service.

"Well right now, he's probably at work." She quickly glance at the watch on her wrist. "Yes right now he's at work, and he don't get home until around nine-thirty tonight. He goes to dinner around four. I can give you his cell number if you want to call him during his dinner break."

"No that want be necessary. I would not feel right disturbing the man's meal time. Just tell him I came by, and that I will try to catch him another time.

I started to come over Friday, but then I remembered that Fridays and Saturdays are the days he is normally at the Mosque. Sundays, well that's a real family day for most people, and I didn't want to impose."

He tried to think of other ways to prolong his visit. When she looked at him it filled him with a warm lustful sensation, and he felt that he would walk to the end of the earth for one of her smiles.

"You can come around at anytime Professor, you'll always welcome. I will tell Raheem that you stopped by, and I am sure that he will be sorry that he missed you."

"Well . . . you both have an open invitation to come up to my apartment, although I must warn you that my place is nowhere up to some people's standard."

"I 'll bet that your place is just fine."

"Trust me modesty is not one of my virtues. You said that Raheem wanted to talk to me about something he read in the Sunday's newspaper?

"Oh yes. It was about a rare first edition copy of the first book to be published by a former slave by the name of Phillis Wheatley. It was published in 1773, and was acquired by the Jamestown Yorktown Foundation. He's interested in hearing your views about this particular article. He knows how you get fired up just talking about the way certain White and Jewish groups are acquiring important African American artifacts."

He was glad for the excuse to spend more time with them.

"I am very familiar with Phillis Wheatley literary work. A lot of her literature she wrote while she was still in slavery. I remember how very gripping and poignant her literary pieces were. It is my opinion, and I put her up there with W.E.B DuBois and Booker T. Washington, that she has played a very important and extensive role in African American history. My favorite of her poems is 'On Being Brought from Africa to America'. Raheem was right I do have radical opinions about things, like the fleecing of our history."

He was glad of the chance to spend time with her, but he wanted to change the subject. She had set him off on his political belief, and he didn't want anything to change his mood.

"Do I smell coffee?"

"I put a pot on seconds after I arrived home. Would you like a cup?"

She was so gracious in her demeanor, very articulate, and he wondered if she had any formal education.

"Sure. That is if it's not too much of a bother."

"How could it be a bother ? Remember I asked you, and besides I would love to have some company right now. I just came home from work, and I need to unwind, and you're just the one to help me fill my time until the kids come home from school."

If all of a sudden the sky would turn black and roared with thunder, and there was a flash of lightening that came crashing through the picture window, and struck him down, he would die happy. All the while watching his heart escape his chest and dance gleefully in the thick of the carpet.

"What type of work do you do?" He calmly asked.

"I work part-time as a billing clerk, and it can be stressful at times, especially when you dealing with people. Whew, anyway I made it a rule not to bring my work problems home and my personal problems to work. Soooo, lets talk about something else."

She poured him a cup of the steaming hot brew, and he accepted her offer of sugar and cream. He lifted the thick mug up and to his lips four times before finally taking a sip. If she noticed she respectfully said nothing.

She removed the Hijab from her head, neatly folded it and put it on the table where they sat. for a few moments they sat their caressing their mugs firmly as if it was some spirited creature that would leap from their hands to freedom.

They glanced at each other quickly, and then again, this time longer. And then all of a sudden it was this magnetic field between them, this pull that was so forceful, that it made their temperature rise and their lungs fight for air. What made her see him in the same light that he saw her was perplexing to him, but the look in her eyes were undeniable, and overwhelmingly with delectation.

"You know there is a certain thing that you do with your face when you take a sip of your coffee. Your nose wrinkles up and your dimples stretches out to a deep vertical line."

She smiled and said. "Are you trying to hurt my feelings?"

"No I think that it's appealing."

It's been a long time since he made an effort to woo a woman, and he was glad that she knew what was in his heart. He wanted to say more, to be more personable with her, but he was afraid that he would be moving too fast. He wanted so badly to kiss her full lips, to hold her so close and tight, that they would appeared to be one solid entity. He threw caution to the wind.

"Every since that last night that I was here, I have done nothing but think of you. I don't want to make you feel uncomfortable by me saying this, but I am very attracted to you. I know that you are a woman of deep faith, and that I don't have a snowball chance in hell in getting to know you more intimately. Yet still, I crave you."

She was in battle with her conscious and she waited a few minutes before responding.

"You and me getting together like that may not be as baleful as you think Professor." She swallowed hard. She was overcome with a sense of truth. "I felt a connection to you on that same night. God forgive me for saying and thinking this, but I felt a kinship between us, that I wished that I had with Raheem. The things you said that night moved me, and made me more politically conscious. The more you spoke, the more you became more attractive to me. That night I hoped to lock those feelings up and never to open that door again, but here you are, beating down my door. And I can't help myself."

He moved towards her, taking her in his arms, kissing her hard, gently forcing his tongue in her mouth as far as it would go.

She teasingly bit his lips, and hotly lick his neck.

He caressed her breast, and her nipples swelled with desire. He gripped the curve of her firm butt, and with feverous fingers he found her crevice, although slightly shielded by her dress and undergarments. She moaned and he knew that he couldn't stop there if he wanted to. She reached inside his pants and stroked his manhood, and he clenched his mouth shut as he tried hard not to eject prematurely. He lifted her up from the floor and pressed her back against the wall. He then moved the crouch of her panties to the side and urgently entered her. His member stroked in and out against the walls of her vagina fiercely, and rhythmically, first slowly then with more urgency, until they both exploded. It was over in a matter of minutes, yet the feeling lingered longer and they held on to each other a little longer.

They arranged their clothing and sat down at the diningroom table, trembling as if there was a chill in the room. She refreshen his cup of coffee, and they both sat there in silence. What appropriate words would they say, it was one of those moments that was best spent in silence.

She started to weep. He felt guilty. They reached across the table and held hands. The phone rang, and broke the silence. She checked the caller ID, and saw that the number was Raheem cell number. It was a sobering moment for the both of them.

"Hi honey. Oh no I was in the bathroom. I haven't really decided yet, maybe something with fish. Why? Was there any thing in particular that you have a taste for?"

There were several seconds of pause before she spoke again into the receiver. "Yes. She still had the sniffles, but she wanted to go to school. I called the school from work and they said that she was doing fine. They should be getting home soon." She whispered inside the receiver. "Ok honey I will . . . me too"

He felt awkward sitting there listening to her talk to Raheem on the phone. When she hung the phone up, he move towards her, and she cringed.

"Do you want me to leave?"

"Yes. The kids will be coming home soon. Before you leave, I want to tell you that it would not be right for us to do this again. I mean what we did was so wrong, so against the teachings of Allah. I don't know why I let myself go this far with you. I have broken my vows, and betrayed my husband."

"I can understand why you feel that way, and if you don't want to see me again, I will honor your wishes. However I want you to know that my feelings for you is strong, and that I cannot will myself to stop wanting you. If you do decide that you feel the same way too, you can come to me. I am always home."

He hated leaving her. She stayed glued to that same spot in the kitchen next to the phone, with tears streaming down her face onto her Abaya, darkening it's shade from a royal blue to a violet blue. Reluctantly he walked to the door. He opened and shut the thick steel cold barrier four times and left.

He kissed her eyelids, brushed his thin lips across her velvet nose, and he then hungrily sought after her hot tongue. They were ravenous with their kisses. They undressed quickly and clumsily found their way to his bed.

His hands slowly took it's familiar tour all over her body, from her neck to down the smoothness of her back, around her firm 'lovely lady lump', and then to her round breasts. He dined on her nipples and areola before softly stroking her clitoris, making her arch her back and groan from the wondrous sensation. Her moans of delight conquer him and he couldn't hold out any longer. He penetrated her, moving quickly and with irrepressible surges inside her, until they both surrender to the intense moments of extraordinary pleasure.

He laid next to her, trembling with delight, holding her close, and smelling the sweat of her body mixed with some light delicate fragrance. He smiled at her with a heavy sigh of relief and he kissed her bedew forehead.

She's been coming to his place for six weeks. When she first show up at his place he was jubilant that she changed her mind about not seeing him any more.

He had promise her that he would leave her alone and respect her wishes if she did not want to see him again. And he tried hard the first week, but then after that he was like a driven lion in pursuit. He sweet talked her and used every means in the 'game' to break down her resistance.

On Valentines day he gave her a single yellow rose and a box of Russell and Stover.

She gave it immediately back to him, in fear that her husband would find the rose and become suspicious.

He would anxiously wait for the time for her to come home from work. He would ignore the risk of suspicion from the tenants and meet her at the bus stop to walk her back to her apartment. He felt that nothing would stand in his way to have her.

He would often compliment her about the way she looked on just about every day that they met, only backing off once or twice when she made a fuss about him being overly zealous. Then one day she relented and came to him. Needless to say he was overcome with amazement to see her standing in his doorway, hugging herself, and looking slight and unsure.

He remembered that on that first day that she showed up. She was nervous, but she tried not to let it show. She looked around his apartment. "Not bad for a bachelor." She said. "Don't get offended, but your apartment is cleaner that I expected. I guess I expected that clothes and newspapers would be cluttering the place."

"I have my moments of disarray. Basically I try to keep things in order so if I need something I would know where to find them, but I am not very religious about it.

See what I mean." He pointed to the volumes and volumes of books that adorned the wall next to the picture window.

"Goodness, you must love to read."

"There's a big mess of books, but yes I do love to read and write."

He went over to the roll-top desk and pulled out stacks of paper. They were stacks of paper that were rubber banded into thick sections, and he dropped them one by one onto the desk top.

"This one is my unpublished manuscript about my time I spent in prison. Which by the way I wrote from my prison cell, and it is the only finished written work that I've done. This one is an unfinished human interest manuscript that I wrote about the resuscitation of the bourgeoisie African American." He slammed down three more thick sections of his literary efforts. "And these along with a few others, that are probably in the hallway closet or somewhere, has taken me thirty years to complete. That in itself should tell you a lot about me."

He tried to resist closing the roll-top desk, but the urge was to strong. He closed and open it four times. He hoped that she wasn't put off by his odd behavior. There was no astonishing look upon her face, just a wide approving smile, and he was relieved.

"What's holding you back from finishing?"

"I can't really tell you, other than I am insecure about some of the material I wrote. It's just I always feel that there is more to be added, more information out there that I have yet to discover."

"It would be good if you had a computer."

"I can't always get the information I need from cyber space, if I need to order a book online I go to the library, however I do think that may be it would be a good ideal to document some of my work onto a disc."

She removed her coat and threw it across the arm of his sofa.

"It's feels like a sauna in here."

"I'll turn back the thermostat." He moved the needle from eighty to seventy, back to eighty, then again to seventy, and repeated it two more times before he left it at seventy.

They spent most of that afternoon talking. They talked about her girls, and the school system. They talked about the economy. They talked about her parents and her siblings, and then they talked about his parents.

"Regrettable." He told her. "Both of my parents are deceased. My mother suffered a heart attack inside her classroom while she was in the middle of a lesson. It was during my first year of incarceration. I blame myself for her death.

My father only wrote to me once when I was in prison, and that was to inform me that my mother suffered a heart attack and had died. He never visited me in prison. He came to the trial and stuck it out through the end, but it was the last time that I saw my pop. I wrote him numerous time begging for his forgiveness, I guess it was to hard on him. He passed away a year before I was released from prison. I didn't come out a whole man, so it was just as well that he didn't see his wreck of a son."

That was six weeks ago, and now here she was lying next to him, and he felt like she was his for as long as the situation would allow.

"I got to go, it's getting close to the time that my girls should be getting out of school."

She kissed him lightly on the lips, quickly dressed, and then left. He ached when ever she would leave him. He was wholly satisfied when they were together, and total tormented when they were apart.

He wondered how she would react if she knew that inside of his maple stain wardrobe he built a small shrine consisting of her photos, the box of Russell and Stover, and the wilted yellow rose. The rose was gradually turning brown, and it's fragrance has long since been depleted by the other odors in the closet. Next to the rose was a small stack of passionate prose, professing his love or his lust for her.

CHAPTER FOUR

Cheryl

The devastating news of the Professor and the Mahdi family did not come in full detail at once to Cheryl, but it came reportedly in segments by reliable and not so reliable sources. Yet gradually things started to add up to a howling fact.

She had gotten a call Sunday evening around eight, that there had been a shooting at the River Front Tower. She remembered thinking out loud, "Christ not again."

It had been an enjoyable Sunday up til then. It was March the fifteenth, her daughters birthday, and they went to the Golden Corral to celebrate. As usual she had over indulged and was felling stuffed and drowsy. She was just about to climb into bed along side of her husband when the police rang her phone.

When she arrived at the River Front Tower, there were several police cars parked in front of the building, with their warning lights still flashing. There were two Ambulances parked next to one of the police units, and crowds of people were gathered under the concrete shelter, and inside the lobby.

She rode the elevator to the third floor, where the police officer had instructed her to go. The elevator made clunking noses, that unnerved to her. It was tiny and she equated the ride up as being inside of a moving casket. She hated that elevator, but the stairwell was not an option for her even though it was just three flights up. She knew that she could not manager her big frame up one flight let alone three. The clunking box made it's mechanical 'ding' and she waited anxiously for the steel doors to slide open.

In the hallway there were curious tenants who lived on that floor. Leaning against the wall next to the apartment was a female police officer who was holding the hands of the Mahdi's two girls. The girls looked frightened and perplexed, but she didn't stop to console them.

Inside the doorway frame was Naema Boone, the tenant in apartment 303, and a plain clothes policeman was writing in a small spiral note pad.

Cheryl approached the officer in the door frame.

"Are you Detective Gilmore? The officer nodded without looking up from his note pad.

"My name is Cheryl Lucas, the manager of the River Front Tower."

"I'll be with you momentarily ma'am. Take a space in the hallway over there." He pointed to a spot several feet away.

When he was done with the tenant he called her over.

"Come with me." They went just a few feet inside the apartment. "As I mentioned over the phone there has been a shooting involving three people, and what we have been able to ascertain is that it was a murder, suicide. What we need from you is a confirmation of residency of the suspect and the victims.

She reluctantly looked at the ghastly scene. There was a body of the woman near the dining area and the body of a man close to hers.

"The woman is Ayeh Mahdi, and the man lying near her is her husband Raheem Mahdi." She pointed to the man closer to them with the small automatic still clutched in his hand. "That's Curtis Jenkins, known round the apartment compound as the Professor. He lives upstairs in apartment 606."

"Do you have the keys to his apartment?"

"Yes in my office down stairs."

"We probably need for you to let us into Curtis Jenkins apartment."

"Sure that will not be a problem."

"Do you know anything about the relationship between the victim and the suspect?"

"No. Not really. I have seen the Professor with Mr. Mahdi in friendly conversation many of times. Also I have seen him with Mrs Mahdi. I thought that three of them were friends."

"Do you have any personal background on any one of them?

"Their leases will have some conducive data and a credit history report. Oh there is this one thing about the Professor tho', and that is he was referred here by the Social Services. I seem to remember that he had some type of emotional disorder . . . . Let me think . . . . Anxiety or OCD, I think that's what it was. Anyway I never noticed anything abnormal about the Professor, he was one of the most polite tenant living here. Paid his rent on time and kept his apartment clean enough to pass inspection. You might be also interested in knowing that he was an ex-con."

Cheryl did not leave for home until twelve o'clock that night, and now it was Monday and she was back in her office filling most of her morning trying to get the complete story from different tenants.

The first thing she did before drilling the tenants for more information was to call the owners and report what happened before it appeared on the news.

The reporters were lined up at the front entrance with their high tech cameras and white vans with call letters, and towering satellites. They were like hungry wild dogs waiting for someone to toss them some morsel of information.

She contacted Naema Boone, the Mahdi's next door neighbor to try and get her to collaborate the story she told the police.

"Miss Boone, the police told me that you heard the shots fired in the Mahdi's apartment, and then called the police."

Naema Boone was a tall brown twig of a woman. She wore a multi color scarf on her head to cover up her dry tangled hair. Cheryl never like her, she thought her to be impudent and a smart mouth. From her ears dangled large gold hoop earrings with her name engraved in fancy gold letters in the middle of the hoop. She was a linguist of expletives and a master at vulgarity and Cheryl wanted to spend as little time as possible in her present.

"Have a seat Miss Boone." She directed her to the small blue upholstered office chair in front of her desk. I know that you spoked to the police about what occurred last night. Can you go over with me what you heard and saw."

"I was sittin' in my fuckin' livin'room watchin' television, when I heard shots fired. It was like pop pop . . . pop . . . pop pop.pop. My little boy and I got on da God damn floor and started crawlin' to da bedroom. Shit I called 911 right away, but dose motha' fucka's took der' motha' fuckin' time gettin' here. I punched dose digit again and ask da bitch where in da hell was da po'lice. I betcha if it was in a White neighborhood, der' ass would have been here befo' I hung up da damn phone. About fifteen minutes later here comes the motha' fucka's."

Cheryl tried not to sound too impatient.

"Did you hear them arguing before the shooting start?"

"I heard some son-of-a-bitch tell anotha' son-of-a-bitch, dat he was not leavin' with out her. I guess he was talkin' about Ayeh, because after da shit went down, she was da only bitch in da room."

Cheryl was becoming very annoyed at the woman's insensitive recap of what had happened. She couldn't bite her tongue any longer.

"Miss Boone you shouldn't speak disrespectful of the dead."

"How in da fuck you're gonna tell me what to say out of my mouth. You called me, remember." She rolled her eyes to the ceiling. "I don't really gotta' tell you a damn thang. I'm doing you a favor." She relaxed her tall thin frame, and slid a few inches to the edge of her seat and crossed her legs. "Shit I already told da po'lice every thing dat I knew. Sounds like da Professor was try'n to move in on Raheem and da poor son-of-a-bitch wasn't gonna lay down and take it. Bam . . . over and done . . . and dat's all da fuck I know, any thang else you wanna know, I guess you're gonna have to get it frum someone else or read it in the news."

CHAPTER FIVE

Elaine

Elaine, the assistant manager came in on her day off to help out any way that she could. She had heard about the shootings on the eleven o'clock evenings news the previous night. It wasn't much information that was reported, just that there was a shooting at the River Front Tower apartments involving three people.

She was approached by reporters, but she knew no more than they did. It was the week for re-certification for some of the tenants, about forty to be exact. She had anticipated a very busy week with paper work and interviews. Now this turn of events lend itself to be more problematic. And if her intuition played through, the owners will be coming in, just to flex their muscles.

When Elaine entered the office, Cheryl was sitting at her desk with a pile of paper work that she knew was waiting for her. She noticed the strained look on Cheryl face, and suspected that she had been dealing with problems all morning.

It was noon time, Elaine went directly over to the small television and turn it on to the local news station.

They both watched as a familiar field journalist gave accounts of the incident.

"It was more than a year ago that a seven year old little girl, who lived with her mother and two brothers on the second floor of this apartment building, was reported missing. For three days the police looked for the little girl. The search ended tragically when they found the little girls body in a huge concrete drain, directly behind this building. Forensic indicated that the little girl had been raped and beating to death.

The River Front Tower has had it's share of lethal violence in recent years. Back in 2006 a woman was found murdered in the parking lot on the eastside of this building. The suspect or suspects in both murder cases are still at large."

The report was obviously edited because the journalist was next seen talking to a few of the tenants.

Elaine pointed to the television at an elderly thin man with a Doberman face, and brown searching eyes. "That's Mister Harper on the third floor, four doors down from the Mahdi"s."

"I heard the shots fired around six or seven, but I wasn't about to go outside my apartment to find out what was going on. I called the police and looked outside my window until they came, and then I came outside my place."

The reporter asked. "Did you know the victims or the suspect?"

"I sure do. Well I didn't know the Mahdi's that well, they only been living here, for, I guess about two years. They seems to be decent folks, religious too. It's a shame what happened to them. And their little girls, real sweet kids, well mannered. Their parents did a good job in raising them. I'm just glad that they have good people to take care of them now."

"Yes. Their maternal grandparents came this morning to pickup a few of the little girls things. It's just horrendous what happen. You said that you also knew the suspect."

"Most people who live here knows the Professor."

"You mean Curtis Jenkins?"

"We call him the Professor because he was an intelligent man, and easy going. I didn't know his given name was Curtis until I heard it on the news this morning. I don't get it, he was a very nice guy, didn't seem the type that would hurt a fly. I thought that he was a retired school teacher even though he didn't look old enough to be retired. You know like they say, black don't crack."

The camera was now focused on the journalist.

"Back to you Shannon."

Sitting behind a mahogany desk, Shannon asked.

"Is there any information leading up to shooting?"

"Right now the most information we have is that it may have been a lovers triangle."

"Thank you Anne." looking stoically at the camera and then the Teleprompter, Shannon reported. "We will have more on the 'lovers triangle' on the six o'clock news, and wait and see what we have discovered about the suspect Curtis Jenkins.

Elaine turned off the television, and she and Cheryl went on with the their tasks that was laid out in front of them like a red carpet.

CHAPTER SIX

Raheem

For two days the news reported the life and crimes of Curtis Jenkins, and the tenants were shocked. Although the Professor's felonious crimes took place years ago, it was hard for anyone to believe that a graduate from Howard University was caught up in such a criminal lifestyle.

After two days the news became stale, and the news reporters proceeded to other news. The tenants went about their days as if nothing out of the ordinary had happened.

What was not reported and what was not known by anyone except the three in the lovers triangle.

What happened was this: About a week ago Raheem came home early one afternoon, after spending all morning in the mens bathroom at school with diarrhea and vomiting. He had caught the bug that was floating around campus.

With just a swig of Nyquil, a hot cup of herbal tea, and a few hours of sleep on his mind, he hurried home to the comfort of his apartment. He did not expect what transpired when he open his front door. Right there in front of him, he saw his wife in the arms of another man.

It was a distressing moment for the three, standing there looking at each other, and frozen in an embarrassing silence.

Raheem's face had taken on a dangerous look, and his eyes were black with rage.

"What in the hell is going on?"

Ayeh started to cry. The Professor made a move to try and calm Raheem down. Raheem could see that he was searching his brain for words to explain why he was there in his apartment, locked in an embrace with his wife. The situation was self explanatory. His inaptness to make an excuse for making out with his wife would have been comical, if the betrayal of the two was not so devastating to him.

He was taken over by anger, and there was no need for useless explanation.

Raheem moved quickly towards the Professor and rendered a blow to the right side of his head, knocking him over the coffee table.

Raheem came at him again before he could get back on his feet. Bending over him he delivered another blow this time to his right jaw and to his stomach.

"Raheem that's enough. Stop it you'll going to kill him."

"You're damn right I'm going to kill him. Fornicator, the both of you. In my home." He kick him in the ribs. "Disrespecting my home with the act of Zina."

The professor managed to roll away before the second kick found his rib cage again. "You'll right Raheem. I was wrong, and I apologies, but hear me out. I chased after Ayeh, she resisted me at first, but I wore her down. We fell in love. Love knows no boundaries."

The Professor undiplomatic confession just enraged Raheem even more. He rushed the Professor throwing wide swings at his head. This time the Professor was prepared, and kept snapping his body forward and back and moving around the room to avoid the flurries of punches that whipped at him in the air. He was thirty years Raheem senior and he knew that he was not his physical match.

The whole scene looked animated and nonsensical, and Raheem got tired from chasing the Professor around the room.

"Get the hell out of my house, before I do kill you. You both not worth me going to jail behind this."

"Come with me Ayeh."

Raheem stood next to Ayeh, flabbergasted at the Professor audacity.

Ayeh buried her teary face in the palm of her hand. "I can't ! I can't leave my children. I can't leave my husband. I still love him."

With a injured pride, the Professor left reluctantly.

Raheem and Ayeah argued and prayed a lot that day. Into the wee hours of the night, and until the break of day they read the holy Koran. They finally decided that they still love each other, and thought that their marriage was salvageable. They also decided to seek out a Muslim counselor and go through the stages of counseling.

Nearly a month went by and they were on the road to mending their marriage. Their lives seemed to be getting back on track. Ayeh was happy, at least she appeared to be, and he was building up his trust in her again.

He had not seen the Professor at all during that month, and he was glad, because he did not know if he could contain the anger he still felt towards him.

He had asked Allah for the strength to forgive and he recited different prayers of the Sharia. Yet still it was hard for him to stop hating the Professor. He felt just as much betrayed by the Professor as he did his own wife, mainly because he had thought highly of him, valued his opinion about things, and had thought him to be a trusted friend.

On that Sunday he was sitting at the diningroom table with Ayeh enjoying pleasant conversation and eating home made almond ice cream, when there was a knock on the door.

Sakeena and Zaina were watching cartoons on the Nickelodeon channel. They had been competing all day about who was the smartest, the cutest, and the fastest. So when they heard the knock on the door they both raced to answer it.

Neglecting their parent's rule about not opening the door unless given permission, Zania gleefully laughed into Sakeena's face, boasting that she was the champion and open the door without first asking who it was.

Raheem shouted at them. "You guys are in big trouble. What did your mom and me tell you about . . . ."

The Professor move smoothly pass the girls. He had a cold menacing look on his face. His whole demeanor and the way he was dressed told a story of hours, days, or maybe weeks of emotional turmoil. So harsh was the truth of his struggle with his emotions, that it eventually disintegrated his philosophy on life, and dissolved all reality and reasoning he may have tried to hold on to.

Although mentally he had already calculated the room, he kept his stare on Ayeh.

"Ayeh" he said with such a wretched plea. "I miss you. I need you, I can't exist without you. You have bewitched me so much that I can't find comfort in food or sleep. I rather be dead in my grave, than to watch another sunset or dawn without the possibility of having you for my own. I grow weak and dispirited in my longing for you."

There was a diabolical heat in the room, and Raheem and Ayeh trimbled with fear, because they could see the pistol in his right hand.

Shakeena and Zania ran to Ayeh, because they too felt the ominous mood in the room. "It's okay babies, go to your room and get dressed for bed, I'll be there momentarily to help you with your prayers."

Shakeena and Zania started to cry and clung tightly to their mother. Raheem desperately wanted to protect them as much as possible, and he yelled at them to obey their mother.

"Do like your mom told you, and go to your room! Right now !

Professor put the gun down and then we can talk."

"Talk! How pathetic you sound."

"Pathetic? I sound pathetic, when you come here holding a gun on me and my wife, frightening my children. Spilling out your pitiful feelings about my wife."

"Exactly. Why would I want to talk to you? Should I say to you, Raheem I am hopelessly in love with your wife and I am not leaving this place without her. And! Will you be saying to me; well Professor I had no idea that you had it that bad, please take my wife if it makes you happy. I am not here to talk to you, but to plea with Ayeh, even though I already know what the outcome is going to be."

Ayeh wanted to try and reason with the Professor, if only she thought that she could control her sobbing long enough to talk to him. She knew that it would be no use though, she could see the determination in his murderous eyes. She regretted ever being taken in by him. Regretted ever finding him desirable.

"Please Professor don't do this." She pleaded with him. "It's over between us. Raheem and me are still in love, and we are trying to make our marriage work. I am so sorry for what you are going through, I truly am, but we are only responsible for our own feelings."

These words that seemed to him too callous, escaped her lips to easily and thrust through his heart so ferociously. They were not the words he wanted to hear, they were the words he expected to hear, and that's the reason he brought his gun. If he couldn't have her, no one will, and then he cocked and released the hammer four times, making his mark, before turning the gun on himself.

CHAPTER SEVEN

'Get Thee Devil Behind Me'

Mabel Jones and her four kids, Tyrese, Sheldon, Christopher, and Myriah(each with different fathers) went to church every Sunday and the kids attended bible school five days a week in the summer time. As a family, they sat all week long under huge white canvas tents on smouldering hot summer nights for Revival meetings.

Mabel Jones testified the same sorrowful condensed story of her life every Sunday during the time that they set aside for testimony. She danced with the holy ghost, shouted and spoke in tongues.

She gave up ten percent of her earnings to tithes and few dollars more to the youth group every Sunday.

She beat her children every Monday for the old and the new, just like her mama use to do when she was small.

Ten years ago she traded her crack pipe for a bible, and now she felt self-righteous. Every chance she got she would curse out the degenerates that atrociously hung around the front of her apartment building (River Front Towers).

She would intimidate some of them, and they would scatter about only to return after she left. For the most part, the majority of them would stay and match her curses and threats.

Even when they threatened her, she was not deterred. She was determined to have the mischief stopped. She called the police and gave them vital information that help made it possible for them to arrest some of the riffraff.

De'Aundre was a business man. He controlled that section of East End, from the ten blocks of the Martin Luther King project to the River Front Tower. When he heard that Mable Jones was interfering with his business, he got two of his soldiers to rough her up. It was a brutal beating, and she spent weeks in the hospital recuperating. It was a lesson well learned, and she counted her self lucky that they did not take her life, or go after her kids.

Now Mabel Jones no longer approach the degenerates in front of her building, but hurry pass them to get to her apartment.

However every Sunday during the time that is set aside for testimony, she added to her regular testimony, her accounts with the devil.

CHAPTER EIGHT

Hellish Hue

Khadeja is black, as black as a starless country midnight sky. She had a beautiful gifted voice, and sang like a nightingale. When she sang before the congregation in church on Sunday, her parents sat listening with tears in their eyes and a glowing look upon their faces. Yet having a voice of a cherub was never enough to fill her with self worth.

She spent most of her life wishing that her skin was any other color than black.

She squandered much of her time thinking about the social significance of having a lighter complexion.

Her color complex grew over the course of nine years, starting at an early age of four and has been cancerous in her brain and soul every since.

No matter what her parents said or did to persuade her of the aesthetic of her African heritage, nothing was more prevalent and powerful than the media, that showed her otherwise.

The media harvested, her brain early on, and she accepted the idea that white was pure and good. She rejected other ideas of goodness to things that were black and dark.

She watched cosmetic commercials where African American women were made to look mulatto with green or light brown eyes, and the Black women that she saw in movies. She also noticed that even in all Black cast music videos that all the girls were light skinned.

Most of her life she was consciously aware of these things, and everything she did was indentured through what society values as beauty in a woman.

She wore bright color clothes to call attention to herself. Her short permed hair was sewn to straight long synthetic hair, that rested on her shoulders and down the sink of her back. Obsessively she would prep and play with her hair consciously and subconsciously all the time.

She use fade cream on her sensitive young face, and masked her complexion with beige powder base. With artistic skill she colored her eyelid s with shades of pastel.

Against her mother's wishes, but with her father's permission, she wore grayish blue contacts.

"All of this cosmetic masquerade was inappropriate for a girl of thirteen." Her mother would say.

At school the boys would not talk to her, and often times laughed behind her back.

73

The girls were crueler. They openly made fun of her clothes and makeup, and left foul messages stuck in the door of her locker for every one to see.

At first she tried hard to shield herself against the frequent hurts and pounding blows of insults by creating a fragile wall of complacency. But the abuse was too harsh and frequent. Subsequently she began to act out her frustrations with turbulence behavior, and expletive outburst in classroom and hallways. As a result she was often expel and labeled a trouble maker.

In the privacy of her bedroom she would cry herself to sleep every night. In the morning, at the insistence of her parents she would drag herself off to school.

Soon enough her relationship with her parents became estranged.

They would argue, and she would tell them . . ."You don't really understand what I am going through."

They would come back with,"you're not really trying. You can do better. You must not let the bad things people say to you get next to you. You should never let such negative things rent space in you head."

She would say, "It's easy for you to say. It's not you that they call out your name. Walk a mile in my shoes."

They blared passionately at each other frequently with one of the three finally submitting to the ineffectiveness of the arguments.

After a while Khadeja shut down. She spent time in her room not talking to anyone, refusing to look at television or look at a fashion magazine, which was one of her favorite things to do. She sat at her bedroom window for hours on end, staring out at the river that flowed into the Atlantic Ocean.

Dangerous thoughts were brewing in her mind as she wondered what it would be like under water. She chewed over if the water would it be cold and serene. She thought how long under water can she hold her breath before the water filled and bursted lungs. She wondered will death come quickly after that.

She imagined that her body after passing of time developing barnacles and fixing itself permanently to a large rock at the bottom of the ocean.

She then wondered if her worried soul be able to free it self from it's organic structure and walk the bottom of the black ocean seeking to explore and connect with the sea scavengers and other ocean population.

What if she thought, her soul became some kind of Plankton, and was able to move on tides, current, and wind, or drift passively with some complex community of living organism. Indulgently she thought these things every day as she sat wasting away by her window staring out at the river.

When she wasn't sitting at her window, she would move through life like a ghost, ignoring her surroundings, and dealing only with life without spirit.

One morning in April she rolled wearily out of bed.

She showered, lingering under the soothing warm water longer than usual.

She put on her tight designer jeans and favorite bright orange sweater—shirt.

She was meticulous in styling her long raven hair, and putting on her make-up.

She adorned her ears with the gold earrings that her parents gave her for Christmas, and made splendid both of her arms with gold bangles and tennis bracelets.

She was ravenous that morning, and she went to the kitchen. She knew that her parents would be, using the allotted minutes of their time to eat a hot breakfast and watch the morning news on television.

"Good morning." She said to her parents." What's for breakfast?"

It was the first time in weeks that she initiated a conversation with them, and they both sat at the small dinetté table in shock.

"There is a little hot oatmeal left on top of the stove." Her mother said in almost a mere whisper.

Over the months she had been so worried about Khadeja. She had stop communicating with them. And she was barely eating enough food to keep a bird alive. She had convinced her husband to let her schedule an appointment next week for Khadeja to see a psychologists.

She noticed that for the first time in months there was an unrestraint look on her daughter's face.

"Do we have any eggs and bacon?"

"Lawdy yes. Praise the Lawd. You want your eggs scramble soft, and your bacon hard and crispy, right?"

Khadeja forced a smile of approval, and watched her mother move swiftly around the tiny kitchen. Her father was watching her curiously over the top rim of his black frame eyeglasses. She avoid looking at him, afraid that he would burn a hole through her brain with his piercing eyes and read what she was thinking. She always felt more connected to him than her mother. Her heart ached at the way she took them both for granted.

It was a school day, but she was in no hurry to leave, and she ate slowly, enjoying every morsel of food that she shoved into her mouth.

"I love you mom." She said, and then kissed her mother on the cheeks.

She went over to her father, whose mouth had dropped open, and his bottom lip was practically touching his chin.

"I love you pop."She said, and kissed him on his forehead. Supposedly she left for school.

They shouted after her. "Have a bless day baby." She did not respond.

Khadeja sat on the wooden bench in front of the building, and watched the children get on the school bus.

She sat there for nearly an hour listening to the birds chirp, and she sang for the first time in years.

She saw a seagull swoop down and claim a crusted crumb that fell from one of the kids jelly covered toast.

She admired the assorted color Tulips, that seemed to her, had pushed up through the mulch overnight.

The sun caressed her plain face and warmed her body, and she sat there for a long while just soaking up the delicious rays. The salty air called her attention to her mission. She walked towards her destination, leaving foot impressions in the thick grass, then in the white sand, and then in the cool welcoming blue water.

CHAPTER NINE

Lucky Joe

Joseph Carson, a.k.a Frank Dillane is a pathological liar, a masterful actor of deceit, and a psychopath hidden behind a mask of sanity.

With quickness of mind, in his lifetime he has been able to deceive and manipulate people.

He has been clever enough to make people believe he is something that he is not. By the time that they were able to figure him out, it was usually to late, and if the real Frank Dillane was still above earth he could give an anguished testimony to that fact.

He spent a lot of his days lately thinking about his past, and in thinking, he realized how lucky he has been in getting away with things.

Today in particular he was not only patting himself on the back for his cleverness in deceit, but was also focusing on his new interest.

With dull blue eyes, he watched her from his apartment window on the first floor. A greasy string of dirty blond hair fell from it's position over his deathly pale and pinched face, and immediately he tucked it back into the pony tail.

She was playing with the other kids on the playground, climbing the multi color monkey bars, and sliding down the hot metal slide.

The warm June sun lit up her ebony skin and made her black hair gleam like onyx.

She was small for her six years. He guess that because her mother was petite, that she had her likeness.

He met Kenya and her mother Regina eight weeks ago, just as they were moving into the apartment across the hall. Two young average looking medium built Black men were trying to fit one of the section from a sectional couch through the door of her apartment.

He waited until they were finished before he wheeled himself to his apartment.

"I'm sorry. Can you get by?" There was still a few boxes in the hallway.

"O' yeah, there is plenty of room." He pointed to his apartment door. "I live there, right across the hall from you. Welcome neighbor."

She looked like a teenager, although he discovered later that she was nearly twenty one. She had a sweet demure look about her with coal black eyes, and a silky smooth chocolate complexion. "Thanks. Is your apartment one or two bedrooms?"

"One, but it's sorta' spacious."

"How is it living here? I haven't heard to many good things about it. The thing is, I can't really afford to live any where else. Some of the nicer places I applied that I could afford there was a long waiting list."

He thought her to be too chatty. Never the least he kept up the pretense of being a caring neighbor.

"It's not to bad. Like myself, most of the tenants stay to them selves. By the way my name is Frank Dillane." He reached out to shake her hand, but the two male movers, move between them and went down the hall towards the main entrance.

He was about to go into his apartment when Little Kenya came out of the apartment and stood next to her mother.

"Mama, I'm thirsty. Can I have a Juicy Juice?"

He immediately became interested in Kenya, it was something very special and familiar about her.

"My name is Regina Dickerson, and this is my daughter Kenya." She looked adoring down at her daughter. "Yes you can have a Juicy Juice. I better get back inside, and face this mess of boxes that need to be unpacked. Anyway it was nice meeting you Frank."

"Sure. Anything you need, just knock on my door, I'm usually home most of the time."

He waited until one week had past before pushing himself into their lives.

"I hate to bother you, I know that you'll probably still busy unpacking and fixing up your apartment."

"No, I'm good, it's just a few things here and there that need to be done, but they can wait."

"My apartment is due for inspection this week, and the girl that I usually pay to help me clean my apartment is not answering her phone. I was wondering if I pay you, could you vacuum my carpet. The rest I can do, it's just that it's impossible to use a vacuum cleaner, and a powered wheelchair at the same time."

She was hesitant in responding.

"It's just the front room and the bedroom. You don't have to move any furniture around, or pickup anything. It shouldn't take no more that fifteen or twenty minutes of your time, and I will pay you twenty bucks."

"Okay. I can vacuum your two rooms for you, and you don't have to pay me nothing."

"I insist that you let me pay you."

"Okay. Let me get Kenya situated and occupied until I get back."

"No don't leave her alone, bring her along."

"Are you sure? She's a typical kid, full of mischief."

"She will be fine, we can keep each other company while you vacuum. Besides I have a few toys left here by my nephews from their last visit."

After she finished vacuuming the rooms. As a ploy to get her to stay longer, he offered her twenty more dollars to wash down the electric stove, and the refrigerator.

"The two front eyes I can reached from the wheel chair, but I found it to be really difficult to reach the two back eyes."

While she was doing the chores, they chatted. She did most of the talking. She boasted about her future plans to graduate from cosmetology school, and then opening up her own hair salon. He pretended to listen, but his real interest was in little Kenya. She was playing with one of the toys, and sitting unconsciously wide legged on the couch, showing the crouch of her yellow printed panties.

He recalled that day precisely. Her innocents and distinctive behavior afflicted his mind.

After that day, Regina and Kenya would often drop by to see how he was doing, or just to chat. Sometimes she would bring over a hot meal or snack food, and they would sit in his livingroom and eat and talk.

He remembered one stormy night, she asked him to come over and watch after Kenya, while she ran to the drug store to pickup some children Tylenol. Kenya was running a fever, and she didn't want to risk taking her out in the rain.

"Please", she said. "She's asleep, and so you don't have to do anything but sit with her until I get back." She gave him her mobile number. "If she wakes up before I get back, and is scared because I am not there, just call me and I will talk to her."

She hurried out the door, and he wasted no time in hurrying down the narrow hallway to the child's bedroom.

Now he sat at his window thinking back on the precious little time he had alone with little Kenya that night. He now waited for another opportunity to get her alone again.

He groped his member as he watch her being pushed high in the swing by an older girl.

"I must not be too impetuous this time", he thought. He continued to have a mental conversation with himself. "Remembering what happen to little Kiesha nearly two years back. You worked hard in winning her over. You even fell in love with her. Then you had to rush things. You went too far too soon, and frighten her. She became hysterical and threaten to tell her mom. You had to shut her up.

There was a knock on the door, he cursed under his breath and he got up from the chair next to the window and walked to his wheelchair.

Elaine stood in the doorway holding onto the black carrying case that housed her bible. She kept her kinky red hair pinned back off her blanch freckle face. She wore a flattering green floral blouse and skirt to accent the color of her hair and skin.

Frank knew that this visit was inevitable, he had complained to her earlier that week that he had been in a lot of pain from his injury that he sustained in the Viet Nam war.

It was one of the blackest of lies he had to tell to keep up the role of a wounded vet.

"Praise God! I was hoping that you would pay me a visit." He lied.

"Glory to God! Praise be the will of God, for I have come to say a prayer over your ailing body." She smiled and scanned the tiny one bedroom apartment. She saw the dust in thickness on the beat up furniture. A sour smell along with the smell of stale tobacco overpowered the place, and she anxiously awaited for her sense of smell to adapt to the odor.

She chose a place on the couch next to some soiled clothing and a multi-color crochet granny blanket.

He wheeled himself to a position in front of her, and tried hard not to show his aversion at her being there.

"As you know that I can't feel nothing from waste down, but the bottom of my back is in constant pain. I was up all night in pain, praying to my sweet Lord for a moment of relief."

She grabbed his hands.

"You know Frank, the soul of the 'just' is in the hands of God." She quoted the verses from Psalm (91: 10-11)." There shall no evil befall thee, neither shall any plague come nigh by dwelling. For he shall give his angels charge over thee, to keep thee in all thy ways."

They both bowed their heads, and Frank watched her through half shut eyelids. "Heavenly Father, we sit here meekly before you, thanking you for all of the mighty blessing you have bestowed upon us. Thanking you for allowing us to get up in the morning and face another day of living, and we ask you for the strength to carry on in the face of trials and tribulations. We ask O' Lord for your healing spirit to touch and heal the tormented body of Frank Dillane. F for as you know he is a good man, with a kind and a courageous heart. We asked that thou will be done, for we know that you have done marvelous and glorious things. Amen."

Frank had managed a few 'crocodile tears'. "Amen. Glory to God in the highest. Thank you Elaine for taking the time to come by, for I have been really sick with pain and depression. You coming here to pray over me, well it's uplifting and comforting."

"Well I am glad that I can be of some help, but as you know all things come through the Glory of God."

"Amen to that."

Compassion flooded her face.

"Frank, I have been meaning to tell you, and I don't know if you know this already, but you can get Social Services to come in and screen you to see if you are qualified for getting assistance around the house. They can have someone to come in and help out with the housework, and help prepare your meals."

"Yeah, well I have been through all that before. The gals that they send to help me out around the place, usually end up stealing from me. No I manage alright for myself, and what I can't manage to do, I get the gal upstairs on the fifth floor, or the gal across the hall to help me."

"I wasn't trying to dig into you affairs, and honestly I thought that since you have been disable for many years, that you probably knew about some of the government programs that you are eligible for. I just thought that I would ask, just to make sure, well you know what I mean."

She got up from the couch, and a puff of dust was released from it's fibers for a moment before settling back into the cotton jungle.

"You are a real angel, and I appreciate your concerns." He smiled charmingly at her.

"Well I better be heading back to the office and relieve Cheryl for her lunch break. Have you eaten lunch? If not I can rustle you up something while I'm here."

"No. Thank you though, I'm gonna stick a frozen pizza into the microwave."

She looked into the kitchen and saw how systematically he had arranged his can goods on the counter, and into a portable four feet tall wooden pantry. She admired his fortitude to be totally independent.

"Don't forget that I will be by Sunday morning around 11:30 a.m. to take you to church. Pastor Fletcher is doing missionary work for six months in Africa, but Pastor Wood will be taking his place. Pastor Wood is great minister, and the church made a wise decision in selecting him. I can hardly wait to hear him preach."

After she left he frowned at the door with disgust, and got out of his wheel chair and walked back over to the window. By this time Little Kenya had left the playground, and he became agitated. He let himself become transfixed to the swing he last saw her on. However his thoughts was not only of her this time.

He thought about the pretentious relationship he had with Elaine and the church they both attended. He became a member two years back, by the encouragement of Elaine.

Joining the Episcopal church that Elaine was a member came about when she came to his apartment one day for a general inspection.

She wore her faith like a shroud. She boasted about the power of God, and she talked about the policy and the bylaws of the church. She talked about things that went on in her church that was all to familiar with him, but he gave his undivided attention as she rattled on. To impress her, but mostly to shut her up he had mention about his membership at a church in Minnesota. A crafty lie based on half truth. As a rule he believed that a good lie is incorporated with certain things that are true, and that makes it strong and believable.

When she asked him why he moved to Virginia. He told her that he had younger brother who was stationed out at Langley, and that he moved here to be close to him and his family.

The truth about Joseph Carson, a.k.a. Frank Dillane is that he grew up in a small town in Minnesota, and for years he attended Victory Life Baptist Church. He live for a while as a decent and respectful person, but there was always a masked sinister side to him.

He made claims to his parents and members of his church that he was planning to attend a Christian college after he graduated from high school to study Ministry. He joined the Youth Choir, and the Usher Board, and taught Sunday School. He made such an impression with the deacons and the minister that he was asked to recite the opening prayer on Sundays and take leadership in some of the church activities.

He was praised and loved by most of the members of the church, and he was pointed out as one of the most outstanding member of the church, and a mentor for the younger members.

'Every man has a rainy corner of his life whence comes foul weather which follows him' (Jean Paul Friedrich Richter).

And so the years passed and were filled with sunshine, in the proverbial sense until one day when the tall husky, rose-cheeked minister visited him and his parents at their modest home. He looked mortified as he reluctantly spouted off accusations that he half heartily believed. It was reported to him by three female members of the church that their daughters claimed that Joseph touched them inappropriately.

So masterly was Joseph refutation to these accusations. He said smoothly,

"Pastor Green, I know those three little girls, they are best friends and every Sunday they conspired together to make my life miserable doing Sunday school sessions. I have been meaning to talk to their parents about their disruptive attitudes, but I decided to reprimand them myself in hopes that the next time they come to Sunday school, their manners would have improve. And so I guess this is their way of retaliating."

The Pastor face looked concern. He wanted so badly to believe Joseph, but he had remember his position in this situation.

"Long before I answer the calling of God, I always thought that I had a six sense in judging people. I thought to myself when these mothers came to me with such outlandish report, that they just could not be talking about Joe Junior. I told them as much.

However as a minister, and to be fair to the little girls, I promised the mothers that I would look into it. I question the girls before coming over here. I questioned them separately, and repeatedly. Their stories were consistent and seemed to prove a certain amount of validity. Now rather or not that their stories were rehearsed, I can't say for certain. There is one thing for certain, and that is Maggie, the older girl, seemed to be more self confident and more adamant. I asked them that prior to the incident did they dislike you for any other reason. Two of the girls said they did not dislike you before, but hated you now. Maggie said she dislike the way you were always staring at her. And so I have come to the conclusion, and it grievance me to say this, but I think that it is best that don't teach Sunday school anymore."

"So you believe that I am capable of doing such a thing." He could see that his parents faces were saturated with embarrassment and disbelief. They tried to convinced the minister that their son was not a deviant, but child of God.

"I am sorry Mister and Mrs Carson, I do not whole heartily believe that Joe Junior could do such a thing, but for the good of everyone involved, my decision is conclusive."

He looked past the swing now, out towards the river. He was now transfixed by the moderation of the tide whipping the shore. A barge carrying a massive crane floated down river, and a tugboat speeded out towards the ocean. However these things were not visible to him, for he was conjuring up memories from his perversive past. Although he was in hiding from the world, he was not in hiding from himself. Despite the fact that he was living the extended life of a dead man, he was in no way that pathetic person.

Never in his life could he be so fatally loyal to any one principle or cause. It was inconceivable to him that someone would volunteer, not drafted but volunteer to join the military and be apart of an aggressive and unwarranted intrusion into a political confused civil war.

He was glad that he was too young during the time the military conscription. Mandating young men fresh out of high school to risk their lives for war that ill fated from the beginning. He believed if he did share their fate, he would be like thousands of draft dodgers and flee to Canada, or get lost among the homeless in New York city.

He thought balefully of the reason he is now living as an impostor.

For years he gotten away with his hungry prowl and ravenous affairs with little girls. He was proficient in gaining their confidence, and convincing them to keep their little secret. He got jobs in elementary school as a substitute teachers or assistant teachers. He once even worked in a school cafeteria, always careful not to stay more than a year in each position.

Most of the little innocent girls he scrutinized then finally chose to enchant, were living constrictive and troubled lives. He was charming and handsome and it wasn't hard to win their hearts. He told them that he loved them, and understood them better than any one else, including their parents.

He did things with them, and he convinced them that those things that they did together is what people do that really loved each other.

In 1981 he was finally caught, tried and convicted for endangerment of a minor, and sodomy. The sentence could have carried twenty years to life, but because it was his first convicted offense. Also because of the weak and inconsistent testimonies of the young victims. He was only sentenced to five years in prison and five years of supervised probation. He was also ordered to pay twenty five thousand dollar fine. The judge also ordered that immediately after his released he was to register and attend a sex offender program.

Although it was hard doing time in State prison, he still felt that he was lucky to only have serve five years, especially since some of the things he did to the little girls were never discovered. He planned his offense brilliantly and covered his tracks well. There were unmarked graves of little girls. They were buried in the most obscured places. Hidden places that helped protect and keep his wicked and evil secret.

Right after he got out of prison things worked out even more favorable for him.

His parents, not understanding why he did the things he did, had given up on him and wanted nothing more to do with him. Although he was hurt by this, he accepted their reasons. In all honesty, earlier on in his life, and for years he struggle for an explanation for his oddity, but not any longer.

He had to find a job and somewhere permanent to live within a certain time span, or he would be in trouble with his parole officer.

It was his lucky day when he walked into a quaint little Irish bar.

After gulping down two bottles of beer, he felt relaxed and in the mood to talk, and the bartender looked in the mood to listen. He unloaded his grievances about finding a job and a place to stay.

He noticed a thin man with translucent skin and blond hair that fell loosely to his shoulders sitting at the end of the bar. He looked as if he was lost in a dark place. Shot glasses and beer mugs were lined up in a row in front of him on top the antique heart pine counter.

When they made eye contact, Joseph perception was that he looked to be around the same age as him, and that he looked lonely, and in need of a friend.

"Bartender, I'll take another Schlitz, and give the gentleman at the end of the bar another round."

They toasted each other.

"Army?"

"Ex-Marine. Fought in Viet Nam, last mission before getting injured was Cambodia." Lines of flesh folded across his forehead, and his face looked tormented. "A lot of empty graves at Arlington National Cemetery with most of my comrades name chiseled on the headstone."

When he poured an ounce of beer on the floor, is when Joseph noticed the folded wheel chair leaning on the edge of the bar.

He moved to the barstool next to him, and they both exchanged names.

They talked for several hours. Near the end of the evening the both of them were fairly inebriated. "Hey man I overheard you telling the bartender that you needed a place to stay."

"Yeah. It's hard finding a place without a job, and poor credit."

"I hear you dude. I'm renting a house about five blocks from here. You can move in with me, until you find something better."

"Nah man, I wouldn't, I couldn't impose. I'll find something soon."

"It won't be imposing. You can sleep on the couch, it ain't much to look at, but it's comfortable."

"Are you sure? I mean you know nothing about me."

"What's there to know? You need a helping hand, and I need a friend, besides you look trust worthy to me."

Looking out at the river he laughed out loud. In retrospect he thought how little Frank knew him at the time. He wondered if Frank had a swift revelation in the last minute of his life.

He can't say in honesty that killing Frank was a hard thing to do. He lost no sleep over it.

The fact that Frank had something dearly he needed to live his life freely, wasn't the only reason that he started contemplating killing him. Frank was always consistent with inconsistency of his loyalties to his country. He was bored with his war stories, and it got so that listening to him tell his war stories over and over again, just rubbed his nerves raw. Living with him was like living on a battlefield when ever he was drinking, and he was always drinking. He had to have a drink first thing in the morning to stop his shakes. Along with his breakfast in the morning he drank his coffee with a hefty serving of Vodka. His idea of lunch was a pint of Gin. His dinner was skimpy and quick and was washed down with more Gin.

The compulsion to kill Frank was at a boil. He waited until it was dark one night, right after he finished a nourishing meal of sirloin steak and bake potato. He approached Frank from the back. Frank was was sitting at the kitchen table, flicking cigarette ashes at his half eaten meal, and half mumbling to himself and anyone in hearing distant, about his heroic feats.

Frank was too drunk to notice the inauspicious deed that was about to happen.

He gripped him tight with one arm around his shoulder and with his free hand he pinched closed Frank's nostril and with the same hand he covered his mouth.

Frank swung weakly at the air, and feverishly he twisted his body to get free, shaking the table, and knocking tableware onto the floor. His eyes were wild and searching as he looked up into Joseph stone face. After a few desperate minutes of struggle, his body became limp. Joseph shook him for signs of life, before removing his hand from his nose and mouth.

Once again he marveled at how easy it was, and how powerful and pious he felt to snuff out a life.

With a claw hammer he lifted the nails from the loose wood slats in the floor, and remove enough board to slide Franks body through. He then sawed through the sub-floor, and dug a deep grave in the harden soil and shoved Franks body in. He covered his body with the loose dirt, repaired the floor, and recovered the floor with the big area rug.

He found the metal trunk where Frank kept his vital records, his army artillery, and his purple heart medal. He grabbed the keys to Frank's father's old Chevy truck, loaded it with Frank's metal trunk, and wheel chair, and left town.

Frank's father's old Chevy truck took him as far as Portsmouth Ohio before breaking down. His only destination was to put as many miles as he could between him and Minnesota.

Settling down in Portsmouth and making the transition from Joseph Carson to Frank Dillane was easier than he had anticipated.

All he had to do was, provide the proper authority with Frank's medical records and identification and he was able to receive Frank's disability check each month. Of course he had to make a few physical changes to past himself off as Frank, but that was no hardship, since he already had similar features to Frank. He just had to dye his hair blond and lose ten to fifteen pounds to make himself look very thin.

He was lucky that Frank had no living immediate family and he hoped that it would be a long time before anyone would take an interest in finding out where Frank was.

The people in Portsmouth were very friendly people, always willing to give a helping hand, especially if you are a disabled VET.

He slid into the lives of the people in Portsmouth, winning their friendship and trust with his skillful role playing.

Convincingly he met with other veterans in the community, got drunk and rowdy with them, and even traded Frank's war stories with them. So well rehearsed in specific details were his stories of combat and comradery, that there were times he thought that he was losing his own identity.

He became close with a particular Marine Sargent, and was even invited to his home. There he met the Marine Sargent's lovely wife, their three month old son, and their beautiful eight year old daughter, Ashley.

The beautiful Ashley made him think of Melissa. There were a bit of Melissa in all the little girls he fell in love with, but it was Ashley's long thin flaxen hair, paper white complexion, and azure eyes, like the arctic sky that reminded him of Melissa the most.

Looking at Ashley he vividly saw the secrets of his unfinished past. His love for his childhood sweetheart, Melissa.

He remembered that although he was just eleven and she was only nine, he loved and adored Melissa. Worshiped the ground she walked on. He was always delighted to be near her. To touch her soft skin, and to smell her girly scent was ambrosia to him. She never objected to his advances, nor did she deny his strange request for her personal items, like her panties and the ribbons she wore in her long flaxen hair.

They were very secretive about their feelings for each other, for fear that no one would understand their innocent patting and kissing, and their puerile curiosity about sex.

Soon enough when she turned ten and he was shoving twelve, she got bored with him, and a little frighten of his urgent demands to be more intimate. She gave him back the sterling silver animal charm bracelet that he brought her with the money he earned selling newspaper. She found ways to avoid him, but that only made him inflamed with persistence in seeing her. She threatened to tell her parents if he came around any more, and that devastated him even more. He took to his bedroom for weeks in despair and anguish.

He just couldn't shake his obsession of her, and he stalked her for weeks. At night he would slip out of his bedroom and walk a block down to her house and throw rocks up at her window in hopes that she would come down and reconcile with him. He even went through their trash hoping to find something personal of hers.

This went on for nearly a year, until fortunate for Melissa, her father's firm relocated him, and he packed up his family and moved to Michigan.

When she left he cried and sank into hellish grave of depression, for what seemed to him at the time to be an eternity.

Ashley was tender and sweet, and so much like Melissa, and like it was with Melissa he became preoccupied with her.

He cleverly attached himself to the Marine Sargent's family, taking advantage of the Sargent's wife good nature.

Ashley copied her mother's good nature, and fell for Frank charming smile, and eyes of forlornness, that supposedly reflected his painful past. She played video games with him, and felt encouraged when he let her win. She sung fork lures to him that was taught to her by her nana, and sat on his lap and read to him classic tales from her modest collection of children's books.

On the rare times that they were left alone, he laughingly fondle and touched her in delicate places, and she naively thought that it was part of their games. He taught her games that was to be kept a secret between the two of them, and he seduced her into thinking that the games that they played were for fun.

There was a playground about several blocks down from where the Marine Sargent and his family live, and Frank talked Ashley into meeting him there on a particular day and time.

When she ask. "Why?" He said. "So we can have more fun together. So we can swing, and slide down the sliding board, and buy ice cream from the ice cream truck."

"But my mother won't let me walk that far alone. Can you come and pick me up and take me there?"

"It's not that far, just down the street from where you live. Remember you have walked there plenty of times with your mother. But if you are scared, you can walk to the end of parking lot, and I will pick you up there. It will just be our secret. We don't have to tell your mother, because she is so busy with your baby brother. We don't want to worry her."

With some difficulty, she climb up into the 1975white Dodge van. At first she said nothing, just looked around at the drab interior, and at the strange apparatus that was connected to the steering wheel. "What's that?" She asked, with bright Amytal eyes of curiosity."It's a specialize gas, break, and steering control, made for people with special needs." "Oh." She said. "Is it made especially for you because you can't use your legs." "Precisely." He responded, and then put the car into motion.

Within a few minutes they were pulling into the long driveway that led to the park. It was close to noon, on a week day, and surprisingly the park was fully occupied with vociferous and jubilant kids, and watchful mothers. She looked anxious to leave the van, and run and join in with the unrestrained pandemonium. He hurried to ask her the question that was needling him.

"Did you tell your mom where you were going?"

"I told her that I was going out to play. She was busy feeding my baby brother, and she didn't seem to care, and so I left."

"Yeah, it's like that with new mom's, they seem too preoccupied with the new baby, and less caring towards their other children."

She looked saddened by his disturbing opinion, and yet she was in accordance with it. "Do you think that my mother love my baby brother more than she love me?"

"I think that she is now more in love with your baby brother, because she feels the need to bond more with him. Hey cheer up, I recognize the need in you, and you got me to spend time with, to play games with, and share secrets with."

He reached inside the glove compartment and pulled out a small square gold box. Her eyes widen at the sterling silver charm bracelet inside the box. "It's a birthday present."

"It's not my birthday."

"I know. It's three months away, but I couldn't resist showing it to you early."

He attached the bracelet to her small wrist. "You can wear it for now, but you got to give it back at the end of the day."

She smiled at the delicate piece of jewelry, pulled on the metal door handle, and shoved her shoulders on the stubborn door. She hopped down on the graveled parking lot, and ran to join the other kids at play.

He remained in the van, looking adoringly out at her. His heart beat thunderous against his chest, as he watch the hot yellow sun gleamed against her corn silk hair. After two hours of play, and the number of kids had dwindle down, she came back to the van, spent and thirsty.

He took her to the drive-thru at McDonald's for a happy meal, and a vanilla soft serve. They parked in the parking lot. He slid open the side door, and they ate in the back of the van. He was thankful that it was between mealtime, and there was little to no traffic going in and out of McDonald's. Afterward he closed the side door and took pictures of her, they got giddy, and started playing some of the games he taught her. He wanted to teach her another game, but she got tired and sleepy, and wanted to go home.

He dropped her off at the end of the parking lot, and he watched her walk briskly down the sidewalk to the end of one unit of apartments, and cross a small grassy patch to get to their building.

He drove home irritated and disappointed that he didn't get the chance to teach her his other game. He could have forged on, make her submit to him, like he did the others, but it was too risky. He had been seen with her by too many people, and the odds of him not getting caught was not favorable. He had to make better plans in getting her alone again.

As soon as he walked into his plain, and inefficient little apartment, the phone rang. It was the Sargent's wife. She sound angry, and was spitting out words to fast for him to follow, but he had an idea what the call was about.

"How dare you to take my little girl anywhere without my knowledge. I'm running around to different neighbors to see if they knew where she was at. I was scared out of my mind that something terrible had happen to her. I was just about to call the police, when here she come nonchalantly walking into the house, like it was okay for her to be gone away from home for nearly four hours." She screamed into the phone. Just what did you do to my daughter?

"What do you mean? I could never do anything that would hurt Ashley. I was heading down your street, after coming back from dropping a friend off at the Naval Medical Center, when I saw Ashley walking alone. I asked her where she was going and she told me that she was going to the park. I asked her did her mother know where she was, and she told me that you did. The playground is just a few blocks down, and it never occurred to me that she would lie about that. You guys have always treated me as one of the family, and so I thought it would be alright to drive her there, treat her to lunch at McDonald's and then bring her back home. I didn't think that it would become an issue. She had fun at the playground, I had fun watching her and the other kids having fun. We both had lunch together and for a quick New York second she help me forget the fact that I will never have any kids of my own."

She didn't interrupt him, and her silence automatically made him think that she was having some doubts.

"I don't want to think awful things about you Frank, I really don't. if it was as innocent as you seem to make it, why didn't you call me, or why didn't you act responsible enough to come to the house and explain things then."

"You'll right. Shit I was in such an hurry to pick up my friend at the Navy Medical Center, of course it was totally irresponsible of me. I told Ashley to tell you that she was with me, what can I say, but that I am truly sorry. Obviously Ashley told you, or we wouldn't be having this conversation. What else did she tell you?" He paused, then stumble in his speech. "I mean did she tell you about the great time we had at McDonald's."

"Yes she told me; that she and her uncle Frank, is what she lovely likes to call you now days. She said that she and her uncle Frank had a grand time at the playground and at McDonald's.

And she also said that she felt sorry for you, that you couldn't get out of the car to play with her because of your legs being broken and all. You know how kids are in describing things. But next time Frank . . ." She trail off. "Well I got to go, the baby's crying."

He knew that there would never be a next time, and he wasn't going to fool himself into thinking that the event wasn't going to put a strain on his relationship with the Marine Sargent and his family. He was relieved though to know that Ashley didn't tell her mother in detail about the games that they played, or else he was for certain that the cops would be knocking down his door that very minute. In conclusion he thought it was time to leave the fare city of Portsmouth, but before he would leave, he was going to make one last visit to the mall, maybe he'll get lucky again . . . .

CHAPTER TEN

The Prowl

Saturday was a busy day at Robert E. Lee Mall. The day started out hot, and at interval he had to run the air condition in his late model butane blue Caravan. When he brought it six years ago, the salesman worked out a good deal, and even gave him an extra ten percent military discount, and made it possible to get a ramp built on, plus other modification for very little additional cost. He knowingly smiled to himself and thought being Frank Dillane had it's perks.

The beaming hot sun rotated around him as he remained parked in that one particular spot. He sipped sparingly on bottle water, and ate a chili dog that he brought earlier from the seven-eleven.

Now the sun was resigning to the shadow of the evening, and he was glad for the cool breeze. All day while sitting there on the prowl, he thought about the past repeated scenario of that day. He recalled that from the time he arrived on this small peninsula how he repeated his routine and habits the same as he did for years in different towns, most of them not much different than this one.

He was in his mid fifties and he really gave no credence to that fact, because for him the years were correlated.

There were several entrances to the mall. However he preferred the main entrance. There was more human traffic there, and a lucky spot for him.

"At last", he thought. He spotted a likely prey, although he preferred to think of them as a potential love interest.

He looked attentively at the smartly dressed teenage girl laboriously pulling on the arm of a reluctant chid that looked to be around the age of eight or nine.

A self-centered teenager with an disobliging younger child, whom he guess was probably her younger sister. It was a stroke of luck.

Greater than his driven sexual desires was the game of chance.

He drove his van to a side street, close to the side of the Mall building, and out of view of the cameras.

He adjusted his baseball cap tightly down on his head, making sure that every strand of his hair was tucked neatly underneath. He put on a pair of plastic black frame reading glasses that he purchased at a drugstore. He was dressed in a famous name brand tan khaki pants with sharp creases, and blue plaid shirt with a famous designers name embroidered on the shirts's breast pocket. He looked gracious and harmless.

He walked through a back entrance of a major department store, in his hand he carried a shopping bag labeled with the major department store logo. Inside of the shopping bag was a stuffed Panda, and a PSP.

He looked in the windows of all the specialty stores that teenagers were likely to shop, until he came upon one in particular. He saw the little girl hanging loosely around the shirt display rack. She was a cute little freckle face redhead. She looked bored and irritated. He looked around the store for the teenager, and he caught a glimpse of her with a arm full of jeans heading for the dressing room.

He took a position on the iron mesh bench in the midway, directly in front of the shop and pull out the PSP and started a game. The musical and mechanical noise commanded her attention, and he looked at her wishfully, hunching his shoulders, and pretending to be an amateur with the game. She came out and sat down next to him. "It's my son's game, I thought that I would try and entertain myself, while waiting for my wife and son to finish shopping."

"My brother has a race car game like that. He won't let me play with it though, he's a real jerk."

"Do you know how to play?" She nodded her head yes.

"Here, you have a go at it, maybe I can learn from you."

He watched her quickly press the buttons and gently veered the small computer game to different angles. She smelled like cotton candy, and his body throbbed to do things to her. He checked to see if the teenager was still in the dressing room. He didn't see her, and he knew that he had to act quickly.

"You're good at that." She nodded her head yes, but never looked up from the game.

"Do you like Hanna Montana?" Again she nodded her head yes.

"I watch her every Saturday morning. My mom promised me for Christmas a Hanna Montana game."

"you don't believe in Santa Claus?"

"No silly, that's for little kids, I'm a big girl."

"Well it must be your lucky day, because it so happens that I brought the Hanna Montana game for my fickle daughter. She once like Hanna Montana like you do, but now informs me that she has moved on. She is now into Zac Efron, iCarly, and Twitter. Her mood changes so fast I can't keep up with them. I have the game in my car, and you can have it. That way you won't have to wait until Christmas."

Her eyes widened with delight, and without any misgivings, she followed him through the Mall and then to his van.

෨

The rain beat against the window, and the dim daylight filled the room. It disturbed his sleep. He pulled the covers over his head and tried to go back to sleep, but memories of last night flooded his brain.

෨

Before curfew it wasn't hard getting on Fort Monroe's base(historical civil war base). The MP's hand signaled permission to enter to anyone who wanted to come on base. There were no real military formalities pertaining to security.

He felt no insecurities when he crossed the bridge and past the security post. He had been there many of times, mostly to park in one of the allotted parking spaces, and stare out at the ocean.

That night he parked in one of those allotted parking spaces near one of the Casemate.

Muffled sobs coming from the back of the van ostracized the thick sea air, and he eased himself next to the little freckle redhead girl to offer her a false sense of comfort.

"Shhhh, I'm not gonna hurt you. Just want to be your friend, that's all."

He removed the masking tape from her mouth and wrist. "I wouldn't have taped you up like this if you had cooperated with me from the beginning. I tried to be nice to you. I gave you a brand new game to play with, and all I wanted in return was to play the kissing game with you. If you stop crying and act nice to me I have another gift for you."

He removed the sterling silver charm from his trousers pocket, and placed it on her wrist. He threw her his most charming smile, but it made no difference to her.

Her light green eyes had turned dark and wild with fright, and her tears soaked her flushed freckled cheeks.

She was sobbing loudly and uncontrollably now. He threaten to slap her if she didn't stop.

He removed part of her clothing, and took snap shots. He then touched and caressed her in places her mother had told her that nobody had the right to touch except herself.

She tried hard not to cry out loud because she was afraid that he would hit her again. However when his breathing became short, and spasmodic, and he did painful things to her, she screamed.

Frantically she kicked and fought in resistance, and little did she know that her weak efforts empowered and aroused him. She cried for her mama.

With absolutely no regards for his victim's desire to live, he pressed his thumbs hard and long inside the sink at the base of her neck. He kissed her thin pink lifeless lips, lifted her precious limp body and carried her to the dark, damp Casemate.

There was no remorse in his recount of last night, just a sentiency of emptiness. He always had a sense of void at the end the game, but during the foreplay of the game it was invigorating, sadistic, and enjoyable. He thought, never again would he reproach himself, never, not since the years of his youth.

He knew for sometime that the evil within no longer owned him, but that he own it, an embraced it.

He gave up to the daylight and encroaching memories of last night. He got out of bed, and went to the bathroom to relieve his bladder.

He turned the television on in the livingroom, and clicked the remote to channel seven for the local news.

He then made for himself a hearty breakfast of two poached eggs, a thick slice of smoked ham, two slices of wheat toast dripping with golden honey, and a cup of hot black coffee to wash it down. He always had a hefty appetite after each successful prowl.

On the way to the kitchen to place his dishes in the sink, the phone rang. On the other end of the phone was Elaine, reminding him that she would be picking him up in the church bus within the next hour to take him to church.

"Elaine, I think that I am going to drive myself there this morning, but thank you for the offer."

"We'll gonna miss you riding along with us this morning. We always enjoy your company along the way.

By the way did anyone call to tell you that sister Simmons past away Friday night?"

"I knew sister Simmons", he said," she sang in the senior choir. I had heard that she was sick. Was it . . . ."

"Cancer. She battled the atrocious disease for over a year. I'm kinda glad that now her battle is over, and she is in a much better place. Remember I told you that Pastor Wood will be giving the sermon this morning. Well I was told by deacon Taylor that Pastor wood is from Minnesota. Isn't Minnesota your . . . ."

"Elaine, I hate to cut you short, but something just happen that requires my immediate attention." He hung up the phone.

His concentration was on the thirty-two inch television. His adrenalin raced through his body when he saw the picture of the little girl. He turned the television volume up a notch. He paid no real attention to the refined beauty of the Black journalist, but registered in his mind every word that parted her lips.

"There is an Amber alert for the eight year old Amy Cross. The little girl was reported missing last night around seven. She was with her older sister Jessica Cross, shopping at the Robert E. Lee Mall." The camera scanned the front of the main entrance to the mall.

"According to Jessica, she went into the dressing room at the Gap to try on some Jeans, and when she came out she couldn't find her little sister Amy. It's been nearly twelve hours since little Amy been missing. The Chief of police has made a statement that the police department are doing every thing possible to find the little girl."

He pressed the power button on the remote, and went into his bedroom to dress for church.

The church is located in Yorktown, nearly fourteen miles from where he live. It took him exactly fifteen minutes to get there. not counting the time it took him to board the van in his cumbersome mobile wheel chair, and stopping along the way to fill the gas tank.

The large beautiful design brick Episcopal church sat back more than five hundred yards from the main road. Inside the immaculate church there was still the smell of new wood, even though the church was constructed nearly ten years ago.

The pews were made from solid oak that was thickly veneered, and thick blood red cushions were firmly glued to the seat part.

Down the center row of pews, the last pew was intentionally design shorter for accessibility of the handicap. Frank took up space there, he arrived just in time for the welcoming of newcomers and the acknowledgment of fellow members.

He shook hands, smiled broadly and played the part of a Christian.

He clapped his hands and mouthed some of the verses to the hymns.

He waved his hands towards heaven in his pretense to praise the Lord.

During the sermon, his voice join in with the wails of hallelujahs and amens. When it came time to testify he stayed silent, except for that one time, when he first visited the church. That day he thought was one of his best performances.

That was the day he told lies about having flashbacks of bout his mission during combat. He wept and lied about being suicidal. And he lied about what may have seemed to be the most obvious, and that was his disability. The lies prompted compassion from members of that immaculate church. The starched and righteous members raised money and brought him one of the best motorized wheel chair that money could buy. It was a testament to his convincing and stimulating fabrications.

However today he had very little time to regress about his first visit to the church, today he was now caught up in his role playing.

At the end of service he felt the same euphoric joy that most of the members there felt. He gotten engrossed with the emotion and the spirit of the room. To him it was like going to a football, or baseball game, and not really rooting for any particular team. He just let himself be submitted to the emotion and energy that surrounded him.

He personally thanked the Pastor for a most spirited and thought provoking sermon, and then he left for home feeling self gratification for his roleplay.

He felt lucky in being Frank Dillane.

CHAPTER ELEVEN

Interruption

He saw her leave the playground with the older girl and come inside the building.

He loved her, he did not know the reason why, she look nothing like Melissa, yet her mannerism, and sweet innocents put him in touch with the memory of her.

The older girl was heading for the stairwell, and Kenya was trailing behind. He softly called out her name. She heard him, and was happy to see him. She hurried to where he sat in his wheel chair, in the open doorway, looking fatherly and trusting.

"Hello Kenya, how have you been doing sweety?"

She threw him a smile that made angels glow from it.

"Fine. You got a present for me again today Mister Frank?"

"I sure do", he said.

"Come on in and I'll get it for you." He closed the door gently behind her. Did you have fun playing with your friend today?

She was anxious for her present, but she answer yes to his question anyway. She remembered that yesterday he gave her a banana moon pie and a twelve ounce bottle of sprite. She told him that her mother did not like for her to have sodas because it was hard on her bladder. He said, "I wont tell if you don't tell."

Two days ago he gave her some costume jewelry that he purchase at a local Dollar Tree.

Nearly everyday that she came to visit him, he always had a gift. They played secretive games too. She didn't particularly like the games, but it always seem to make him happy. However she did like him taking pictures of her, although she never got to see any of them. She felt special when he took pictures of her.

She was loyal to her promise to him, and she never told anyone about their secret games. She had no desire too, because their secrets also made her feel special.

"You know Kenya, you mustn't swing to high up in the swing you might fall off, and that wouldn't be to good, you can get really hurt that way."

His tender caring voice made her feel warm inside, and she imagine what it would be like if he was her dad.

"Is your friend's mother watching you today, until your mother gets home from work?" She nodded yes.

"Do you like playing with your friend?"

"Yeah . . . . But sometimes she tries to boss me around, I don't like that."

"Do you tell her about our secret games?"

"No, because she don't share her friends secrets with me. She say's I'm too young to know about what she and her friends talk about."

"Let's have some fun, and play our games."

She agreed, but she wanted the games to be over with quickly so she can get her gift.

Always when they finished their games, he was sweaty, and out of breath. She noticed that many times after their games he would wet himself. There was a bottle of beer on the end table and she thought that it was a soft drink. She wanted to tell him that he should stop drinking sodas, because it hurting his bladder.

She considered telling him that for a quick minute, then decided against it because she learned from experience, that grownups had a type of freedom that was not afforded to her. They seemed to always do the things that they tell her not to do.

She eagerly grabbed the coloring book, crayons, and the small package of ball and jacks. She left feeling exuberant. She never receive three gifts at once in her visits with him. She was so anxious to show her friend her new gifts and boast about how special she was to Mister Frank, that she didn't notice the attractive placid White woman with a stern look on her face. Neither did she notice the tall Amerindic looking man walking next to her.

Frank didn't have time to freshen up or change his pants, when there was an urgent knock on his door. He thought first to ignore the knock, to pretend that he wasn't home. He thought of Kenya leaving, and he knew that whoever it was at his door, must have past her in the hall, and knew that he was home. He cursed and put the bible on his lap to hide the wet stain, and steered the wheel chair to the direction of the door.

"Mister Frank Dillane?"

"Yes, that's me. How can I help you?"

"I'm Agent Marlene Phillips, and this is Agent Yuma Haag, we're from the Federal Bureau of Investigations. Can we come in?" Their demeanor was confident and postulating. They moved slowly past him without waiting for an answer.

Agent Phillips walked over to the wide window, lifted the blinds and looked out at the playground and at the surrounding area. She paid no attention to the fascinating view of the James river. Or the fast moving motor boat that brutally cut a cascading path through it. Her attention was to one particular perimeter of the demesne.

While Agent Phillips observed the limited view of grounds from his window, Agent Haag took the position of a sentinel between Frank and the door.

Agent Phillips turned to face Frank. "Mister Dillane, I see that you have a good view of the playground from your front room window. Do you often look out of your window?

Frank tried to control his breathing, he could feel his blood rush to his head, and he started sweating profusely.

"I stay busy in the confinements of my little apartment. As you can see I am disable, so it takes me a while to do my daily chores around the house. I also spend a lot of time reading the bible, and certain times of the day I look at my favorite TV shows. Sometimes when I'm in the mood I might look out the window at the river."

"Do you sometimes observe the kids on the playground?" Her face looked stoical, and her hazel eyes were piercing.

His throat felt constricting and dry, and it was hard for him to swallow. "Sometimes I look out at the window at the children playing on playground. Why do you ask?"

"I apologize Mister Dillane, I neglected to tell you the reason for our visit. In 2007, a seven year old little girl by the name of Kiesha Brown went missing for several days before the police found her body in huge concrete drain, located at the back of this building." She showed the picture of cute light skinned girl with long auburn twisted pony tails, adorned with fashionable barrettes. "Do you remember ever seeing this little girl at the playground ?"

He made a pretense of trying to remember. "No, I don't remember seeing her."

"Think hard Mister Frank, I know that it's been a while, and there were a lot of kids over the span of two years that played in the playground area. I know that it would be exceptionally hard to try to remember someone if you had no particular reason too."

He gave it a few more seconds of pretense to recall. "No, I'm sorry, but I don't remember ever seeing that little girl. But let me say that I think that it is deplorable that someone could hurt a child like that, or any child." He patted his bible. "It's terrible, and horrendous."

"What about this girl ?" She handed him another photo.

He looked at the photo of ebony girl who looked to be in her early teens.

"Her name is Khadeja Jones, she was reported missing in April this year, four months ago. Some of the kids that live in the building claimed to have seen her last, sitting on one of the park benches, when they were boarding their school bus."

He recognize the girl, and recalled seeing her sitting on the park bench, and he remember this because he thought it peculiar that she did not board the bus with the other kids. Instead she walked in the direction of the beach. He lost interest and went back to what he was doing. "No I don't remember seeing her either."

"You don't remember seeing her coming in or out of the building?"

"No I do not, if I did I would tell you. Again I am sorry that I am not able to provide you with the information you so desire."

She looked unconvinced of his sincerity. She gave him her card. "If you remember anything in relations to the two girls don't hesitate to give me a call."

Assuming that they were leaving, the pulsating veins on both side of his in his head subsided, and he felt some relief.

"Mister Dillane do you mind if I take a look out of your bedroom window?"

She was halfway down the hall heading towards the bedroom, before he answer.

He trailed behind her, and Agent Haag followed him.

She looked out of the window, and then turned and looked past Frank and stared at the black filing case on the top shelf of his bedroom closet. She made no remark about it's existence, but he could tell that it evoked an interest. She also saw the metal trunk resting on the floor of his closet.

"You were in the military, is that correct Mister Dillane?"

"Yes ma'am the Marines. Got injured in combat, and as a result lost the use of my legs."

"Where's your home Mister Dillane?"

"Minnesota."

"How long have you live in Virginia?"

"I don't know I guess maybe I have been living here at River Front Tower about ten years."

"Have you lived any other place in Virginia other than here at River Front Tower?"

"No. After I left Minnesota, I moved to Portsmouth Ohio, then to a lot of towns in the mid-west.?"

She pulled out a small spiral note pad from her pants pocket.

"Isn't it true Mister Dillane, that you did an extensive amount of traveling from the mid-west to the south-east. First moving from Minnesota to Portsmouth Ohio, stopping at cheap motels along the way. You stayed in Portsmouth for several years before moving to Altoona Pennsylvania, lived there for three months, before moving on to Harrisburg Pennsylvania, then to Baltimore and Wilmington Maryland. You did a lot of traveling Mister Dillane, why was that?"

"You did a profile on me, does that mean that I am a suspect?"

"What it means Mister Dillane, is that I am thorough in my investigation. It just struck me as odd, that a disable man would do that much traveling.

Another thing that strikes me as odd, is that you told Elaine Tisdale, the assistant manager here at River Front Tower said that you had a brother stationed at Langley. I did a lot of research under the name of Dillane, and although the name is not particularly common, I could not find any military person with that last name stationed at Langley Air Force Base. Do your brother have a different last name?"

He tried to calm his nerves, and not let her see his hands shaking. He held firmly to the bible that was in his lap covering the wet stain still on his trouser.

"I did tell Elaine that I had a brother stationed at Langley, and that he was the reason that I moved to Virginia. But that was ten years ago, and my brother has since then left the military and now has a civilian job back in our home town in Minnesota."

"What is your brother's name?"

"Gilbert Dillane."

She looked sternly into his cloudy blue eyes.

"And the name of your home town?"

"Litchfield Minnesota. I haven't heard from my brother in some number of years, and I'm not sure of his exact address. Before he left, we weren't exactly on speaking terms. We had a big misunderstanding. He was always getting into my case about my drinking, and I was always telling him how much of a pompous ass hole he was."

She moved past him, taking one last look at the black plastic file case holding all of his victims photo and precious keepsakes, and at the metal trunk before exiting the bedroom.

He trailed her, and Agent Haag followed. She was cool and calculating, and Frank had the impression that she was good at her job. He also thought that she suspected him of something. She turned slowly to face him for the last time.

"Mister Dillane, do you know Mister Charles Richardson that live on the third floor, apartment 303? His apartment faces the front of the building, in fact you both have the same view of the grounds, except his view of course is higher up."

"I don't know a tenant by that name, perhaps if you were to describe him to me."

"He is a thirty year old African American with medium brown complex, medium built, about five feet and eight inches. He wears his hair cropped close, and has a distinguishing large keloid on his left ear lobe."

"Yes I have seen him frequently coming and going. He is a quiet man that stay to himself."

"Have you ever seen him with any kids, or near the playground?"

"I may have seen him walking once or twice walking in the direction of the playground. I don't remember seeing him stopping and talking to any of the kids in the playground."

"Have you ever had a conversation with Mister Richardson."

"We speak to each other when we past each other. He held the door open for me once when I was having trouble trying to open the door. Other than that, no, it's like I said he was a man of few words. He'll speak, then continue on to where he was going.

Nobody bother him, and he never bother anybody, at least from my point of view."

"I wouldn't be so sure of that Mister Dillane. Mister Richardson is a convicted child molester and sex offender, who has been living here for years without registering his address with the police department.

In the last two years, there have been a lot of very young kids, being abducted, raped, and even murdered in this city and in the neighboring city." She handed him her business card. "Five young girls were abducted, raped and killed in this neighborhood alone. If you remember anything that relates to my investigation, you have my card please give me a call."

Agent Phillips and Agent Haag walked smoothly and arrogantly towards the door and left.

After they left his apartment, he wondered if Agent Haag had a tongue. He also wondered if they would be coming back.

As Agent Phillips said, she was thorough. Maybe she will trace back to the cities he lived and try to connect him to some of the missing girls in those city.

He concluded that his luck in being Frank Dillane was running out, it was time to move on, and find a new identity.

PART TWO

CHAPTER TWELVE

Reunion

The lines on Ruth Ann Sedley face and the slender folds of flesh hanging loosely from her neck are in conformity with her silky white hair, and the brown liver spots that are like suntan kisses over most of her translucent body.

Five years ago she had problems swallowing her food, and had to get her esophagus stretched three times during the course of those five years. The first time that the doctor performed the dilation, he found a malignant tumor in her stomach, which had to be removed, along with part of her stomach.

The narrow esophagus and small muscular sac are the contributing factors in her having frail frame. Yet she still remained optimistic, cognitive, and agile for a woman who has lived seventy years.

She had a clear memory of her life that stretched across the distant of time for more than three scores. Most of her life was filled with strife and misery, and with the grace of God she championed these burdens for she believed that God never left her side, not even during the blackest of days.

The mid-morning summer sunlight beamed through the wide picture window and bruised the skin of Ruth Ann Sedley and the obese woman that sat awkwardly on the stylist tan couch next to her.

Thirty minutes ago the woman was at her door claiming to be Maureen, her oldest daughter that she hadn't seen in more that forty years.

The sight of her daughter elicited a lot of emotions; love, happiness, and contrition. She wanted so badly to embrace her, but the woman was stiff and her face showed no signs of exuberance.

The woman was dead set in making sure she had found the right person. The last time that she saw her mother was on the night that her father had badly maltreated her. Her mother was in her early twenties then. She looked at Ruth Anne strangely searching for familiar features.

That was thirty minutes ago. Now after a few awkward minutes of diplomacy, they sat starchily facing each other, waiting for one or the other to break the cool silence.

Maureen took a quick look around the immaculate apartment. Everything looked new and lustrous even the vintage furniture.

"Have you lived here long? She asked. It was not the question that was burning on her tongue. She felt that she had to hold off until the right moment to ask the question she came there to ask.

"Lester and I moved here in seventy-six. Before then, we use to live with his mother"

"Lester?"

Ruth Ann pointed at a beautiful sterling silver frame, holding a photo of a handsome brown skinned man, with light brown eyes and a charming smile.

Maureen could not hide the disheartening look on her face. Nor could she stop the loathing thoughts she had of her mother for being with the man who stared back at her from the classy frame.

"God rest his soul." Ruth Anne said. "He died ten years ago, colon cancer." She shook her head and fought back the tears. "It was devastating watching the man I love slowly melt away in front of my eyes. Oh Lord he was in so much pain, so much agonizing pain.

I prayed to God to take him to Glory soon. I just could not bare to see him suffer."

Ruth Ann then pointed to the other beautifully frame photographs. There were photos of light brown faces with resemblance of her and her late husband. With a glowing smile upon her face and a loving melody to her voice, she named them.

"Are they your children."

"Yes, well Jeremiah and Isaiah are our sons. If you look closely you could see my resemblance in Isaiah' face. Jeremiah is the exact replica of Lester. The others are our grands and great grands."

Maureen looked at the photos of happy and contented faces, and she could hardly contain herself. She felt sickened and the question that she was burning to ask set vilely against the back of her throat. Now she could no longer repress her feeling.

"Mama you had three other children. I don't see their faces among your proud pictures. I understand why you left daddy, but I want to understand why you left us, and never came back. Why didn't you come back mama?"

The word mama tasted bitter on her tongue. She said it with such scorn that she was certain that Ruth Anne felt the cut of it.

Ruth Ann looked straight and hard into her daughter's face. She could see the likeness of herself. But there was no kindness there, just determination and hatred. So emanate was the fierceness of her look that it spoked out loud and it was deafening. She could almost hear her say, "I have been waiting for this day all of my life."

She was certain that her daughter's visit was not a purpose of a joyous reunion. She was sure that her daughter's motive was to try and bruise her conscience by calling forth her past sins. She knew that one of the greatest sin of a mother is to abandon her child.

She could have told her daughter right then and there that she tried hard to find them, instead she decided to fill her estranged daughter in on some gruesome details that she may not know about her father.

If it was retribution that ate away at her daughter's encephalon, so be it, because it was guilt and the longing for redemption that hounded her for years.

She got up from the couch and went to the wide picture window and looked out at the James. The tide was calm, and at a distant she could see two barges moving sleekly over the ripple water a distant shore. A middle age White man with dirty blond hair, and a precarious look upon his face steered his motorized wheel chair across the parking lot towards a blue van. She closed the blinds to shut out the sun and then went into the kitchen, and brought back a pitcher of ice tea, and two tall tea glasses.

"You said that you found my name on the internet?"

"Yes ma'am."

"Then I'm glad that I didn't change my name."

She wanted to tell her daughter that she was not the Same Ruth Ann, that she knew so many years ago. She was not weak and submissive like she was with Matthew. She was now more secure about herself, more confident in the things she did. She wanted to tell her daughter that she owed it all to Lester. She didn't tell her daughter this because she felt guilty that she had started a new life with out her and her son and other daughter. She didn't tell her daughter how grateful she felt to have found Lester, because she knew that she would start to mourn him anew.

"How old are you now Maureen? The question was rhetorical, for she spent many hours of the day recounting all her kids date of birth, their accomplishments, their failings, and flaws. She spent hours in prayer over them. They were her life, and her whole reason for breathing.

Her daughter's eyes became like narrowed slits of sapphire and her lips drew up into a thin roll. She responded to her mothers question through clenched teeth.

"I am fifty-four mama. You don't remember that I was born April the twelfth, nineteen-fifty-five?"

"Of course I remember. I remember clearly that it was a rainy cold day in January, not April. I remembered that the cold rain had washed away the first frost that was sweetening the many rows of collards and turnip greens. I can still smell the wood burning in the old black pot belly stove in our bedroom. I had been labor with you for nearly six hours, and I was growing strained and weak from trying to push you out into this world. When you finally came, there was no stress on you blush face. You looked tranquil and beautiful. It was one of the happiest day of my life."

"Are you sure that it was January and not April?

She caught the annoying tone in her daughter's voice, but she ignored it. She smiled weakly at her daughter. "The day that you bring a child into this world is something a mother never forget. I had a mind to correct the error that was made on your birth certificate, but never got around to doing it. The midwife that helped with the birthing did not turn in the information of your birth to the State of Mississippi vital records department until four months later. I don't know why I didn't get around to making the correction. I was young and ignorant and there were so many distractions during the year that you was born."

She saw the disappointing look on her daughters face. It pained her to think that her daughter may have to make some adjustment or correction in her life because of neglect.

"You were born in a small town called Lampton in Marion County, Mississippi.

I was only sixteen at the time and we got married less than six months before I had you. The hushed pregnancy and the quick wedding was what the old folks called back then, 'a shot gun wedding.' Your father, Matthew Lee Sedley was a tall handsome man with sandy color hair and sky blue eyes. He was the heartthrob among most of the girls Marion County. They were always swooning over him and throwing themselves at him.

He could have had his pick of any girl. I was surprised and happy when he asked my pa permission to date me. I was petite and pale with freckles across the bridge of my nose. There were a lot of girls that were prettier than me. I knew that I was plain, and I use to fret about it. My mama use to say to me;" You just hush that nonsense Ruth Anne. Ain't no flies swarming around my little gal's face. As far as looks go, you can hold your own against any gal in the County."

She sigh and took a few moments before she continued.

"Our families were dirt poor farmers, and your father and I had that in common. However it was the only thing we had in common. We were as different as night is to day. They say that opposite attract, and I think back to the time we met, and I am prone to believe that. We were physically attracted to each other. I won't go into details, but we were hot and mad for one another.

On the day that he brought me to his parents home to live, the desire we had for each other fizzled out. I did not regret having you, but I sure as hell regret ever marring your father. He let me know just about every day how much he resented being forced into marrying me.

He stayed mad at me for a long time, and he made my life miserable. I didn't know this before we got married but soon learned it when I came to stay with his parents. Your father was a mean son-of-a-bitch, just like his father, and his father's father. So I guess you can say that he came by it honestly."

She freshened her glass with more of the cooling beverage, as she contemplated rather or not she should be explicit in her accounts of her life with Matthew.

She wondered is she should tell her daughter about the nights he would brutally rape her. The only thing that would save her from being savagely ravished, was when she was pregnant or menstruating.

She thought maybe she should tell her daughter about the morning while sitting on the front steps of his parents modest home she tried to breast feed her. Maureen was just a few months old. She was screaming at the top of her lungs to fed. She pull out her breast to feed her. It was a natural reaction, and she didn't think that she was breaking any primal rule. He got up from the porch swing and came over to where she was sitting and slapped her hard against the side of her face. The slap was so forceful that it knocked her and Maureen down to the hard dusty ground.

"Don't ever do that in front of me again." She remembered that he yelled so loud that she fathom to think that people could hear him in the next County. "There's a lot of niggers that past this way of the main road. Unless you want one of them bastards lusting after you, try not to act like a whore."

She thought about the many similar times during their marriage that he would knock her around for one empty reason or another.

"During the first year of our marriage, we went through some real difficult times. Farm life was hard enough, but Matt's father was behind several months on the rent. We were faced with eviction. It was nearly impossible to compete with the bigger farmers in the area. Matt decided that he had enough. His exact words were; "I am tired of living no better than some common nigger."

She wanted to give her daughter some insight about her father's people. To tell her about the history of her grandfather, his father and brothers and sons of brothers. She wanted to tell her how they carried on the family tradition of hatred and prejudices against Negroes and Jews. She decided against it. Besides she thought, Matt did not keep it a secret among their children about how much he hated people that were different from him

"Your uncle Nick moved to Virginia during the was to get a job working in the Shipyard. Matt called Nick up one day, and arranged for us to go Virginia and live with your uncle and aunt until we could afford a place of our own.

My hopes were that once we got away from the poor life we had in Lampton and move to a city that offered mor job opportunities that things would be right between him and me again.

Surprising enough, not more than a month after we came to stay with your uncle and aunt, Matt found a job working in the Shipyard. Things were looking up. We moved into a nice two story house on Pine Avenue. You remember the house we lived in on Pine Avenue?"

Maureen nodded and looked away.

"When Junior came two years after Annabel, I made up my mind that I wasn't gonna have any more children. Without your father knowing I marched myself right down to the Health department and got some free birth control pills.

City life did change your father in a way that I probably would have never guessed. He started drinking, and hanging out with his brother until late at night. Not only was he out drinking into the wee hours of the night, he was also out fornicating. I could smell the other women cheap five an dime toilet water on his clothes. Not that I was all that broken up about his cheating. I was in fact relieved that the ravishing attacks on me had stopped. However the name calling and physical abuse continued.

It was nothing I could ever do to placate Matt. The only time that Matt act like he was pleased with something I done, was when I gave birth to Junior. He was bursting with pride in having a son. He boasted and kidded his brother Nick about having all girls. For a little while he treated me half way decent, then he went back to being the same old ill tempered fool that I grew to hate."

Maureen sigh impatiently, and adjusted her massive size to a more comfortable position on the couch. Ruth Anne looked quickly at her daughter and wondered why she let herself get so fat.

"If you're hungry I can offer you a slice of home made carrot cake. I remembered that you use to love my home made cakes."

"After you left, I stopped liking a lot of things, especially memories of you homemade cakes."

"I realize that you're anxious for me to tell you about the night I ran off from the house. I don't know what lies your father have been telling y'all over the years about me. You came to me wanting to hear my side of the story. To make sure that you understand the reason why I left I need to tell my story in it's entirety.

"You might remember that when we first moved to the house on Pine Avenue, we joined a Baptist church. not far from where we lived. At first I was hoping that if I could get Matt to join the church, that he would accept Christ into his life. Then soon enough he would realize that he needed to change his ways. Matt refused to go to church and was against me going, but during that time he wasn't that adamant about it Church was my salvation in more ways than one, and I will tell you about that later.

Like I said before, your father was cheating on me something fierce. As I said before I wasn't too unhappy about who he spent his time with, but I was sure as hell pissed off about how he spent his money. Especially since most of his money was used on whores and whiskey. It got worse when he started seeing this one particular woman on a regular bases. By the time I heard about her, he had been seeing her for nearly two years, and he even had a baby with her."

She wasted no time with long pauses. Incessantly her narrative of the weeks that led up to the night she left Matt and their kids were pressing.

"When I got up the nerve to ask Matt about the other woman, he didn't deny that he was having an affair. In fact he boasted about his love for her, and his live for their love child. I didn't know what to do after that. I was too much of a coward to demand that he stop seeing her. I just prayed about it, hoping for some kind of divine intervention.

Just when I didn't think that things couldn't get any worse, they became more desperate. He would sometimes leave and wouldn't come home for days. He gave me very little money to pay the bills and to feed and clothe us. I knew that most of his money was going into keeping his mistress and their child. Finally I decided that I wasn't gonna to just sit around the house waiting for him to come to his senses. I got a job working as a waitress in a Greek Family restaurant over-town(cross the bridge). I didn't know much about waiting on tables. I had no experience at doing anything, except housekeeping and taking care of y'all. And of course picking cotton, but there were no cotton fields around here.

I left y'all with the neighbor across the street. You remember Miss Rosa?"

She look Maureen in the face, but she didn't wait for her to answer. "Miss Rosa went to our church. She was a good old soul. She didn't have any children of her own. Well she had that one son, but he was killed in the war. He husband had passed away several years before. She lived in that big house all by herself, and she was overwhelm with joy when I asked her to look after y'all while I was at work. When she agreed to keep y'all she refused any pay, but I had already made up my mind that I was gonna insist that she take some pay

I only worked several weeks before you father found out. One day when I came home from work, there he was standing in the front doorway with his belt in his hand. He had a murderous look on his face, and he stood their waiting for me to come pass him, so he could beat me down like I was some rabid dog.

I tried to reason with him, but he didn't care to hear anything that I had to say. He beat me so badly that night that I was too afraid to go back to work. He wanted to keep me tied down to the house. He wanted complete control over me. I was not allowed the luxury of feeling independent any more. I wasn't even allowed to go back to church. Church members came by the house and wanted to know why I hadn't been to church. I would lie and make excuses. What little food we got he brought home, and if the bills got paid, he paid them.

At one time Miss Rosa, God bless her, would bring us loaves of bread, flour, and fresh meats. Matt found out about that and he chewed me out about excepting hand outs. I think that he went across the street and said something to stop Miss Rosa from bringing us any more food.

In the fall when papa died, Matt refused to take me home to his funeral. I beg him, and pleaded with him. I knew that one of the reason was because he still hated papa for making him marry me."

Her fingers tremble when she touched the gold cross that hang from the folded flesh of her neck. "After that I hated your father. For years I tried my hardest to please him, and I was grateful for any crumb of kindness he threw my way. He would beat me and rape me, and I forgave him. It was hard to do, but after a while I forgave him. Because I knew that his ways were part of his upbringing. I could not forgive him for not letting me go and comfort my mother. I could not forgive him for not taking me to my father funeral to say my last goodbyes.

I wanted to pack our bags and just leave. I wanted to go back home and live with mama, but I had no money. I thought to go to the pastor of our church. It had been so long since I attended church, that I felt too embarrassed to go to him and ask for help.

I use to pray that Matt would change, and then I found myself praying that he would die.

When he wasn't around I would spend my days in bed depressed and weak with sadness. I was having myself a grand old pity party. God forgive me for neglecting y'all. I just did not have the right state of mind to pull myself out of that well of self-pity.

Your father was living two lives. One with us and one with his other family. To tell you the truth Maureen. I was confused as to why he bother coming home to us. He certainly did not love me, and he rarely showed y'all any attention."

She could see that she had Maureen's full attention. She was not sure as to how Maureen was feeling about her side of the story. Although she was listening attentively, there was a unappeasable look on her face. She wondered if her daughter remembered any of the things she just told her. She uttered a small sigh and continued.

"Anyhow on one of those nights that Matt decided to stay home, he was in one of his usually foul moods. Nothing suited him. He complained about everything. He made comparison about the way I was keeping house, and the way his mistress kept her house. He compare my way of cooking meals to her way of cooking. He complained that I was skinny and ugly, and that I was an embarrassment to him. He was yelling and complaining so much that night, until finally I just lost it. I just went bonkers. I told him straight out, that he could go to hell and take his bitch with him. I told him that I was tired of taking crap off of him. My words inflamed him, but I didn't care. At that moment I was inflamed too. Within seconds though I regretted my moments of retaliation. He raced towards me to hit me. I quickly duck the first swing, but I caught the punch to the head from the second swing. My poor head was used like a punching bag. I was feeling dizzy and weak, but I fought back.

I remembered that while he was hitting me, I didn't feel that I was really there. It seemed as if my soul had floated away from my body. It must have known that my life was about to end. I could barely feel the pounding to my face and stomach. I remembered striking out at the air wildly, and then hitting his chest. My small, childlike fist didn't even make him blink. He then grabbed me by the throat and started choking me.

I could see you and Annabel tugging at his clothes trying to get him to stop. I could see the tears running down y'all sweet young faces. I could not hear your cries. The sounds around me were muted.

My face felt hot and swollen, and I couldn't breathe. There was a ringing in my ear, and the this bright light took over the room."

A door slammed in the hallway outside her apartment and the sound delivered a brief distraction. Sounds of footsteps past her door and moved down the hallway towards the elevator.

Ruth Ann hadn't realized that she had been crying until she felt the wetness on her cheeks and saw the water stains on her summer thin blouse.

She looked into Maureen's teary eyes, and realized how the spin of that past night was also a loathsome memory for her. She reached to touch her daughter's hand, but she pulled away as if her touch would burn her skin.

Maureen stared down at the green plush carpet.

"I can't believe that until now I did not remembered all that happened that night. Maybe for some reason I blocked it out of my mind. Now I remember, and the memory is clear, liked it just happened yesterday.

You and daddy were fighting as usual. I remembered that I wasn't frighten out of my mind that night. I remember that daddy was brutally beating you, and Annabel and I was trying hard to get him to stop. Matt Junior had went to a corner of the room and faced the wall crying. It was too much for him to take.

I remember seeing you laying stiffly on the floor. I thought for sure that you was dead. Even after you had collapsed to the floor, I saw him kick you two, or maybe three times. It was horrible to watch. I just covered my eyes and wept into the palm of my hands. When you finally came around, you jumped up and ran desperately from the house. I wanted to run too. I want to run and find you, and stay with you wherever you were that night. I thought for sure that you would come home after daddy left for work the next day. I waited all day, but you never came home."

She wiped at her runny nose with the back of her hands. Tears soaked her plump cheeks. She hummed through her teeth. It was one of those things she learned to do when her father was abusing her and demanding her not cry.

I lived from moment to moment each day hoping that you would come home."

Ruth Anne felt stabbed in the heart.

"I know that it was a terrible thing for you, Annabel, and Matt Junior to have to witness. Believe me when I say that I would have come back to you that night if I was physically able.

I ran from the house that night, hard and fast, never risking any delays in my step by looking back to see if Matt was following me. I was in pain, but I didn't let that stop me, not for a minute. I was not particular in what direction I was running, just any direction from the house. I never in my life ran that long and hard before, and I was surprise at how I was able to do it. I ran wildly from street to street. I hadn't noticed that I had ended up in a Black neighborhood.

I heard singing and shouts of praises coming from the direction of this huge brick church that sat on the corner of one of the streets. The double doors were wide open and the light streamed out to the sidewalk, inviting me to come in.

By this time the adrenalin was subsiding, and the pain in my stomach and sides were becoming unbearable. I climbed the steps and stumbled into the church and collapsed again.

I remember waking up from the hospital. I was told by the nurse that I was unconscious for two days. I was treated for a ruptured spleen, fractured ribs, and massive bruises. I was to weak to stand and walk.

I laid in that hospital bed for weeks afraid that he would find me, and hoping that he was taking care of y'all. He was a mean son-of-a-bitch when it came to me, but he was never cruel to any of y'all. I tried to convinced myself of that.

When I got well enough to have visitors, this warm and wonderful Black woman and her son came to see me. Her name was Martha and her son name was Lester. They brought me home grown Lilies and Daffodils, and warm rice pudding with raisins. They came to see me nearly everyday. When I was released from the hospital they insisted that I come and live with them until I could figure out a way to take y'all back.

I went downtown and had charges filed against your father for assault and battery. I thought that once I got Matt out of the house, I could safely go back and get y'all.

Martha promised that we could live with her and Lester until I got back on my feet. I figured that if things didn't work out at Martha's that I would write mama and ask her to send me enough money for train tickets back home.

The sheriff called me up two days after I had filed for a warrant, and said that they were unable to locate Matt. He said that he went to the house and the house was vacant. He said that he put out an APB (all point bulletin) out for Matt.

The news frighten me and I was worried sick about y'all. I called up your uncle Nick to find out if y'all was with him. Your aunt Kathleen answered the phone. She said that she hadn't seen y'all. Your wretched uncle was there, I know he was there, but he would not come to the phone. I knew he knew where Matt had taken y'all.

Lester advised me to go down town and talk to a mediator, and try to file for custody of y'all. I put it off for a bit, because I was afraid that the judge wouldn't grant me custody of y'all, because I had no job or permanent place to stay. With the pastor and a few members of my church support I got the nerve to go before the court. I was happy with the outcome.

I decided to go to the house. Lester and his brother Earl accompanied me to the landlord office to pick up the key to the house. The Sheriff was right, the house was empty except for a few broken down pieces of furniture, and few toys scattered about.

I was devastated, everything seemed so final. He had taken y'all from me, and I didn't know where to start looking for y'all. It was no need for me to go to the Shipyard because the Sheriff had said that he no longer work there. It thought of his mistress, but I didn't even know her name, or where she lived."

The phone on the kitchen wall summoned her from her world of misty colored memories. She excused herself, and moved promptly to answer it. She spoked softly into the receiver

Maureen could not hear what she said, but she guessed that part of the conversation was about her.

Ruth Ann ended her conversation over the phone. She sat back down next to Maureen.

"That was my oldest son Jeremiah. Everyday during his lunch break, he always call up his old mama to see how well she's coming along." She smiled and her mind wondered off.

"Both of my boys are special, but Jeremiah got a lot of his father's endearing ways. They are you brothers, and I would so much like for you to meet them."

Ruth Ann could see that Maureen became tense and stiffen when she suggested that they meet. She decided not to push the issue, at least for now.

I got back my job waitress at that I moved back into the house. I brought a mattress and placed it on the naked floor in y'all bedroom. I refuse to sleep in the same bedroom that Matt and I shared. I brought some dishes and cookware, a few chairs. I didn't buy much for the house, just the things that was necessary.

117

Every evening after work I would come home and sit by the phone. I knew deep in my heart that he had only taken y'all just to get back at me. I shouted at the walls, and cursed his name every lonely night. It did no good, it didn't bring y'all back to me.

I hoped that you remembered our number, and I prayed that you would find a way to contact me. I said to myself; 'Maureen is a resourceful child, she will find a way to call her mama.'

Weeks had past and I was going out of my mind worrying about y'all. Then months came and went, and there was still no clue as to where y'all were. Y'all was so small, especially Junior, and I knew that y'all needed me. It just drove me crazy thinking that I may never see y'all again. All sorts of crazy thoughts were going through my mind.

If it hadn't been for Lester and Martha, I think that the worration (worrying) would have killed me. We knelt before God many nights, praying that my babies were okay, and that Matt would forget his foolish scheme to get back at me for calling the police on him. I knew that he knew that the police was after him, because what other reason would he have to pack up and take off. I feared that he had left town. I prayed that he didn't abandon y'all.

I went home to see mama and to talk to the Sedley's. Talking to the Sedley's was like spitting into the wind. They had closed themselves off to me. I suspected that Matt had told them a bunch of lies. I just couldn't figure out what those lies were. I was a good mother, and dutiful wife.

Then one day out of the blue, your aunt Kathleen called me up. She said that she overheard a phone conversation between Nick and Matt. She said that Matt was bragging to Nick about his new life in a small town in Washington. She said that he told Nick that he and his woman, and the kids were getting along just fine. Matt claimed that he had a good job and that Loretta was a good mother to his kids.

When I heard that y'all was doing okay, it was like God had shined his ever loving light on me. Before Kathleen hung up she told me that she had been struggling a long time with her conscious. She knew the way that Matt had treated me was wrong, but she was afraid to say or do anything, because Nick had warned her. She said that Matt had told them lies about me having an affair with a member of our church. 'I told Nick', she said,' that Matt was full of it. And that you didn't have a cheating bone in your body. But you know how the Sedley's are, knuckle heads the whole lot of them, including their mother Mittie. I never could stand that old cow.'

As soon as I finished talking to Kathleen, I dropped to my knees. I cried and prayed at the same time. I thanked God for keeping my babies safe.

I then called the police and gave them the information that Kathleen had given me.

I waited and I prayed for them to call me back with some promising news, but it never happen. They still couldn't find y'all. I was beginning to have my doubts about the police methods in finding y'all. I hired a private detective. It burned a big hole in my pocket book, but I didn't care. I was willing to do what ever I could to get more money if I had to. Yet even he came back with no leads, and no information.

For years I was obsessed with finding y'all. When I shut my eyes, I could see y'all little faces. I could hear y'all calling me. Every time the phone rang, my heart would jump out of my chest. Before I answered I would say a prayer, hoping that it was you or someone with news of y'all."

Her throat was hurting now from the strain of holding back the tears.

"My whole existence was limited to going to work, coming home to a lonely house. A house that was absent of voices and laughter. I existed on in waiting. I called Kathleen all the time, but as soon as she heard my voice on the phone, she would hang up. I could not figure out why she had suddenly turned against me.

I went down to the Shipyard, and waited at gate 49 for Nick to get off from work. I was determined to make him tell me where Matt was. He insulted me. Called me every name but the child of God, but I didn't care. I had a few choice words for him too. He warned me to stop sending the police to his house looking for Matt.

Although my life seemed dark and bleak, I kept my faith in God. I thank Lester for helping me with my faith. There were times I grew weak, but Lester stood by me, and prayed with me. Except for my pa, he was the most kindest and loving man I have ever know. God worked his miracle through him.

Love knows no boundaries, and yet I fought hard not to fall in love with Lester. I was surprise that I could love a man the way I love Lester. We loved each other madly, yet I was afraid that there would be too many more harsher problems for us to deal with if we continued on in our relationship.

There were a lot of heavy tension between the races back then. A lot of horrendous and frightening things were happening down in Alabama, Mississippi, and even her in Virginia. I didn't want to add those social problems to my plate. I believed that it was God's will that we be together, because he kept providing patches of light between us, and it made my resistance seemed weak and empty.

We were careful not to display our love, or friendship openly among a mixed society. We were free to be together in his home with his family and among our small group of friends.

It was suggested to us that we move up North, but Lester was against the idea. He didn't want to leave his family and the good job he had working for the city. I didn't want to leave because I still had faith that one day someone would contact me with information about y'all."

"The mechanical clicking of the air-conditioner pulled her back to the present Within a matter of seconds the temperature in the room started to drop. The thermostat was set on seventy-five. It was the lowest she was willing to set it, because her body temperature was always low. What may be comfortable for someone as frail as Ruth Ann, was certainly uncomfortable for someone that was not so frail. Sweat rolled off Maureen face and her cotton sleeveless dress was wet and clung to her round body. She removed an embroidered handkerchief from her fashionable straw purse. She wiped away the sweat from her brow and face.

"I remember our old phone number to the house on Pine Avenue. It was Chestnut 45789.

When we moved to Washington, I remember calling that number all the time. After a while I gave up. I thought that you never went back to the house on Pine Avenue."

She gave Ruth Ann a wicked look. "I don't see why the police couldn't find us. Our name and number was listed in the phone book. Daddy drove the same car for almost a year, with the same license plates.

When we first moved to Washington, we moved to a small town. We only stayed there for less than a year, and then we moved to Spokane. Daddy got a job working in a paper mill. For eighteen years, he worked at that paper mill, until he passed away in 2004.

He's was laid to rest in Spokane Memorial Cemetery. He was a cantankerous alcoholic and an abusive person."

The room hadn't cool down much, and she was still unbearably hot. Yet she was determined to stay and say what she came there to say.

Ruth Ann felt no sadness in hearing that Matt had passed away. She did express her condolences to Maureen, and hope that she sounded sincere. It was hard for her to put her hatred aside for Matt, even after all those years apart.

"Years abo I had a premonition about Matt," she said. "I don't know why he crossed my mind that particular day. I guess one often thinks about the good and evil things that happens in their life. I had this eerie feeling that something bad had happen to him. I didn't get any satisfaction from this feeling, nor did I feel any sorrow. The intuition passed quickly through my mind.

Five years before I had a premonition about Matt, I had one about Lester. One thing did sadden her about Matt death, is that she imagine that their children must have grieved a lot over his passing. Especially Junior. He was like Matt's shadow when he was small. Annabel was so much like Matt in so many ways.

"I know that by now that you, Annabel, and Junior must have kids, maybe grandchildren.

For so . . . Lord so many years, I tried to imagine what life was like for y'all with your father.

I just prayed that y'all was healthy and happy.

I could never forgive your father for taking y'all from me." She started to cry again.

"Now," she said. She expanded her lungs and then proceeded. "You must tell me about Annabel and Matt Junior. Lord when I think about how much of your lives I have missed out on, it just ate away at me like cancer. I had no photo of any of y'all and I was scared that the images of y'all would fade."

Ruth Ann folded her arms around her thin body and rocked back and forth. And she openly moaned and grieved for the missed time without her children. Her cries were doleful and piercing, and it rocked the tempered air. However Ruth Anne mournful wails laid a cold finger on Maureen's heart, for she remembered the agonizing years she spent under her father's roof. She remembered how she was forced to fill her mother's role. Her heart was heavy with contempt for her mother, have been for years. There was no clinical therapy that has proven to be helpful with her mental contamination. She blamed her mother for her, and her siblings pre-borderline personality disorder. She thinks that because of their childhood detachment experiences, It definitely lead them to an inadequate sense of self worth.

She believed that Annabel would not have been such a wild and promiscuous teenager, and maybe Junior would not have gotten involved with drugs, if they had a nurtured and normal life. Of course she thought that their father played a monestrous and antagonizing role in the equation. She learned later on in her youth, that the only reason he taken them from their mother, was like her mother said, it was an act of retaliation.

He had expressed on numerous occasions how much a burdensome bother they were to him, and that he wished that he would had left them with their mother.

She looked at her mother's tear streak face, and she fought back the tears. Not for her mothers pain, but for her own painful memories of a stringent life with her father.

"Mama you can take comfort in knowing that Matt Junior is a high ranking Marine officer. Although for a while I had real concerns about his future when he was doing drugs.

He married a local girl, but unfortunately they only stayed married for less that five years. Three good things came out of the marriage; their two little girls, Lindsey and Beth Ann. Their marriage was righteous to me because it started Matt Junior back on the right road.

The same thing could be said about Annabel, when she became pregnant with Taylor. I would also like to think that it was also my diligent interventions, that made her realize that she was better than some man's trash.

She pours all her love into little Taylor. He is a well adjusted little tyke too, and he loves his mama dearly. Nobody knows who Taylor father is, and Annabel swore that she will take that secret to her grave. I have my suspicion who he is. Anyway she got her GED, and she went on to earn a degree in nursing. I'm so proud of her."

Her bosomy chest rose and fell like a turbulent tide.

'When you ran off that night, daddy sat in his easy chair for hours, sipping on uncle Nick's homemade corn liquor. He sat there in a drunken state, staring at the walls. We knew that he was waiting for you to come back home, so he could finish you off. Annabel and I sat in the corner with Matt Junior, and we cried and waited too.

The next day he went to work as if nothing bad had happen between you and him. He left us to make do with things until you or him came back home.

For three days we managed on our own. When he finally came home he looked frighten. He acted desperate as if the devil himself was coming for him. He then made Annabel and me pack up a lot of our personal stuff. He loaded us all up in his chevy sedan and took us to a two family tenement house in a sub-division of Warwick.

We were rushed over there. Actually we were dragged over there. There were a lot of things going through my mind on the way there. I thought that you was dead, and that he was in a lot of trouble with the police. I thought that he was taking us to this house to leave us with some stranger.

I was shocked to see him pull out a key and unlock the door. Shocking two was what was waiting for us inside. This very attractive woman holding a little girl in her arms stood there in this very immaculate livingroom. This little girl strangely enough looked a whole like Annabel., when she was that age.

I looked at my father for an explanation, and I could honestly say that I did not recognize him. He looked so adoringly at this woman and her child. It was a look that I had never seen on daddy's face. It hurt me deeply and brought tears to my eyes.

He spoked softly and with such devotion to this woman. He spoked her name Loretta and then the child name Jessica as if it their names were butter on his tongue.

There place was nicer than ours, everything through out the house was neat and clean. And the house was always filled with the scent fresh baked bread and cookies.

Daddy left again for a couple of weeks. When he returned he packed us up again, including Loretta and Jessica. He moved us to Ritzville, this small town in Washington that I was telling you about. I had an idea that daddy was running from the cops, but I had no idea why he chose Ritzville to live. I heard him tell Loretta one day that aunt had let the cat out of the bag. I figure he was talking about you or the police, and so he packed us up again and we moved to Spokane.

When I heard that you might know where we were I became hopeful and happy.

We were not allowed to use the phone, but one day when daddy and Loretta was not around I pick up the phone and call the operator. I gave her uncle Nicks address, and she placed the call for me. I was relieved that aunt Kathleen answered the phone. She admitted to me that she had talked to you. At the time when she talked to you she didn't know what town in Washington that we were living. I was happy knowing that you was looking for us.

She promised me that she was gonna go and tell you that she had talked to me. I waited for weeks for aunt Kathleen to call me back I wondered what was taking her so long.

I tried to call her again, but daddy found out that I was on the phone, and he beat so hard that I stayed sore for days.

One Spring day uncle Nick, aunt Kathleen and our three cousins came to visit. I was glad to see Mary Beth, Kathy Lou, and Willie Mae. It had been a long time since seeing them and it was always a fun time in their company. Most of all I was glad to see aunt Kathleen."

She wiped at her face again. She picked up the glass of tea and took a big gulp.

That same year, before Spring and the few months in the previous year, we were having a hard time trying to adjust to the climate in Washington. We were always coming down with colds. Matt Junior almost died from pneumonia the first year we were there. Annabel and I didn't get registered in school until the late Fall after we moved to Spokane. Daddy wasn't gonna bother about taking us to school to register, and so he left it up to Loretta. Loretta dragged her feet, because she needed us around the house to help do the chores.

Your name was forbidden to be spoken, and so I had to wait for an opportunity to get aunt Kathleen alone. She wasn't to happy with me pressuring her about information about you, but I was persistent. 'Forget about your mother', she said to me. 'What's so awful about your life here with your father and Loretta. You living well, and you couldn't ask for a better place to live.' What she knew or didn't know about our situation with daddy and Loretta was at that time irrelevant. Even if I were to tell her about the way we were treated, I doubt that she would believe me. I said to her; aunt Kathleen, Matt Junior cries all the time for mama. Loretta has not been motherly to us at all. We need to know if mama is okay, and if she is still coming for us.

She then said ; ' I doubt that your mother is coming. I saw your mother one day over-town at Grant's department store. She did not see me, but I sure as hell saw her. She was picking out baby clothes. I knew that she had moved from y'all house on Pine Avenue, because after our little talk over the phone I went over there looking for her. I heard that she was living in the Colored section of town. I heard that she was living with some Colored man and his mother. I did not believe it at first. When I heard it, I rebuked the dog that brought me that bone. When I saw her buying baby clothes, and looking as if she was happy living the life she was living, I was taken back by it. That's all I'm gonna say about the matter.' It was all she wanted to tell me.

It was a hard blow to the stomach to hear that our mother had started a new life, and had seemed to erase us from her life. Something inside of me died that day. The hope that I had in you coming for us was gone, and it's place was hatred."

She did not look at her mother. She stared out into space.

"After uncle Nick and his family left, our lives returned to a bleak and miserable existence. Loretta put away her mask of a loving step mother after they left, and only wore it when ever daddy was around. She was a superficial woman, who was use to having her way. If we got in her way or made things a little distressful for her, we were beaten or punished. She once locked Matt Junior in the kitchen pantry all day, just because he tracked the floor with the mud he had on his feet. He was young, and he couldn't remember all of Loretta's rules. She made him stay in the pantry all day, without anything to drink or eat. He pissed on the pantry floor because she wouldn't allow him to go to the bathroom. She punished him for that.

When I tried to intervene she slapped me hard across the face, and made me mop the floor. Matt Junior cried for you the whole night. It was nothing I could do or say to comfort him. We all had to face the sad truth that you wasn't coming for us.

Birthdays and Christmas were all special days for Jessica's. Annabel and me adapted to the way things were. Matt Junior was the same age as Jessica, just a few months apart. It was sad seeing him being neglected during Christmas and birthdays. Well that's not altogether true. We did receive a shoe box filled with hard candy, fruits and nuts on Christmas eve. There was never enough money to buy the things we needed, because Loretta took what money they had to spare and spent on her and Jessica.

There was this house about a half mile down the road from us. It's construction was similar to our house except for the magnificence porch and tall white pillars on the front of the house. Loretta had a hissy—fit about not having a nice porch to sat on in the evening and watch the sky turn purple when the sun went down. She nagged daddy for months, until he finally agree to having a porch built to the front of the house.

Here Annabel, Matt Junior, and me were walking around with thrift shop clothes on and Loretta spent thousands of daddy's loan money he got from the bank and built this extravaganza of a porch. I brewed about that one for a long time.

Loretta after that became a real hog about material things. She spent money like it was water on stupid and foolish things. One year she went out and brought a set beautiful Tiffany floor lamps. They were the most grandest lamps I had ever seen, but it looked odd in the livingroom. Loretta went out and open up line credit in the most expensive furniture store in Spokane. I thought now she's gone and done it. I thought as soon as daddy get home and see all the expensive furniture he was gonna shit

That day was the only time that I could remember, of him ever raising his voice at Loretta. Daddy temper tantrum didn't last long, because Loretta had her ways of making him happy."

Maureen could hear her mother steady intake of air through her nose. She could smell the fruity fragrance her mother was wearing. She remembered the scent, and she wondered how she was able to ascertain the fragrance. She thought that it was no longer on the market.

Before continuing, these were the things she thought about during her short moment of composure.

Daddy didn't have much use for me and Annabel, but I truly believe that he loved Matt Junior. He just didn't know the right way to show his love for him. He was cemented with old ways and ideas about how a boy was suppose to act. The things a boy was suppose to do. The things a boy should show an interest in. He forced Matt Junior into sports. Brought him a rifle and a powerful crossbow and arrow set, and taught him how to kill. All the time he was pushing his ways and ideas on Matt Junior, he never once cared about the things that really interested Matt Junior. Matt Junior liked and wanted learn how to play a guitar. He also had an interest in fixing things. He loved to take apart things, and time himself in putting it back together again.

I tried to be there for Matt Junior. After all I practically raised him. It was a hard battle for me up against a boy's excessive love for his father."

The sun had floated across the sky to the other side of the building and the room became shaded. The reddish brown tea in the pitcher and tea glasses was weaken by the melted cubes of ice. Although the tea not as tasty as before the ice melted, Maureen sipped at it anyway. It felt cool against her dry throat.

For the first time since she came, she took time to really scan and study some of the items her mother had on shelves of the corner curio. She noticed that her mother had compassion for collecting thimbles. There was a picture in the center of the wall of president Obama and his wife Michelle. She quickly looked away.

When she got out of her rental car and crossed the grassy lawn. She became apprehensive about the group of Black people standing around the front of the building.

She could not understand why her mother would want to live here or be around people like them. She was however, impressed by the majestic towering building with the beautiful backdrop of the James River. She curled her lips up at the wasted beautiful venue for a bunch of degenerates. Her negative views she had for African American, and Native American, were the views she had in common with her father. She thought how fortunate she was to live in Spokane, because there were not that many African American living there. They made up about two percent of the population. The demographics of where she lived made her feel at ease.

A skinny White man in uniform, who looked to be in his early twenties, let her into the building. Although he did not look intimidating enough for a security guard, she still felt some comfort in seeing him.

The building smelt of sour garbage and mildew. The black floors were lumpy and uneven. She did not trust the elevator, but she was not in perfect health to climb the flights up to her mothers apartment.

Her thoughts dismissed the clanging sounds of the elevator. She tried to, as she had tried so many times before to picture in her mind what her mother must look like by now.

When she reached her mother's apartment and knocked on the door. She was surprised at the sight of the tiny frail woman that answered the door. This woman lent nothing to the memories and dreams of her mother, nor did this woman's face look anything like the small black and white phot that she clung to over the years. She kept this picture of her mother, safely tucked under her pillow for so long. Nearly every night she would pull her mother's photo out and she would talk to it.

Her mind was wondering off track, as she often found herself doing lately. She thought the reason for this was because of the type of drugs the doctor had her on. Then she thought that perhaps it was the fact that she was getting old, and it was getting harder for her to stay focus. She continued where she left off.

"Loretta left years before I started high school. She took up with some real-estate joker. Before she left she boasted to daddy that this guy had ownership to a lot of property in Spokane.

She packed most of the things in the house, including the fancy Tiffany lamps, and she and Jessica left. She was gone, and I was glad. I did miss Jessica, I practically raised her too.

After Loretta left daddy became a monster. It was impossible for us to be around him. We walked on egg shells when he came home. And many nights he came home stinking drunk and ill tempered.

He forced me to take Loretta's place in more ways that I care to talk about at this time. I got beatings and punishments for things I dare not try to remember, because some of the memories of those dark days are too painful."

She thought to herself, 'Too many explicit things'. Too many perverted and explicit things that a daughter should not have to be submitted to. They were horrendous things that she could barely speak of to her psychiatrist. No matter how much she thought that she hated her mother, she could not bare to hurl the details of these repulsive things at her.

The specific reason for her coming there was really a therapeutic approach recommended by her psychiatrist. It was suppose to be her first step towards recovery.

During her sessions with her psychiatrist, she disagreed with his analogy in making her mother as a victim too. For years she hated her daddy, but she hated her mother more.

It was hard for her to erase the measurement of time she spent hoping and wishing for her mother to save her. She was deeply hurt knowing that her mother had given up in finding them, and started a new life, replacing them with other children. Her hatred for her mother was like a luscious fruit, and it was going to be hard to stop her cravings.

She remembered that when she finally left her father's house, and strike out on her own. She had a difficult time functioning normally, and socially with people.

For years she suffered with depression and with hypomanic episodes. She managed to put herself through college, and achieving a degree in business and finance, but she often found herself jobless.

She was now weary from purging herself. She had said most of what she wanted to say. It was out there in the air like a heavy fog between them. She could not say the real hurtful things she wanted to say to her mother. There was no need now.

Maybe the psychiatrist was right, maybe she needed to stop blaming her mother, and graciously wipe the slate clean between them. That way she could move forward.

She looked straight into Ruth Ann tear stain face. She wanted to utter the words of forgiveness. After all she contended that she was not the same young and beautiful mother that she felt abandon by so many years ago. She was not the same woman she imagine herself confronting. She thought how could she be abradant to this frail, and piteous woman that sat humbled next to her.

She looked at her wrist watch and got up from the couch.

"I got to be going if I'm gonna be in time to catch my flight back home."

She made no attempt to touch her mother, not even a gracious hand shake.

Desperate and unsure words fell from Ruth Ann lips. "Do you think that you might becoming back to see me again ? I want so much to spend more time with you. Maybe we can rectify some of the wrong between us.

I want so much to see Matt Junior and Annabel again. If you could just give them my phone number and have them call me, it would mean so much to me."

"They have your address and phone number. We've had it for more than a year now. I honestly tried to get them to come, but they just wasn't to keen on seeing you again. After all these years, I guess that they still have some abandonment issues. Then too, you got to understand they didn't have it easy living with daddy. I tried to tell you about some of the things that went on over the years, but it would more time than I have today to tell you about. I really would like to spare you of some of the things that they had to endure."

As she spoke, flashbacks of Matt Junior being struck in the head with their father's fist, when ever Matt Junior didn't perform well in sports. She remembered that her father would give Matt Junior jobs around the house that was imperceptible for a boy of his age and body size.

At once her mind became flooded with memories of the beatings, the abuse, the missed school dances, and the dates that they were never allowed to go on. The memories of the monestrous things he did to her in the bottom of their basement was pounding against her brain.

She stood there trembling and regressing for what seemed to her to be a long period of time.

"May I have a glass of water?"

The time it took Ruth Ann to bring back the glass of water was not noticed by her. She was still in a deep drop of retrogression. She popped two tiny pills into her mouth and washed it down with the tepid water. She resided in the comforting fact that it would be just a matter of minutes before the pills take effect.

"Are you sick?"

"Somewhat. I'll be fine once the pills kick in."

She moved towards the door. "I will be contacting you again. I can't really promise you when. The day has been emotionally draining for me, and I'm sure it has been for you too.

She reached inside her stylist straw purse again, this time she pulled out a piece of paper. "This is my address and phone number. I have also included Annabel and Matt Junior's phone number and address. If you decide to call them, don't expect it to be a pleasant experience."

Ruth Ann stood motionless with the piece of paper in the palm of her hand. She silently watched as her daughter left her apartment.

Maureen walked swiftly back to her rented car. She wondered if the reunion with her mother had proven to be beneficial. She did not feel the satisfaction of retribution she was hoping for. Yet there was something new that took place in her heart and mind, and it was warm and inviting. It was forgiveness.

Before getting into the car, she looked up at the window to her mother's apartment. She could see her mother's thin white face peering down at her. She did not wave a final goodbye.

Ruth Ann held tightly to a flora octagon box as she watched Maureen get into her car and drive off. Her face was soaked with tears. Her bony white fingers lifted the top from the box and fingered the few mementoes. The box held for her waiting a lavender silk ribbon, three very tiny pink buttons, that once was sewn to an infant sweater, and a small wooden toy train. Children playful laughter, and loving and compelling phrases echoed through the windmills of her mind. She placed the paper with the addresses and phone numbers in the box. She closed it lovingly and placed it back in it's special place.

CHAPTER THIRTEEN

The Shine

His sweaty stubby forefinger trembled on the curve of the cold metal trigger. His ashen thick black lips blanked the barrel of his automatic. Tears rolled down his ebony balloon cheeks. He was forced to think long and hard about the set of circumstances and events that led him to this terminating moment in his life.

His wide and heavy body pressured the mattress and box spring closer to the floor, cracking the lid of a plastic shoe boy underneath. The box housed several stacks of paper money, and two large blue plastic bags of Gen 13, and small packages of superb cocaine.

Loud gangster rap music hogged the atmosphere, canceling out the clamourous noises in the hallway, and the exuberant sounds of life from the play ground five stories down from his apartment.

The stench of the cannabis and malt liquor stifled the air.

Coffined inside the top draw of the 'tall boy' were mounds of letters from his father in State Prison. They were letters of adoration for his one and only son. They were letters of encouragement. They were persistent letters for him to keep his focus on school and football. They were demanding letters for him not to follow hin in his foot tracks. They were crisp pages filled with thunderous, and redundant testaments of his father's sins and regrets.

In the kitchen of the modest apartment that he shared with his mother was a short note adhered to the refrigerator door. In neat whirling calligraphic were written details of his chores and other peremptory requests for her one and only son.

He felt like an Island, for he was alone in his trouble. It was circumstances of gruesome trouble that placed him there.

Death was cold and still while it waited for this nineteen year old boy to make his final move.

So filled with sorrow and regret was the mind of this youth, that he now wishes that he had a second chance at life. He thought; 'if only I had stayed strong and regarded my father's advice.' The advice his father gave him seemed so far and lost to him now.

"Stay in school." His father would often say to him. "Use your God given talent for sports to your advantage, and earn yourself a scholarship. Stay off the streets, and mind your mom. I wished that I had listen to your mother, probably would not be where I am today. At that time I thought I had all the right reason for doing the things I did. I think back on how foolish I was. I think about how much of a know it all ass hole I was.

Since I've been here in this God awful place, I have found God. I know that you're probably heard convicts claiming to be born again Christian, and that it was all a put on.

Believe me when I tell you son, that I am a change man. I feel that God has welcome me back into his bosom and he has forgiven me of my transgression. God willed me to believe in myself, and he has enlighten me about the righteousness in every man. God's holy words have compel me to make prophets of other men. I am not just saying this, because I wish to impress upon the Warden, or members on the parole board that I am a born again Christian.

I know that I am a lifer, I have accepted that fact. I cannot take back what I have done, I can not bring back that man's life. I know that the family of this man is still grieving over him. I pray for their forgiveness. I pray for you and your mother's forgiveness.

He urged him to write him more often.

For a long while he wrote letters to his father, giving him news of his triumphs as an offensive lineman on the high school football team. He shared news with him about the neighborhood and the maleficence of his father's old friends. He did not want to write too many disparaging things about the 'people around the way', and so he mostly wrote about his accomplishments in sports. He wrote about his desire to be the greatest linebacker that ever lived, and that maybe one day he would be inducted into the Football Hall of Fame. It was his desire to 'shine'

His dreams to 'shine' motivated him to be masterful in his efforts to becoming an outstanding football player.

His hunger to 'shine' made him powerful, and he was like a stone wall, a raging bull, and a violent storm on the football field. His fortitude and passion for the game set the bar for his fellow team members, and it boosted their morale.

He was lovingly called the 'Big Mac' by the student body and faculty at his school. The moniker soon caught on around the city and was mentioned in the city newspaper. It was shouted out, and chanted at his games, in the classroom, and in the hallways of his school.

He had the 'shine.'

During the football off season, he worked hard at keeping the 'shine' nurtured by competing in wrestling tournaments. Although his weight and height may have been an disadvantage for him at first, it wasn't long that he learned the philosophy of wrestling.

Where he lacked swiftness, he made up by expediting skillful and specific maneuvers, and strategic battle holding techniques. His teammates started calling his methods of wrestling; 'The Mac Attack'.

He earned his team trophies and he it appeased his desire to 'shine'.

Parents pushed their kids into wrestling and football, in hopes that the 'shine' would wrap a halo around their kids ambitious bodies.

His popularity grew strong. When ever his peers planned parties, he was at the top of their list. His present at these many wild raves made these events magnetic.

At these parties, he exercised no restraint. He went wild with the consumption of drugs and alcohol. The girls threw themselves on him, and he greedily took what they offered.

The cycle of time soon pitched him into a downward spiral, as the tokens of his sins choked and smothered him. The 'shine' became elusive, and slippery like wet soap.

His senior year playing football was to be his final test for a real future, but the Scouts representing different colleges showed no interest in his weak, and fumbling performances. His fans chanting for the 'Big Mac soon faded out. His coaches tried to incite him.

Coach Benson said to him; "I don't know what's gotten into you son, but you' not giving us your all. You was once burning with passion for the game. You was like a brick wall out there on the field. Now you show up late for practice, and you don't have the stamina like you use to. Get it together son, or you will be benched for the rest of the season."

Malcolm defense was watery. "I know Coach that I have not been on the top of my game. I have been battling this cold for the longest time. I promise you I still have the drive, and I will get back my staying power."

Nothing really changed in his performance after that. His promise to get back to his old self had become repetitious and artificial. So ended his one chance at becoming a pro-football contender. That same year he stopped writing his father.

Like Malcolm, 'Sixty' had a bright future in sports. He was a track star at their high school. Running track was why he was branded with the nickname. He could run four hundred meters in just sixty seconds.

Like Malcolm he lost his dream to be successful sports, after he injured his knee.

He and Malcolm now shared a different dream to success. They had become runners for De'Aundre. They were 'bull dogs' when it came to getting De'Aundre's drugs out to the streets

For nearly a year, things went, what they would describe as 'ghetto. Until one day they met up with their friend NuBlac at the Congo Nightlife (night club).

The Black Eyed Peas, 'Boom Boom Pow' song vibrated the walls at the Congo Nightlife. The patrons crowded the floor and danced themselves into delirium.

NuBlac was a short scrawny fellow, with gray black skin and tar black irises that spilled over onto the white part (sclera) of his eyes. His real name was Earl Jones, but very few people remembered his name, including Malcolm and Sixty. He was a hyperactive person and everything he did and said was if he was racing the clock. He had more intelligence that people gave him credit, and he had to admit to himself that this misconception sometimes worked to his advantage.

NuBlac washed down the drinks that Malcolm paid for. He had smoked a 'blunt' before coming, and he was now feeling euphoric. He felt that he owed his friend Malcolm and Sixty something in return. He also thought that it would be to his advantage if he told them what he knew.

He wore a black cotton shirt and he looked almost invisible under the low beam lights. He gave them toothy smile as if the information he had would make their lives golden. He looked around and lean forward.

"I know this White dude from up north, who calls himself Monk. He lives up in Denbigh, and we met through a mutual friend." He paused and let that little bit of information enticed them into listening. "Hell man, the truth is he was boning Millie."

Malcolm eyed him with disbelief. "Fine Millie that went to school with us? Fine White, Miss Valedictorian Millie ? The bitch, who walks around school like she got a stick up her as.?"

NuBlac smiled boldly, and nodded his head in agreement. "Yeah the same stuck up bitch we knew in high school. Only thing is, she not so stuck up anymore. Not since she got hooked on Meth."

Sixty laughed out loud. "How in the hell you become friends with that stuck up bitch?"

"Man, shiiit. I got my ways in hooking up with people."

Malcolm asked; "Why in the hell would you want to hang with that bourgeoisie anyway? I didn't even think that she was into Black men."

"That goes to show how much you think you know a person. I thought the same thing until I got to know her."

Sixty scuffed at his friend. "Fuck you NuBlac, ain't no way you got any of the pale bitch's pussy."

"Sixty you and Malcolm both can kiss my black ass. Besides man, that's irrelevant right now. I'm trying to tell you nigga's something important. Something that can improve your motha. Fuckin' life."

133

He pretended for a short moment that his feelings were hurt before he continued. "Like I was said, this White dude, named Monk was looking for recruits."

Malcolm was feeling the jovial mood in the club, and he thought to tease his friend again.

"Recruits for what motha fucka?'

"Suck my dick nigga. You know what the fuck I'm talking about."

Malcolm lightly hit NuBlac on the shoulder. "Spit it out, you short limp dick motha fucka."

NuBlac rubbed at his shoulder. "Monk told me that he was new in the area, and that he was looking for recruits to move this 'premium blend' he's got at first I was suspicious of the motha fucka. I thought that maybe he was a cop, and so I played it cool for a while. I checked around to see if I could find out some information about this dude. I found out that he already had a small crew. I don't think that this 'cat' is here for the long run. I think that this 'cat' is just her to make it rich quick and move on."

"I smell pork." Sixty said.

"I don't think so." NuBlac offered up. "Why would the police set up a few 'bull dogs with such a premium blend. I've seen and tasted the White Lady', and I'm here to tell you that shit is the shit. It's righteous shit. Made my dick get hard the first time tasted it. I ain't looking to hook on that shit though. I'm a hustler with ambition to become rich.

Nah man, ain't no vice squad is gonna throw shit like that out on the street, just to catch a few minnows. I just started to push the shit, and there's a real hunger for it."

The music change from hip hop and rap, to rhythm and blues and a lot of the people on the dance floor went the bar or back to their perspective spot.

Malcolm casually asked. "Why are you telling us this?"

"Because 'dog', I know that you nigga's want to get large, just as much as I do. Because I trust you nigga', and I need your help.

I know that Monk have a connection in Canada, that's where he getting his Gen 13(potent marijuana). He gets the 'White Lady' from a group of Merchant Seamen. I have not seen these motha fucka', but I overheard Monk talk to them on the phone.

I figured once we get our dicks wet, well you know the score."

They did indeed know the score and they was happy about the prospects.

A few days later they made it out to Monk's place in Denbigh. They wasted no time seeking out this fellow call Monk and subsequently the took their first step to becoming entrepreneurs.

With the money they earned running drugs for De'Aundre, and the money Sixty inherited from mama Lorraine (his deceased foster mother), plus the five grands NuBlac gave them. They were able to put together enough money to buy several bricks and several pounds of Gen 13.

They left Monk's place thinking that they was glad for the business relationship that they had developed with Monk. They came away thinking that Monk was a very intelligent person. And it was like NuBlac had said, that he was only in the game for a short while. He revealed to them that he had dreams and plans to invest his money else where.

They cut only a third of the cocaine and named it the 'White Virgin'. It was their plan to only do this for a short period of time, just long enough to get themselves a good reputation.

With in months, and as they had anticipated the potent cannabis, and the cocaine earned them a reputation.

They discounted the reaction this would have on De'Aundre.

They felt like caesars.

They were impaled with the 'shine'.

Despite the fact that it was like opening up a convenience store next to Wal-mart. Regardless of how small the lost of sales it was for De'Aundre, it still pissed him off.

The rules to the game. One rule was that there was no tolerance for betrayal. This rule was so defined that hippest, and the not so hip in the neighborhood knew of this rule.

The burning fact that ate at De'Aundre was the treacherousness and audacity of Malcolm. and Sixty to sell their product right there at River Front Tower, and other real-estate that belong to him. According to the rumors, their product was superior than his, and this really made him snap. He had a reputation to keep, and he needed to put out a message to the community.

He called Jordan and Lucas into his confidence. With a grand a piece to burn their palm, and more promising accolades in the future, he laid down his demands to "exterminate the nestling mahogany wasps. Try and catch wasp in the bush, away from their nest. Send out a message to any other ambitious motha' fucka's out there."

In the great depths of the night, the warm summer rain pounded the roof of Malcolm's black early model Cherokee. They were parked on a side street near a housing project. They sat solemnly sipping Bud Lite, and listening to Tupac's 'All Eyez On Me'. Malcolm would occasionally snort a line of cocaine. Both of them were lost in their own thoughts. They were thoughts of being weighted down with the inscrutability of life.

One by one a famished soul from the ghetto would appear like ghost in the night. Each one would press their dark wet faces against the car window. They held tightly in their hot hands wrinkled paper to exchange for a little piece of heaven. Each one had their own agenda, their own reason for their hunger. To Malcolm and Sixty, their motives were not so significant as it was the fact that they were there as patrons. Pawns and a means to get rich and 'shine' again.

Between listening to Tupac, and servicing their patrons they planned ways to double their earnings.

The rain was at a steady downpour. The illumination from the distant light post cut through the heavy rain and darkness and exposed their faces.

Sixty was a good looking brown skinned boy with dark brown eyes that looked nearly ominous under the beams of light. His real name was Prince Rogers, but he prefer that people use his nickname. He didn't remember much about his mother before she died, but he remembered how he hated hearing her call out his full name in front of his friends. He was teased about his name all during his childhood and adolescence. He wasn't much of fighter, when he was coming up. He spent most of his time running away from fight, and so he was proud and glad when his peers started calling him Sixty.

He looked at Malcolm dark severe face. He recognized in his companion a kindred spirit, and he felt lucky to have him as a loyal friend. He knew that if things went wrong, that he could always rely on him to cover his back.

He broke the silence between them.

"Malcolm . . . man, I know that we're just getting started in this business. And I know that the road to success is long and hard. But fuck man, I got the 'beast'. We made more money than I ever thought we would. And now I'm ready for us to step up the game.

I say that we combined all of our money with NuBlac and increase our inventory. We can can increase the variety of inventory, to include 'smack' and 'crank'. Next thing you know Bro' we will be' mackin 'it. The 'rag' will be rolling in."

Malcolm like being in business with his pal Sixty. He had unbending faith in him. He knew that what ever Sixty set his mind in doing he would succeed. He knew that Sixty was not the type to waste words about plan unless he was sure that he could see it through.

"I am extremely excited too about all the possibilities of this business."

They pounded(knock fist).

"Tomorrow we will go to Denbigh and hit up Monk for five more kilos. I been doing the math in my head, and the way I figure it we should have enough money for the'snow'. I know fellow that running a lab, and I'm sure we can get the 'smack' and 'crank' almost wholesale.

Hopefully by next week we can organize a reliable crew for distribution. I got my eye on a place that's up for rent in the seven hundred block of thirty six street. It's a 'shot gun' house but it's perfect for a 'chop shop'.

Malcolm released the back of his seat to a reclining position. He let the cocaine and alcohol seize him. "I thought that the five hundred to seven hundred block, running from twenty fifth street to thirty fifth street were Tyson's real-estate."

"Tyson doing time. He pissed off the local cops. He 'roll over'on a few 'whalers' hoping that the D.A. would convince the judge to reduce his sentence. Don't do no good if pulling one or one hundred years if you're a 'dead man walkin'.

The word on the streets is that Tyson is trying to run his business from the 'joint', but his streets are not organize. He lost respect, and nobody trust him. We'll soon have the amount of product to step in on his turf.

Koto and Bowelzer are two fierce niggas I know I can count on them. I know a few of Tyson's boys that are waiting around for a good organization. I think we can offer them that. Soon we can buy Monk out. Get the names of his suppliers.

The two fell deeply into discussing there future plans. They did not notice the low beam headlight approaching them from the rear. Before both men could realize what was about to happen, the quiet night exploded with powerful sounds of gun shots.

Malcolm had no choice but to get him and his friend to the hospital. It had occurred to him that there would be questions. He tried not to concern himself with that for the moment. He tried to stay focus.

The windows were shattered and glass was everywhere inside the car. Pieces of glass had blanketed Sixty's limp bloody body. Blood was gusting from the hole in his chest and from the side of his head. Malcolm felt the side of Sixty's neck and there was a faint pulse.

He started the car.

"Hold on Bro. I'm gonna get you to the hospital. Just don't fucking die on me."

There was a nagging ache from his right shoulder, and it was then that he realized that he had been shot. He remembered that things happen so fast. He saw the shadowy figures behind the exploding gun. He acted quickly and was able to grab his gun and fire off several shots. He thought that one of his bullet made contact with one of the assailant. He shouted out loud. "I think I got one of those motha' fucka's. Man . . . I'm sure that I made a mark on one of those son-of-bitches."

He looked wildly into the night. The rain was still pouring down which made it even more difficult to see. He began to fear that they were still out there.

"Who do you think they were? Do you think that they work for De'Aundre?"

Sixty did not respond. He really didn't expect him to.

"Well I think that they were De'Audre's soldiers."

His head was feeling fuzzy. He was swaying all over the road. He tried to stay focus on his driving. It was three o'clock in the morning and he was grateful that there were very few people out on the road. He took the most convenient route, where the speed limit was higher than the alternate route, and the stop lights worked in his favor if he kept to the mandated speed limit.

He pulled around the back of the hospital. Before he pulled up to the emergency entrance, he made a stop in front of the Medical Center. There was a man made pond across from the Medical Center. There was a neat row of rose and azalea bushes. He buried their guns, the drugs and the money beneath a wide Azalea bush.

He left the hospital tormented with guilt and sadness for the lost of his best friend. The pain in his shoulder was nagging him like a bad tooth ache. They tried to keep him there, but he wasn't having it. His head and heart were pierced with thoughts of vengeance.

Still resinating in his mind were the questioning of the police. They did not buy his story about the shooting, but he stuck to his story.

"Where were you when it happen?" One cop with paper white complection and pale blue eyes asked.

"We were driving down Marshall avenue."

"Were you driving?"

"Right."

"Why were you out that late at night, driving down Marshall avenue?" Another cop asked. He was tall and too heavy for the job of a policeman. His face turned red as he approached Malcolm. He was smug and cynical when he questioned Malcolm.

"I was taking my friend home. We had been watching basketball at my house. He had too much to drink. Hell we both had to much to drink, and we fell asleep. When my friend awoke, he told me that he was still wasted and asked me if I would drive him home."

The cynic cop restated some of his story. "So you were driving down Marshall Avenue and this car came out from one of the side streets. Turned on Marshall and pull up parallel with your car and stated blasting away at your vehicle, killing your friend and wounding you."

"That's right."

"And you have no idea who this assailant or assailants were, and why they would target you?"

"No."

"could you make out the make of the car?"

"No."

"Did you get a chance to make out the license plates?"

"No. I told you, all I saw was this dark color car pulling up beside us. The windows were tinted. It was pouring down rain and I couldn't tell if it was one or more than one person in the car. That's all I remembered seeing other than smoke and sparkle coming from their ' hard iron'."

"So there was more than one gun?"

"I guess."

"So it stands to reason that it was more than one person shooting."

"Yeah . . . I guess . . . I'm still bugged out about it."

"Malcolm", the cynic cop flipped his small notebook with his thick wide fingers. "Malcolm James that's your full name correct?"

Malcolm knew that the cop already gotten the information about him from the nurse or doctor. He thought; 'here we go with the bull shit. The mouse and cat game. How fuckin' dumb do they think I am.'

"I thought the nurse gave you my name and address."

The cynic cop kept his eyes on his notebook. "How old are you Mister James?"

":What's my age on your notebook?"

"Mister if you don't cooperate we can run you in for obstruction of justice. Now I am gonna ask you again. How old are you Mister James?"

"Nineteen."

"Where do you reside?"

"River Front Tower, apartment 1012."

"Do you live alone?"

"No I live with my mom."

"Do you work Mister James?"

"I'm still looking. Nobody's hiring. Must be the recession."

The cynic cop snorted. "We gonna need you to come down to the police station to file an official statement."

"Do I have to go right now?"

"Well as soon as you are able to be release. I personally will drive you down to the station. Since you're not able to drive your car, because it has been impounded for evidence."

Malcolm wanted badly to serve the obnoxious cop with a hard blow up against his globular head, but he knew that he would be playing into their hands. He knew that they were looking for a reason to arrest him, and hold him. They would have him in a place where they could, harass him for the information they wanted to hear.

"Am I being arrested?"

The other cop wanted in on the questioning.

"Why would we arrest you Mister James. We don't arrest victims. We ran a check on you and there are no warrants out for your arrest. you're squeaky clean. We just want to make sure you get to the police station safely, since it appears to us that somebody is out there wants you dead."

"No thank you officer . . . ." He looked closely into the pale face of the blue eye officer. He then scanned slowly down tot he badge to read his name tag below his badge. "Officer Bob Haggard, I can get a ride from one of my friends. It was nice of you to ask. I just need to get home and change out of these bloody clothes."

The cynic lashed out at him. "We need you to make it a.s.a.p. Mister James, say within the next two hours, or we will be coming for you."

Malcolm thought:' You fat fuck. He knew that he was heavy, but he was solid and muscular, not like the cop he saw before him. He was soft around the shoulder, and his belly hang over his belt.

He wanted to say, fuck you officer Krupke. Instead he said; "No problem officer."

A loud clamor and screams came from down the hall, and Malcolm recognized Sixty sister Portia's voice. She was crying out in pain and disbelief.

He knew Portia since grade school. At one time he held a secret crush for her. She never gave him the time of day. Not even when he was one of the most poplar person at school.

Her foster mother, mama Lorraine warned her about boys like him. Mama Lorraine had her every since she was a toddler. Sixty was only a year older. She loved them like they were her own. She kept close reins on Portia. She wanted her to go to college and make something positive out of her life

Hearing her moans he realized that he maybe still carrying the torch for her. He wanted to go to her, and console her. He wanted to make promises of revenge on their behalf. His thoughts were interrupted by the cynic cop.

"One thing seems a bit puzzling Mister James. You stated that the car came out from one of the side street and on to Marshall Avenue and the assailants inside the car fired upon you, it that correct?

"Yeah."

"That's strange, because the officers on the scene, claims that there are no signs of the incident happening there. There is no broken glass, no skid marks to support your story.

When you come to the station, bring a clearer memory with you."

At that moment Portia screams had fallen to a heavy moans and prayers. Malcolm soul burned with compassion for her, and his mind for his own plans for justice remain firm and relentless.

It was the type of day that the afternoon sun blazed the sky and toasted the earth.

It was a hard day, that sent people and animals alike hurrying to find shade or other ways of comfort from the riding sun.

It was a day that even though there was a heavy rain the night before there were no signs of moisture anywhere.

It was a day that even the crow gawked and dry-flies timbal'd their complaint about the sun's ferociousness.

It was the day that potent scents of Magnolia trees, Azalea bushes singed the still air, and blended with the odors of the salt and seaweeds in the ocean. Also with different cuisine flowing freely from restaurants and homes. And their odors were distinguishable depending on the direction in which one was traveling.

To one person in particular it was a good day for wasted souls to die.

Malcolm drove his friend NuBlac forest green Taurus to parking lot of River Front Tower. He was hoping that he wouldn't be recognized by using his friends car and parking it in an obscured place in the parking lot. He did not see De'Aundre's sentry standing in front of the building. He guessed the reason for this was because of the heat.

He held tight to the right side of his body his automatic, that he had retrieved from the place he buried it the night before. He gave NuBlac the drugs and money and instructed him to use a portion of the money for payment of their friends funeral. He knew that he may not come back, and that he made NuBlac a rich man. There was still a good portion of money hidden in a hole in the wall of his bedroom closet. The hole was made obscured by a cardboard shoe rack. He was hopeful that if anything happen to him that his mother would discover the money and use it to get out of the River Front Tower and find a decent place to live.

The sun trounced the building and the heat burned his shoulders as he move swiftly and sleekly along the side of it. He had guessed right about De'Aundre's sentry, but he knew that they were waiting in the lobby of the building, enjoying the comfort of the air condition.

His defensive strategy was to enter through the two sets of double doors and shoot up the place. He entered quickly. He saw the two men alone at the security desk. He fired off a several rounds. He fatally wounded Pee Wee. Spivy tried to make it to the elevator and he took him down with one shot to the head. He was glad that there was nobody else in the lobby, but he was pretty sure that Cheryl and Elaine was in their office, several feet down the hall. He was prepared to take them down if they came out.

He decided to take the stairwell to the twelfth floor. He opted not to go to his apartment on the tenth floor. He knew that De'Aundre spent most of his time in the twelfth floor apartment that he had arranged to be rented in the name of one his whores. He used the apartment to 'wack' his drugs.

After popping Pee and Spivy, a case of remorse threaten his need to carry out his plan. He forced himself to move on.

He approached the apartment and stood to the side of the apartment door, out of sight of the peep hole. Inside he knew that at least one of De'Aundres boys would be standing in front of the peep hole. He was hoping that it would be on of the two men that came after him and his friend Sixty.

He shot inside the peep hole, and waited a few seconds, listening for a painful yell or a body falling to the floor. He was in luck. He rammed the door with the full force of his weight. The door yield with just one forceful charge. He thought he heard a whispering chant. "Big Mac". It was his imagination.

He realized that he had taken down Jordan, and he quickly burned Lucas before he could pull out his piece. De'Aundre stared at Jordan and Lucas bodies in disbelief. The stupor that De'aundre was in gave him the time he needed. He shot De'Aundre in the chest and then the head. It was the same way that his best friend Sixty was killed.

Female bodies were rushing past him to get to the door. He recognized most of them. They were De'Aundre's whores and 'crack heads' and he cared nothing about their escape.

He noticed Gloria on the tan section couch stone out of her mind. He popped her because he never liked her. She had sassed him a couple times in the past, about matters he couldn't quite remember at the moment. At the time he remembered that the things she said to him made him feel humiliated.

Afterward he felt drained and soulless. It was the first time he killed anyone and now it all seemed surreal. He moved passed the bodies in a dream like state.

He did not hear any police siren, but he knew that by now Elaine or Cheryl must have called them.

He did not remember walking the two flights down and entering his apartment.

People who were heading or leaving their apartment saw him walking down the hallway with the gun still clenched tightly in his hand. There was a numb look upon his face. They stood there, not knowing what to do. They were not able think which way to run. Should they scream. Should they dropped to the floor.

Agonizing moans burned at his throat. His arm grew heavy, as he tried to find the courage to pull the trigger. Mindfully he wished that he could turn back the hands of time. He wished that he could be the son that his father had encouraged him to be. He wished that he could have been the son his mother prayed for him to be.

He squeezed the trigger, and blackness came, and there was no more regrets, no more longing for the 'shine'.

CHAPTER FOURTEEN

A Mind In Hostage

Every morning no matter how little sleep he had the previous night he got up exactly zero-five-hundred hours. For nearly forty years Terrence Major is still stuck in a time warp. It started when he was in boot camp at Parris Island.

Today was what he considered a promising day. He was grateful that he didn't awake in the middle of the night with chills and night sweats. Yet he wasn't going to fool himself into thinking that the haunting nightmares wouldn't return the following night.

The earth seemed to have moved further from the sun, and the sky was a grayish blue. It was the season where the sun went unchallenged through Virgo, and it was a glorious time for harvest and comfortable cool weather. The fall and winter are his favorite season. He hated the spring because he suffered constantly with allergies. He despised the summer time because it brought back too many memories of the heat exhaustion he suffered while in the jungles of Vietnam.

After meticulously making up his bed, making sure that the sides and the ends of the sheets and blanket were tucked neatly between the top mattress and the box spring. He moved his tall thin frame towards the kitchen.

At sixty-three he was not the striking figure that he was twenty years ago. Very visible was his limp and twisted swagger. He smoked at least a pack and a half of cigarettes a day. Which was most likely the reason for his hacking cough and bothersome thick yellow phlegm that he was compelled to spew into the sink, or onto the ground.

His thick wavy salt and pepper hair made his reddish brown face sophisticated looking.

His dark brown eyes told stories of an excruciating lifetime.

He fried up some hash brown potatoes and onions, and six slices of crispy bacon. He gave no rational thought to his high blood pressure and high cholesterol.

"Fuck it." he would say to himself often enough about the matter. "If the Vietcong, and the streets of D.C. couldn't snuff out my life, what the fuck do I care about few crispy slices of bacon clogging my arteries. Besides, you gotta die of something. Might as well die from something you love."

He sat down at the small dinette and strategically spooned modest amount of the hot food between his thin ashen lips, washing it down with a gulp of hot black coffee.

He flipped the pages of the local newspaper from time to time, lingering for a few minutes or more on any articles that peaked his interest.

He checked his battered watch. It was zero—seven—hundred hours. The sun would peak out from the cloud from time to time. It was too early to make his way down to the park, and to his favorite bench. He turned the televison on, but it was also to early for CNN news room. The urge for a drink of alcohol gnawed at him, but he resisted.

He turned the channel to watch GMA, but the show could not hold his interest. His eyes left the television long after his mind and it was now focusing on the drab beige walls. He had a conversation with himself "if these walls could talk they would probably have some gruesome tales to tell, but then again I have a few gruesome tales of my own."

Many of nights he shouted those tales out in his sleep, or while he was in a drunken stupor.

His thoughts now drifted back to nineteen-seventy-eight. It was the year that he was honorably discharged from the Marines. The Marine didn't have a job for him any more.

'Nine years', his thought blasted at his brain. Nine gruesome years of my life I served my country. "Almost got my fuckn' leg blown off," he thought he heard himself say out loud.

He rubbed at the hard scars on his chest. Next to the scar was a F UNIT tattoo. He moved his hand down to the grotesque splattered scars that mapped his left

He was on his second tour and they were hunting down Vietcong guerillas, when he stepped on a land mine. The last thing he remembered hearing before losing consciousness was the dreadful click. When he regain consciousness his commanding officer was leaning over him.

"You're one lucky son-of-a-bitch gunner. If you had put the whole weight of your foot on that mine, we wouldn't be having this conversation"

He remembered seeing the flesh of his left leg hanging from the bone. The medic was having little success trying to tape up his leg. "You gonna be okay Marine, just hang in there." The medic's voice sounded confident, but his eyes gave him away.

The commanding officer gave him and encouraging smile. He remembered feeling special, that his commander officer was taking a few minutes of his busy time to show him support. He waved at two young Marines. "You two 'grunts' get your ass over here, and load the Sargent onto the 'Huey'." "Get yourself patched up 'gunner', and bring your ass back here, you're the best damn sniper we got in this unit.

The year before he was on his first tour near the border of North Vietnam when he was shot in the chest and back by a Vietcong sniper. So when he went on his second tour he felt like he had his own personal blood feud with the Vietcong.

Now almost forty years later, in his head he could still clearly hear his Captain shouting orders. "Stick with the plan, and follow my orders 'gunner', it could save your life.

Sharp and quick taps on the door, pulled him back from his regression. He was thankful for the intrusion.

He could see the petite statuette of Shanita through the peep hole. She had her back to the door, and she was looking up and down the hallway as if she was afraid that someone would see her.

He opened the door to let her in. She moved passed him as if she was in a hurry to come in. He observed the state that she was in. Her hair although was styled tightly in micro braids was matted. Her face and lips were gray and ashen, and she looked as if she did not have a good night sleep in days.

"What in the hell happen to you."

"What do you mean?'

Terrence glared at her.

"Never mind. What do you want Shanita?"

She made a move towards the door as if she had made a mistake in coming there. But they both knew that she was not about to leave until she got what she came there for.

"Shit! . . . Terrence I need a 'pluck'."

He lit a cigarette. "I gave you twenty yesterday. I'm not a bank. I can't be giving you . . ."

She cut him off. She was sweating bullets, and her stomach was cramping.

"Look here Terrence I wouldn't ask if I didn't need it. I'm hurting bad sweety. I promise that I will pay you back."

"Shanita, I can see that you're hurting. I can see that, but like I said you can't keep coming to me all the time for money, I ain't got it like that. You and I both know that you is not gonna pay be back, and I ain't your sugar daddy."

He hated that she made him feel sorry for her. He hated her for reminding him of his own wretchedness. He knew what it was like to be a slave to drugs.

"I can spot you a 'sawbuck', but don't come asking me for another motha' fuckin' dime for a long while."

"I need twenty bucks."

"What the fuck do you need twenty for. Can't you be satisfy with getting a dime bag for now."

"I owe Ray Jay ten from the last time. He won't sell me any more shit until I pay him the 'sawbuck' I owe him. Come on Terrence don't be such a hard ass."

"Oh so now I'm a hard ass."

She laughed. Come on Terrence you know I was just joking. I tell you what, I'll suck your cock. I will suck it so good and hard you would think that a dirt devil had a hold of that motha' fucka'.

"For twenty bucks I want the bearded clam."

"I'm riding the 'cotton pony', but I don't give a fuck if you don't."

Terrence unbuckle and unzipped his pants, and let them drop to the floor.

"Blood don't brother me, I've seen oceans of blood in my lifetime."

"If you don't want the front door, you can go into the back."

"I got a mind for both.

The sun warmed his face as he rested his full weight on his favorite bench. He felt comfortable under the orb of the sun, resting on his favorite bench located on his favorite spot in the small park in front of River Front Tower. It was a good spot to watch the children at play. It was a good spot to watch the devilry of some of the people who entered and exited the building.

He was feeling particularly good after having sex with Shanita, and drinking a quarter of pint of cognac. Except for what he called 'chokin' the monkey', he would frequently warm the canal of some female 'crack head'. But cognac was his one and only mistress.

He was first introduced to cognac when they brought him into a medical facility in Vietnam. He had scrap metal enlarged in his right leg. They had ran out of anesthesia and so the doctor flushed down his throat nearly a half of bottle of cognac, before digging at the metal in his leg. Not long after that cognac became one of his passion.

"What's up old timer?"

Terrence looked up at the stout honey colored man. He grabbed at the crouch of his pants.

"I got your old timer. Young blood."

They both grinned at each other, it was the common greeting between the two. He rested his large frame next to Terrence, slightly shaking loose the large rusted bolts that held the bench legs steady in the concrete sidewalk.

"Can I bump a 'cancer stick' off of you?"

"Terrence handed his friend one of the unfiltered cigarette, and lit it for him. He then lit one for himself.

"I always know where to find you when the sun is shining."

"Every since 'Nam', and living on the streets for so many years, I can't stand being cooped up inside. Even when the weather is bad, I try to find someplace to go. The mall, the Space Center, somewhere, anywhere with lots of open space."

"I feel you 'dog. I'm the same way. I needed to get out and enjoy nature. Just how long did you live on the streets?"

Terrence looked into the face of his gentle friend. Three years ago is when he first met Gregory. He immediately took a liking to him. He sensed right from the start that he was a common man with a gentle soul. He was tall and heavy set, but there was nothing antagonistic or intimidating about him. He like talking to him.

"Right after I got out of the military I messed around for a few years, working at odd jobs. I could never stay on a job for to long before I got into some kind of trouble. One thing led to another, then another, and the next thing I knew I ended broke and homeless."

He saw in his friend eyes a hunger for more details, and so he shared his story with him.

"When I came back to the States, I came back with a monkey on my back. I remember like it was yesterday. We (his unit) landed on the Binh Dinh Province, in central Vietnam. It was my second tour. I had this weird feeling when I first saw the place. Other than the regular jitters and fear of dying. It was something else that made me feel uneasy about being there.

We set up our base in Qui Nhon. It was a quant ancient city in the Binh Dinh Province, with banks, schools, and pretty petite Vietnamese girls. The lifestyle was totally different for what we were use to. It was described by one White Marine, as being a Bohemian lifestyle.

In Qui Nhon there was no inhibition about sex and drugs. Cargo' of opium were being shipped frequently, and it was made very accessible to soldiers and citizens.

I don't know much about the politics of South Vietnam. I think that the sale of opium was used to help finance the war for South Vietnam."

He took a strong pull from his cigarette. He looked at it as if he was seeing it for the very first time.

"Cigarettes were laced with opium, and even the beer that was shipped there had opium in it. I thought that I was strong minded enough not to get hooked, but I was wrong. I was wrong about a lot of things I did during that time."

He closed his eyes for a brief moment, as if he was trying to conjure up some spell to repress his memory. He heard once that some soldiers who came back from the war in Vietnam had suffered with psychogenic amnesia. At times he wished that he could block his memories of the terrible things that went on in Vietnam.

He reached inside his tan cardigan and pulled out a pint of cognac and took a sip. He offered his friend a sip.

"Nah man. Go ahead and knock yourself out."

"We were caught up in an intense battle and raids, a lot of our comrades were killed. We walked miles on a mission to search and destroy guerillas. It's true that in our efforts to successfully complete our mission, a lot of innocent women and children were hurt and killed. Casualty of war is what our C.O. would call it. We went right along with, even though we knew that it was wrong, we did as we were told. Some soldiers didn't give a fuck, to them they had been given a ticket to kill niggers. I just tried to stay focus

On the task at hand and stay alive. Just counteract and follow orders soldiers is what was shouted at us, by our commanding officers.

I stepped on this land mine, that nearly blew my leg off. I spent nearly three months in a military hospital. Sometimes at night I would be woken by the sounds of other wounded soldiers, calling out the names of their comrades. Many nights I would wake up with the shakes and in a cold sweat after having dreams of mutilated bodies of women and children. I got some help in the military hospital for PTS (post traumatic stress), but it didn't do any good. For one thing, I just couldn't tell about all the wrong I did. I just couldn't bring myself to tell a military doctor about all the terrible things we did there in Nam. I just couldn't say, oh by the way 'doc' while we were out burning villages and raping women. While we were killing little children and taking home a finger or a ear as a memento from some Vietcong. We were constantly getting high.

I got myself hooked on 'smack' and marijuana. I was high the whole time I was in Binh Dinh "He smiled to himself. "Marijuana was everywhere, it grew like weed there. We harvested and dried it like they do on tobacco farms. We smoked it from makeshift bongs and from the barrels of our M-sixteens. We smoked it in the rice fields and the mountains of Binh Dinh.

But it was like I said, I couldn't bring myself to tell the 'doc' about those things even though I knew that he knew. It was in the news. The world knew. People here in the States were demonstrating and protesting against the war, and the travesty at My Lai village.

We were beginning to doubt our reasons for being there. Hell the South Vietnamese soldiers gave up long before we did. Then there was the 'fraggin' that the soldiers dare to speak of to anyone. Even now I won't talk about."

He took another swig of the cognac. He shook off a ghostly chill. He looked at Gregory and saw a strange look on his face. He was listening attentively, but his eyes placed him somewhere else. He wondered had he said too much. Was his friend trying to imagine what it was like for him in Vietnam?

Terrence turned his attention to a pigeon, that had swooped down and picked up a luckless earthworm that had wiggle his way onto the sidewalk.

Two small souls left their position on the monkey-bars, and headed toward Terrence and Gregory. The girl in measurement was somewhat several inches taller than the boy, who trotted unsteadily behind her. With strong similarity in facial features, it was obvious that they were siblings. They looked dirty and their hair was dusty and kinky. Terrence had spotted them long before they noticed him sitting there. He knew that from their habit of seeking him out, that it wouldn't be long before they would come to him. It gave him satisfaction to know that they liked his jovial way with them.

"Hi Mister Terrence", they said in unison.

"How come you two Gremlins not in school today?"

They both snickered. "We ain't no Gremlins. You always call us that."

"Do you know what a Gremlin is?"

They responded gleefully in chorus. "No."

"Then how do you know you're not Gremlins?"

"I'm boy." the smaller of the sibling intensely protested.

"I'm a girl." shouted his sister.

"See, that's exactly what I mean. You know nothing about who you are, because if you did you would know that you Raquan (he pointed to the little boy) is a boy Gremlin, and you Journey, (he pointed to the little girl) is a girl Gremlin."

They looked at him with excitement and full of wonderment. "What do Gremlins do?" Journey asked with adrenalin pumping away at her heart. She knew it was a game he was playing, and she liked playing games.

He made an ugly face. "They eat . . . . fart . . . . and sleep all day, but mostly they eat. They eat nearly anything that you put in front of them. They eat you out of a house and home if you let them. But then again these are the things you do, so stop teasing me. You're terrible little Gremlins trying to pull my leg again." He laughed out loud, and they join in. "Stop pretending that you don't know. You didn't answer my question. Why you two Gremlins are not in school?

Journey smile faded from her small appealing face and a swelled tear took forever to leave her dark brown eyes, and roll down her sad cheeks.

"Mama is sick again. She said that she is too sick to get up. She told us that we could stay home today."

Terrence knew their mother, and he knew of their mother's sickness. "Did she tell y'all that you could go outside?"

"No. I told us we could go outside." Journey felt strong and independent enough to make decision for them. There were many times that she had to take care of herself and her brother while their mother laid sick in bed. She felt sorry for her mother, because she knew how sick she would become. Sometime she would lay in bed for days. Yet there were good days when their mother was well enough to take care of them, and she wished that those days would come and stay.

It pained Terrence to see their needy little faces, but he had seen worse cases of suffering children in Vietnam.

"Was your mother too sick to feed you today?"

Journey remembered seeing eggs, and raw bacon in the refrigerator, and some fresh meats in the freezer, but she did not know how to cook them. Besides she was not allowed to mess around with the stove. The night before she and her brother shared the last corn dog that was left in the freezer. It was not enough to satisfy them. It was hard and dried out, because she had cooked it too long in the microwave.

That morning she pulled the chair up to the counter and grabbed a can of corn. She could not get the can opener to work for her, and so they settled with two pieces of toast and drank the last of the kool-aid.

Journey and her brother Raquan looked at their dirty sneakers and answer Terrence question with a nod of affirmation.

Terrence and Gregory looked at each other knowingly and shook their heads.

Terrence handed Journey a five dollar bill. "You take this money up to Miss Bernice up on the fourth floor. Her apartment number is 406. She's a nice church going lady, so you don't have to be scare to go inside. You give the money to Miss Bernice and you tell her that Mister Terrence sent you, and that for her to cook you up one of her nice hot meals."

Journey grasp the bill and held it tightly as if it might escape through the fingers of her tiny little fist. She raced towards the building with little Raquan trailing behind her.

Terrence looked down at his trembling hand. Beads of sweat curtained his brow. He reached inside his cardigan again, and pulled out the now half filled pint of cognac. He quickly released the cap with his nimble fingers and let the warm fruity blend flow down his throat. He and Gregory just sat for a minute or two just listening to the sounds around them. Finally Terrence spoke. "I don't know man, the more things change, the more things stay the same."

He felt that it was the phrase that could settle the discouraging look that was on Gregory face.

Gregory shook his head. "I got to find another place to live, this place is depressing. It's not a place to raise a kid. If I had kids, I definite would not let my kids play on the playground, not since those kids came up missing. Man, it looks like every fuckin' day it's always some kind of drama. Women getting in fights over men, or trouble with the kids not getting along on the playground. Sometimes you see or hear about somebody getting shot. It just don't make no fuckin' sense why our young brothers are killing each other. What make it really bad is that the kids are caught smack dead in the middle of all the violence. It's crazy. Just senseless. You remember that dude they called the Professor?

"Man, shit, of course I remember the Professor. We use to chew the fat all the time, right here on this bench. I thought the 'cat was cool. I was shocked about what happen."

"See that just goes to show you, sometime you could spend a lot of time with someone and really don't know them. The poor fool got himself involved in some twisted love triangle. He must of had mad love for the woman. I mean mad motha' fuckin' love. I ain't gonna never let no 'chic' put chains on my heart and balls like that."

"Never say never 'dog'. Love is a powerful drug."

"Trust me 'old timer', it ain't gonna happen."

Gregory wave his hands in the air at a medium built woman with thick silky black corn rows, that helped to shape her round face.

"How you doing Mrs. James?"

The woman nodded and hurried off across the lawn towards the parking lot.

"Poor Mrs. James. I feel sorry for the lady. It had to have been rough coming home and finding her only child in his room laying in a pool of blood. She must have gotten there a few moments before the police, because it wasn't long after 'big mac' shot up the place that the police came."

Terrence lit another cigarette and passed one to his friend.

Gregory tapped the cigarette a couple of times on the back of his hand. It was a habit he picked up from Terrence. He put the cigarette between his full lips and lit it. He took a moment to enjoy the sensation he felt with the smoke when it went down his throat, into his lungs, and back out through his nose.

"That day was wild. I counted eleven police cars including the unmarked ones, and one SWAT unit. I think that there were around six of those special weapons guy lined up against the side of the building ready to go inside and take down the brother, and maybe a couple other innocent people that got in their way."

With the lit cigarette between his index and middle finger, he pointed at the front of the building. "The police had the whole front of the building marked off with that yellow tape, and they were telling people to leave the area, or move several yards away.

Tenants were talking about 'big mac' shooting up the place. A lot of them were speculating as to why he did it. No one knew that Mrs. James was in her apartment at the time the police arrived. When the SWAT team stormed the apartment. People were saying that she was so shocked by her son's death and the sight of all those men with armor and rifle that she had a mild heart attack. I'm glad to see that she's doing better.

Not long after that every tenant got notice on their door, stating that they were under new management and that there was now a stricter policy. Remember that?"

"Yeah I remember."

"But you know that it don't mean a motha' fuckin' thing. Because those drug dealers are like cock roaches, they come in leaving a trail of shit behind them for other drug dealers to follow. It's like you said 'old timer', the more things change, the more things stays the same.

Now some other motha' fucka' by the name of JaiBo done come. Some tall tar black, Mandingo looking motha' fucka' done claimedDe'Aundre's turf. I ain't never seen this motha' fucka' around the way. This nigga' just showed up from out of nowhere, binging his two goons with him. He look like he don't play, and he got the tenants spooked."

Terrence pinched off the burning ashes of his cigarette and put the butt in his shirt pocket for later. "You right 'young blood' it's a terrible place to bring up kids. I been to worst places, and I've seen worst things happen. But if you think hard about it, some of the people that live here are just poor hard working people. Just like you 'young blood', they are hoping that things get better for them so that they can find their up out of here.

If you also think about it, there drugs and violence everywhere in this city. You could move any place in the city, and I guarantee you that you're gonna run up against somebody selling drugs in the neighborhood. Maybe somebody living next door to you or a few doors down from you. That's just the way things are now in this city. People are always looking for a way to make a fast buck I'm not condoning it you understand, but the fact is that most people that's making minimum wage, don't make enough to pay rent and put food on the table. The cost of living is just to fuckin' high.

If you think that this city is bad, try living in D.C. Worst yet try living on the streets of D.C."

"How long did you live on the streets?"

"Too fuckin' long. Longer than I care to remember."

"I heard you often speak about it."

"Yeah man, but it's a time in my life that I wish that I could forget. I wish like hell I could forget the streets of D.C., and the war in Vietnam. But I can not stop these memories from hunting me, no more than I can stop the rain from falling.

I spent most of my time strung out. Even when I was stone on drugs and alcohol, I would see the crimes that happening around me. Drug dealers poppin' one another, pimps murdering their whores, cops beating up on young Black boys, and corrupt cops raiding drug houses, and killing off the witness. Just like you see in the movies. "He smirked. "Art imitating life. To survive and feed my habit I hustled aluminum cans, empty soda pop bottles, and scrap copper. If I didn't make it to churches or food centers in time, I ate out of garbage bins. I had no pride. I sat on corners and begged for money."

He looked up at the towering apartment building. "This place is like the Taj Mahal in comparison to some of the places I lived. At least the wharf rats around here are just afraid of people as people are afraid of them. Shit, the rats in D.C. are as big as Pomeranians, and twice as fierce. Those son-o-bitches ain't no joke. They would come up to you, and climb up your pants and bite the crap out of you. There were many of nights that I slept in rat infested alleyways and sewers. The worst thing was I had these blackouts, at least I think that they were blackouts. I would snap and go wild, and the next thing I know I was in the hospital. This happen quite a few times. The last time I woke up in the hospital I let them talk me into going into 'rehab'. I did the whole twelve step bull shit. You know the shit like; believe in a power greater than yourself, turn your will and life over to God, meditation, spiritual awakening, bull shit, bull shit and more bull shit. Some of that shit must have penetrated my stubborn mind because I got better. I rolled over like a frisky pup and got my ass out of there and came back home. I didn't fall off the wagon until my father die.

When I came home I could hardly recognize the place. All of the Jewish own stores were gone, burned down by rioters in nineteen-sixty-eight There were scarcely any place to shop.

I couldn't find any of my old stumpin' buddies. I learned from different ones that I went to school with that most of my old pals got drafted and died in Vietnam. The one's that made out of Vietnam, I was told that they were now living up North.

My parents were old and feeble. They were like strangers. I wished that I had kept in touch with them more. They were proud of me though, they thought that I was a hero because I had a few medals. Not quite a year after coming home my father died, then my mother three years later. At least they died thinking that their son was a hero. I buried my purple hearts with them. I thought that it was only right for them to take my medals with them to heaven. I was glad that they never found out what type of person I had become.

"You never got married?"

"No. That's one thing I can say that I did right in my life. I had the good sense not to mess up some woman's life. I met this woman not long after I got out of the service. I thought that I was in love at the time, but she couldn't deal with my depression and violent fits."

He sigh heavily and took another sip of the cognac.

I think I got a daughter though. She might be in her early forties by now, if she's still living. She was born in Vietnam, and her name is Kaiya.

For a minute I had this relationship with this Vietnamese girl in Binh Dinh. She was petite, sweet and shy. I knew that she was young and to be honest I think that she was in her teens. It didn't matter much to me at the time, because I knew that in their culture they married at a very young age. We made out for a few months, and then one day she came to me and told me that she was pregnant. I thought that she was trying to trap me into bringing her back with me to the States. It had happen often with many military men. I had made up my mind that I was not gonna let it happen to me.

I told her that I didn't believe that the baby was mine. I had a feeling that the baby was mine, because when she came to me the first time, I knew that I was her first. I was determined that I wasn't gonna be tied down.

I had heard before I got injured and was shipped by home, that she had a little girl and that she named her Kaiya. I heard this from a buddy of mines, he also said that her people put her out because the baby was biracial. Ain't that a kick in the head. Some of those bastard were darker than me. The fuckin' gooks. We were over there fighting for their freedom and they had the nerve to be prejudice towards an innocent mix child." he choked back a tear. I think about her from time to time. The way I handle that particular situation, I'm not proud, not proud of at all. After the war was over, I should have went back to Vinh Dinh and looked for her."

Terrence sensed that Gregory was uncomfortable. He realized that he was weighing Gregory down with too much dismaying information about his life. He had gotten emotional and he feared that his friend, like most men were not sensibly equipped to handle such a situation.

"Man that's wild." Gregory appeared nervous and anxious to go. "Hey Tameka, where you going girl. Bring your fine self over here." He looked at Terrence and winked. "I've been trying for weeks to get a piece of that ass. She's seeing some 'dude', and she got this notion that she's in love. I think that I can wear her down."

The young woman hesitated for a short minute, and then turned to walk into the building.

"Girl hold up. Stop playing. Don't act like you don't know nobody. Wait up. I got this serious bug to put in your ear." He got up to chase after her. "Check you later 'old timer."

Terrence knew that he was using the girl as an excuse to leave. He slapped his friend lightly on his back.

"Go for 'young blood' do some damage."

They bumped fist. Gregory cocked his head like a prideful rooster. When he moved toward the girl he used his smoothest swagger to impress both the girl and Terrence.

Terrence took another drink of cognac, and he noticed that the golden substance was getting near the bottom of the bottle. He drowned the rest of it, wiping away the spilling from his squared chin. He was feeling the effects of the liquor, had been feeling the sensation since the third sip.

He started to feel that he had no control over his head. It felt light as if it was floating away from his body. His body felt cased to the bench. A feeling of nausea overwhelmed him. He tried not to vomit, but the repulsive matter shot out fast from his lips and onto the sidewalk. He was mindful of the mess he made and he was inclined to look and see if any body was watching, but at that moment he didn't have the strength nor balance to do so.

"Fuck it!" He shouted out loud, disturbing the crows that were perching on the limbs of an old maple tree behind him. They gawked and flew off. They circled their roost several times before returning.

He was beginning to feel irritable and disgusted with himself. He mumbled to himself. "You damn drunken fool. You drink too much and you talk too much."

He looked at the repugnant spew on the sidewalk again, this time he looked at it as if he was seeing it with new eyes. It no longer appeared to be vomit, but blood.

Flashbacks of Vietnam electrified his encephalon. He tried hard not to let it happen for fear that he may end up in the hospital again. The flashbacks kept coming. He could hear the firing o M-sixteens,'redeyes', and the deafening explosion of a grenades. He could hear his comrades yelling out in pain. He could see dismemberments of arms and legs, and the blood was everywhere. The small holes that were dug by the Vietcong were like pools of blood. There were puddles of it on the roads and foot path they walked. He could hear

from a distant someone yelling repeatedly, "come back". He thought at first it was his C.O., and then he realized that it was his own voice. He wondered why he was looking up at the sky. Was he looking for a rescue chopper, or was he looking for sparkles from a deployed missile. He couldn't think sensibly why his nose and eyes were burning. He was hyperventilating and then all of a sudden his face felt numb. The light of the day precipitated into blackness.

There were flashes of lightness, then darkness, and then light won over darkness.

Strange stern faces dressed in blue EMS uniforms were hovering over him. People he recognized from the tenement were standing in back of them.

"Are you okay sir? Do you know where you are? Can you tell me how many fingers I'm holding up? Can you tell me your full name?" The questions raced at him, giving him very little time to answer.

One of the person in EMS uniform was holding his wrist trying to measure his pulse. He then lifted his eye lid and with ocean blue eyes peered at his pupils.

He peered back. "I'm alright, just blacked out is all."

One of the men in EMS uniform stood up. He was short and had skin of bronze. "Do you have blackouts often sir?"

"No, well just a couple times when my blood pressure goes up."

"It's pretty high now sir. Two—hundred over ninety." Terrence made a move to get up. "Just sit still sir, we're gonna get a stretcher and transport you to the hospital, and let the doctor take a look at you."

"I ain't gonna go to no hospital! I've had my fill of hospital.".

"Sir we can't make you go to the hospital, but you got know that it's most likely that something is seriously wrong when your blood pressure is so high. Are you taking blood pressure medicine?"

"Yep. One Benazepril every morning with my breakfast."

"Have you been drinking Mister Major?"

"Yep, only a little though." Terrence tried again to get up, but he was held down by another man in EMS uniform. This man look younger than the other two men. He had an intelligent look about him, and he said nothing the entire time.

The man with the bronze color skin said with a tolerant tone.

"Do you know that it is dangerous to mix alcohol with blood pressure medicine? By touching and feeling your skin, I can tell that you're dehydrated. Consuming too much alcohol could be one reason why you are dehydrated. Losing consciousness the way you did, there could be a number of reason for that. Why don't you let us take you to the hospital and let the doctor take a look at you."

"I done told you I ain't gonna go to no damn hospital, and that's that. Let me up. I'm going back to my place and rest-up."

"Like I said before Mister Majors, we can't make you go against your will. At least do me a favor and let us take you to the truck and get some fluid in you. That way you can rest up a little and hopefully your blood pressure will go down. If you still adamant about not going to the hospital, then we will let you go. It will be against my better judgement, but what else can we do. Is it a deal?

Terrence felt renewed after his short nap and hot shower. He tried not to dwell on the past events of the day. He fried up two fillet Tilapia. He also clumped in a couple of tablespoons of butter into an iron skillet and saute thin slices of sweet potatoes, that was sprinkled with brown sugar and cinnamon. He had a taste for homemade cornbread, the way his mother use to make it with sugar, buttermilk, and just a pinch of nutmeg. He didn't have the cornmeal, so he settle on frozen biscuits from a bag. He then opened a can of seasoned collard greens, and emptied it into a small pot and poured in some vinegar and sugar, and put it to low heat on the back of the stove. He lifted from the overhead kitchen cabinet one of the three pints of cognac that was left, and pour himself a hefty shot into a small glass tumbler. He sipped at the liquor while tending to the food.

After he ate, he lit a cigarette, and poured himself another glass of the liquor. This time he increased the amount. He strode over to the wide picture window and gazed out at the alluring blue river.

A woman cried out from the hallway. "Will somebody please call the police, my child is missing." she whimpered," call the police please. I can't find my little boy. Lord help me."

She shouted down the empty hallway."help me to find my little boy. O'Lord pleas, please help me.

I know some nasty man got my boy." She now sobbed uncontrollably. "You bastard, leave my boy alone. What are you doing to him.? You evil and nasty man, stop what you're doing. Get away, you monster. Get away from my boy. Lord make him stop. O'Lord he's watching me, putting his evil spell on me. Give me back my soul. Give me back my boy.

Osa toigbalamo waa, osa toigbalamo waa(Ga language). I curse you. You evil man."

"Go back inside Miss Adele, you're having another one of your spells." A woman yelled from a short distance down the hallway. "Go back inside before someone calls the police and they come and take you away again."

"You Jezebel, I know you. I know what you done with my husband. Keep him cause I don' want him back, but bring me back my boy."

"Suit yourself, you crazy old woman. I was just trying to help you out." A door slammed, and another open. There was loud clicking sound of a woman's heels in the hallway. Soft whispers of comfort was directed to the disturb woman and she went back into her apartment and closed the door. Then there was the same sound of a woman's heels clicking back down the hallway. The clicking sound was then muted by the slamming of a door.

"Osa toigbalamo waa" is a native tongue of the Ga tribe in Ghana. It's translation: You deserve severe punishment.

Terrence listened to the commotion apathetically and continued to gaze at the blue alluring water. He whispered to the river, just before taking another sip of the fruity golden brew. "Taj Mahal." It was a nonsensical phrase used by many people, he thought. He thought what else in his life he could make comparison. Living here in the River Front Tower apartment could be compared to a cut on the hand to stabbed in the back, or lying awake all night in the heat of the jungle in Viet Nam while the bugs ate him alive, and pulverized with fear of a surprise attack. Or maybe lying on a concrete sidewalk or in the alley kicking at the rats who ate at his shoes, while fighting off the pain in his stomach in need of a "fix".

CHAPTER FIFTEEN

Fervent

Felicia hurried across the grassy lawn away from the tall looming apartment building, away from the scrutiny of any curious beings. She was tired of people judging her, talking about her behind her back, and calling her all sorts of names.

For years she did what she thought was right in life. At one time she even had a good paying job and a man who claimed to love her. But he died, and all he left her was a case of HIV. But that seem a life time ago for her now. Now when she wasn't feeling so sick, she did what she had to do to make money.

The sky was black, and there was no moon or a heavenly body of stars to put a glow to her chocolate skin, and curvaceous firm body.

The night air was brisk and snapped at her skimpy thin garments of clothing. She increased her pace a little and continued on her way towards the back of the parking lot in search of an old nineteen-eighty-seven gray Monte Carlo.

She left Raquan and Journey alone in the apartment in front of the television watching some show. She couldn't remember the name or type of show they watch. She had left them so many times before. She felt slightly ashamed, but she figure that she had to do what it took for her to provide for her family.

Her mind stayed steady on the man she was going to meet. For two days she had converse with him online, finding out about his likes and dislikes, and about his life in general. It was risky talking to him about the nature of their soon to be relationship, but they both took that chance. She was careful not to divulge too much information about herself, and he only knew her as KeKe.

She made arrangement for them to meet in the parking lot. She tried to set up a meeting with him on the first day, but he was reluctant. She had a feeling that it was because she was Black, and that she lived in the part of the city that was often reported to be a high crime area.

Near the parking lot there was a lamp post. The lamp post modestly cascaded it yellow beams over the grounds and the parking lot, and she was thankful for that.

She spotted the old model car. She peered hard and was able to make out the outer state license plates, and the battered condition of the car. She remembered that he had said that he collected old cars and fixed them up, and made them into a classic. She was now feeling doubtful about the man she was going to meet, because the car looked in bad condition. It showed no signs that there were any reconstruction work being done on it. The car was a faded gray. Rust was on the roof and the trunk of the car. There were no hub caps on any of the almost tread-less tires.

She fought against the feeling of vulnerability. She had been doing this job for a long time, and she was confident that she could handle any sticky situation.

The car windows were rolled up, and it impressed upon her that it was because of the night air, or maybe it was his way of preparing to leave quickly if there was any danger to him. None of these reasons were particular disturbing to her. She was use to her dates feeling uneasy with the neighborhood. What was unnerving was the tobacco smoke that was entrapped in the car. It hid his face.

From the passenger side she tapped on the glass. The window made a soft squeaking noise when he rolled it down.

"Roland?"

"KeKe?"

She opened the door and slid into the car. The cigar smoke was staggering, and she cough several times.

"Are you a cop?"

"No I am not a cop. Why? Do I look like a cop?"

"His voice was low and rough sounding. His frame was thick, and his face was white as snow, except for the red blotches on his cheeks. His soulless eyes were what really made Felicia uncomfortable.

"It's cool baby, don't sweat it. I just had to ask." She shook off the foreboding warning that nagged at her senses. "So Roland what do you want KeKe to do for you? She spoke of herself as a third party.

"Do you want straight sex? Do you want KeKe to suck your cock?"

She spilled out a list of things as if she was reading off a menu

"Do you like having your butt licked? Do you want'two in the pink'? What's your fancy baby? You name it and KeKe is ready to do the do. Keke don't do S and M, but if you want me to pee on you, I'm game for that."

"Lift your skirt, I want to see your cunt.

"Good! You're a man of few words. I like quite men, they usually know right from the start what they want."

Felicia swung her body around to face him. She leaned against the car door, and lifted her skirt, and opened her legs wide.

. She smiled.

161

He didn't smile back.

She noticed the small red and white flag with a maple leaf hanging from the rear view mirror.

"Where you from baby? You don't sound like you're from around here."

"Up North. Put your legs up on the seat and bend your knees."

Felicia hairs on the back of her neck stood up, yet she did as he asked.

"You want to lick KeKe's pussy?"

He didn't answer. He released his penis from his pants, and moved closer towards her. He rubbed at his penis and inserted his middle finger inside her vagina and moved it back and forth until it became moist.

Felicia groaned in a pretense at ecstacy. "Yeah baby, you fuckin' know how to please a woman." She licked her lips and rolled her eyes. He groaned, and then brutally increased the back and forth movement. Felicia pretended not to feel the pain. She looked at his erection, and she moaned louder, hoping that he would climax soon.

He removed his finger and licked away her milky discharge.

"Honey you're one kinky motha'fucka' ain't you? That's cool baby. Different strokes for different folks I always say.

KeKe will do what ever you like, just as long as you know that it's gonna cost you more than twenty bucks. If you want the six and nine, I can accommodate you on that, but we're gonna need to move to the back seat. That's gonna cost fifty bucks, plus the twenty for the 'one in the sink' that we just did. I need my money up-front sweetie.

He shoved a red stain fifty dollar bill between her large breast, next to the razor sharp blade that she had hidden there. He didn't disturb the blade, and so she was confident that he ignorant of it's present.

"I want you to suck my cock."

"Okay sweetie, you got it, but just so you know, KeKe don't swallow. If you insist that I do, you gonna have to come up with more than the fifty you just shoved down my titties."

She could see that he was angry, and his eyes grew darker and more sinister looking.

"Chill out baby, KeKe is gonna to take good care of you. I'll make it worth your time and money."

Right before she started to service him, she noticed that he took off the black leather belt from around his pants and strapped it around his neck.

She licked at the head of his penis to lubricate it before putting the entire member inside her mouth. Skillfully she massage his scrotum with gentle fingers while slowly guiding his penis deeper and deeper down her throat

A few minutes later his entire body relaxed, and he let his head fall back against the head rest.

She wiped at the semen around her mouth with the back of her hand. She then reclaimed her seat next to him, and removed a piece of bubble gum from her skirt pocket and stuck it in her mouth.

"You good ? You held my head down when you knew that you were gonna discharge. I understand that you was caught up in the moment. Remember I told you I don't care to swallow, so I'm gonna need an extra saw buck. I like you so I'm giving you a discount."

He threw a ten in her lap. He mumbled some inaudible response and then turned his face away from her. He fixed his stare out passed the window, and into the stillness of the night.

KeKe didn't like the look on his face. That uneasy feeling griped her mind again.

"Well, I got to go. You know how to contact me if you want another date." Although she was doubtful that she would setup another meeting with him, she felt that she had to say something to end the night on a pleasant note.

Ash she turned to open the door, he moved swiftly and with great intent towards her and wrapped the belt around her throat. There was only a few moments of confusion before she realized that he was trying to choke her to death. She withdrew the knife from her bosom, but it was hard for her to swing the blade at him, since he was on her from behind. She tried to twist her body around, but he was to strong and held her steady against him as he pulled tighter on the belt. She couldn't breathe and her ears were popping. All the blood left her face, and she was in a state of panic as she continued to twist and fight against his weight. She tried slipping her fingers between the belt and her neck, but the belt was to tight. She was coughing uncontrollably and her throat was in excruciating pain.

Her face felt the size of a pumpkin. Her body was weakening.

She lost the strength of her arms and legs and she felt helpless.

Her mortality was like an epiphany to her now.

Tears flooded her cheeks as she thought about her two kids waiting for her to come home what will happen to them was the last thing on her mind as she slipped into nothingness.

CHAPTER SIXTEEN

In God We Trust

Bernice Lewis, a fifty-five year old widow, with six adult children.
They were all on their own and were spread though out the city. They were of
strong body and strong mind. They were the product of their mother's nurturing and
righteous ways. She raised them in the ways of the Lord, and like herself they became lambs
of God. She was proud of the type of men and women they became. She patted herself on
the back for their success as responsible and loving human beings. But it wasn't easy raising
six kids after her husband died. However she never felt alone, she always had the church, and
she knew that God's footprints were along side her's in the sands of life.

She communicated with her children everyday, either by phone or with a visit.

Everyday she found ways to let her children know how much she loved them.

Everyday she would say to them;"I love you." She would also say to them; "God forbid,
but one never knows when it would be their last day on this earth. For it's a failed mother if
she don't let her child know that she will always love them unconditionally, no matter what."

There came a day that she did not get the chance to say to her children that she
loved them.

This particular day was breezy and sunny, and she was glad that the long hot dry
summer was over. She let the breeze comb through her shoulder link gray hair, and kiss at
her caramel oval face, and it felt heavenly.

It was the end of her workday, and she was tired as usually, but her spirits were high.

She happily thought of her children as she waited for the city transit to pick her up and
take her home.

She rode the same bus home everyday, and everyday she sat beside her friend, Honey.

They met on that same bus several years ago and discovered that they had so much in
common that they became fast friends. They were compatible in nature and enjoyed each
other company everyday on their way home.

Their conversations were entertaining and interesting during their thirty minute ride.
Sometimes they talked about their jobs. Sometimes they talked about life in general.
Sometimes they would talk about the bible. And then sometimes they annoyed the younger
crowd on the bus by singing gospel. Often times the older riders would sing along, and they
would have a grand old time. It was a good way to shake off the stress of the day.

At the end of her ride that day in particular, she got off and wave goodbye at her friend the way she always did, and proceeded to walk the three blocks home.

She was still high in spirit and so she hummed her favorite hymn. It helped to lighten the load from the bag of grocery she had enfolded in her arms. It also helped in taking her mind off her aching feet during her short walk home.

She inhaled deeply, filling her lungs with the cool breeze. She was getting close to home. She could smell the salt from the James river, and she could imagine the gentle waves hitting the shore.

"Hallelujah and glory to God. What a blessed day." She shouted to the breeze. And the breeze whispered back "Amen." She thought if she didn't have a arm full of grocery she would fold her hands in prayer.

"Hello sister Bernice. How are you doing?"

She was caught off guard when she heard someone speak her name. She usually looked for her fellow member of the Ivy Avenue Baptist Church, when ever she approached her however today she was busy praising the Lord.

"Hello sister Martha. How you doing this glorious day?"

"I'm blessed. God is good."

"All the time."

On sunny days Martha was always perched on the same thick wooden rocker. She looked swallowed up by the huge old white two story Victorian style house, with it's beautiful constructed turret, and handsome dormers.

Every time she came upon the house, Bernice always looked at it with new eyes. Devouring it with her hungry stares at the artful construction of the wide A symmetrical porch, and the light green decorative wood trim that was meticulously attached to the edge of the gable roof. She fell in love with the corbels on each corner of the house that was architecturally design with an acanthus leaf. It was a well kept house, but it looked awkward among the other simply designed homes on the block. It had many owners over the years. When the neighborhood became predominately Black, and the homes in the neighborhood started to deteriorate, it's value went down. When the house went up for sale again, Martha and her family put the money together and brought it.

Martha loved her home and everyday, every chance she got she sat smugly on her wide porch.

Although Bernice chastised herself many times for feeling envious of her friend for living in such a magnificent house. Even though she has told herself time and time again, that envy was the workshop of the devil, she just could not seem to fight the feeling whenever she came upon it. She was invited inside the house many times, it was just that one time that she took her friend up on her offer. Once inside the house she was immediately smitten with it's charm, the high ceilings, crystal chandeliers, and the warm and inviting fire places. She now rated her experience in seeing the inside the house as bitter sweet. Having been inside the home made her feel sad that never in her lifetime will she own such a magnificent home. In all honesty she had to admit that not even when her husband was a live, and there was two income were there any real chance that they would own a home like it.

"I noticed that you'll reading the bible. What book?"

"I felt in the mood to read a couple of chapters from Psalm. It is one of my favorite books in the bible, especially the twenty-third and thirtieth chapters."

She quoted a verse from the thirtieth chapter, as if Bernice was not familiar with it. "I will extol thee, O Lord, for thou has lifted me up and has not made my foes to rejoice over me."

Something came over Bernice. Maybe it was the wonderful free breeze that made her spirit feel free, to say the things she been wanting to say. Or maybe it was the green eye monster that squeezed her heart, and made her tongue recite the quote. Irregardless she said she said it and now she couldn't take it back.

"I also like to read the chapters of Psalm, and I particularly like chapter seventy-three, verses three through five; "for I was envious at the foolish, when I saw the prosperity of the wicked. For there are no bands in their death, but their strength is firm. They are not in trouble as other men, neither are they plagued like other men."

Martha had a perplex look on her round coffee colored face as she tried to figure out why Bernice would recite those particular verses.

Bernice smiled nervously at Martha, and pretended that it was an unrelated reason why she quoted the verses.

"I made a pot of hot lemon tea. I brought out an extra cup, hoping that you would stop by and visit for a little while, and rest those weary feet."

"I would love to sit and chat with you today, but I'm having company over tonight. I want to go straight home today and start cooking." She lied and whispered for God forgiveness.

"Maybe tomorrow if the weather holds up." She turned and walked away.

Martha shouted at her back.

"Well if not tomorrow I'll see you at church Sunday, sister Bernice."

"You can count on that sister Martha." She waved goodbye and continued her walk home.

She did not notice the dark skinned man with an intent stare. He sat still on the narrow steps of a old one story house. The house was ugly and run down, and his whole physique seemed to blend in with it.

The fact is that she had seen him a few times on her walks home from the bus stop, but he seemed invisible to her. Mostly because her mind was usually being entertained by thoughts of her children, or the events of that day.

When she did see him it was with uninterested eyes. She never noticed his scrutinizing stares, and never did she think of him as a threat. And so today, this particular day, she was so intent to end her short journey home, that she did not notice that he was trailing behind her.

He was of average height, but taller than Bernice. He looked thin and sickly.

Nearly forty-eight hours had past since his last fix. For two days he had to hustle desperately trying to come up with some money.

He was soon to be evicted from the rat and roach infested house that he lived in, because he was two months behind in his rent.

He thought about his so called friends that stuck to him like flies to shit when he had money to party, now avoided him like he had the plague.

He was shaking horribly now and in a lot of pain. The craving for his drug of choice was monstrous.

He looked at Bernice as she lively walked towards her destination. With great irritation he thought to himself; "For an old bitch, you sure can move fast. Slow down bitch, you ain't running no marathon."

He quicken his pace, and was able to trail just a few feet behind her. When she crossed the grassy lawn and went up to the front entrance of River Front Tower, he made it in time to catch the door before it closed.

She never even suspect that he was following her. He was confident in thinking that she most likely thought that he was a tenant or visiting one of the tenants. He was so close on her now, that he could smell the soft flowery scent that she wore next to her skin, and the coconut pomade that shined her hair.

He slid in the elevator behind her and watched her press the button for the fourth floor. To avoid suspicion he pressed the button for the fifth floor. She hardly glanced his way. He fought against the strong urge to overtake her while in the elevator. He convinced himself that he would not have enough time before the elevator reached the fourth floor. She started to softly hum a hymn that was unfamiliar to him. Yet the familiarity of the type of woman he perceived her be reminded him of his mother, and he hated his mother. The thought of his mother inflamed his heart, and heighten his ill feeling for Bernice.

The elevator rattled it's way uninterrupted to the fourth floor, and when the doors open he follow her out.

When she came to apartment 406, she placed the bag of grocery down on the floor, and reached inside her black vinyl purse for her keys. When she found her keys, she fumbled at the lock, and that's when he made his move.

∽

When the lock finally gave way, she opened the door and breathe a sigh of relief.

"Thank you Lord. It's good to be back home," She sang out loud.

"whew! I'm tired and I'm hungry and I'm sho' nough' ready to relieve my aching feet of these worn out work shoes."

When she reached for the bag of grocery, a heavy weight came down upon her and strange hands shoved her inside her apartment. Mere seconds before it happen she caught a glimpse of someone approaching, but it was to late for her to really realize what was about to happen.

He threw the bag of grocery on the floor next to her, and shut the door behind him.

He moved quickly towards her, kicking cans of vegetable and packaged chicken out of his way. He hovered over her. In his hand he held a long Bowie style knife.

"Oh my God. Mister don't kill me," she yelled. "What do you want? Please don't take my life. I give you anything I have, just please Mister don't kill me."

"Shut the fuck up. Do you live by yourself?" He stayed steady in his stance and cautiously looked around the apartment.

"No," she lied. "My oldest son lives with me." Her answer caused him some concern, and he tried to look pass the livingroom and down the hall.

"Is he here now?"

Her body shook with fear and her voice spoked unconvincedly through her sobs.

"Yes. He works the night shift, so he sleeps during the day."

"Don't move, stay your ass still, or I will kill you."

He picked the handbag up from the floor, and searched the inside. He removed a small wallet and lifted the few bucks from the narrow compartment.

"Thirteen bucks, that's all there is?" He dumped the loose coins into the palm of his hand and put the money in his pants pocket."

He put the knife up to her throat. "Get up, and you better not try no shit, or I will stick you." She stumbled to her feet, and the knife dug into the flesh of her neck. She could feel her blood run down her neck. She tried to control her sobs, but fear had a tight grip around her heart. In-between sobs she tried to reason with him.

"Look you got all the money I have, and you frighten an old woman nearly out of her mind. Just leave while you still have a chance. Leave before my son comes down that hallway and make you sorry that you ever came here."

He grabbed her by the shoulder and shoved her down the hallway, and through the open bedroom door. The room was very tidy, and the bed was neatly made. There was a satisfied look on his face. "I had a feeling that you was lying. Just like I have a feeling that you are lying to me about the money. Old bitches like you always have money hidden somewhere. Probably under the bureau draws, or wrapped up with newspaper and stuffed between the mattress, or under the rug."

He thought again of his mother. He thought how she denied him a few bucks to help feed his addiction. He thought how she knew how bad he was hurting, and she still turned him down. ' Well to hell with her', he thought. "You old hags are cunning in hiding money, it could be anywhere."

He looked around the room.

"Maybe it's sewed into the cushion in that chair in the corner, or in a lining of an old purse. All I know, is that you better move your ass and find it, because I mean business."

He shoved her again into the center of the bedroom.

Thoughts were rushing her head. She thought maybe she should try to run pass him, and make a mad dash down the hallway to escape out the front door. Should she grab for anything she could get her hands on, and try to fight him off. should she just scream and hope that he would panic and run off. Fear made her doubtful that she could do any of those things. Besides she thought he was right about the money, and it wasn't worth her life.

She walked over to the walk-in closet, and pulled out the white hamper. She dumped soiled clothes onto the floor. She then removed a white cardboard from the bottom of the hamper, and pulled out a long white envelope stuffed with currency of twenties, and fifties.

Her eyes glimpsed the wooden bat behind the hamper against the corner of the closet wall. It belonged to her youngest son, who left it there for her protection. She remember that he tried to convince her to get a gun, but she argued that she was to frighten to have a gun in her home. She now regret her decision and she thought that at least if she owned the gun, he could use it to spook him off.

He snatched the envelope from her hands. He marveled at the amount of money that was ide.

She suddenly realized that he may not just take the money and leave, that he may still try m her. She had to act quickly in an effort to save her life.

She whispered a short prayer, "Yeah though I walk through the valley of the shadow of death, I will fear no evil for thou art with me." She grabbed the bat and hit him across the right side of his face. The force of the blow forced him to stagger, and dropped the money and knife. He quickly recovered and made a move towards her, and she brought the bat down on the crown of his head. She did it several times as if pounding a nail into the floor. The blows rendered him and he fell to the floor. Blood erupted from his head, and his body laid still.

She looked to the heavens and said, "thank you Lord for delivering me from evil."

Her expressions of relief was premature. Just as she tried to run to safety, he grabbed hold of her leg and pulled her to the floor.

He knelt over her with the knife in his hand. His face was blanketed with blood and rage.

She slapped at his face and scratched at his black evil eyes. He brought the knife down into her chest, breaking the sternum, and missing her heart by a few inches.

He yanked it out from her chest and brought the knife down again, this time puncturing her right lung. She tried to scream again but she could barely expand her lungs. What little strength she had, she continued to struggled to get free. She dug her nails into the side of his face, and he sliced off her thumb and index finger.

She was out of her mind now with pain, fear and the foreboding realization of death.

"Why O Lord ?" She asked.

She was choking now, choking on her own blood.

He brought the knife down again to the center of her chest.

Her spirit escaped and hovered over them, as he continue to stab at her limp body.

RIVER FRONT TOWER

The Tower of Souls

RIVER FRONT TOWER is a twelve story high-rise apartment building. It sits majestically on five acres of land, on the bottom east-end of the city, and several hundred yards off the bank of the James River. The story takes place there. It is a fictional depiction of the rigorous, and torturous existence of the people that live there. It is a compelling story of love, sex, crime, and violence.

Mary E. Stephenson is a native of Newport News, Virginia. She graduated from Huntington High School and briefly attended Hampton Institute as a student in the Adult Nursing program. She worked for over sixteen years as an Office Accounts Clerk. She is an Author of five novels, River Front Tower (the tower of souls), Afloat with Memories, Torsional Storm, Halona, and Labyrinth of Life.

authorHOUSE®

ISBN 978-1-4918-4167-9

51995

9 781491 841679